the
# BOOKWORM
box

Helping the community, one book at a time

# Behind the Bars

BOOK ONE IN THE
MUSIC STREET SERIES

BRITTAINY C. CHERRY

Published: Brittainy C. Cherry 2017
brittainycherry@gmail.com

Editing by Ellie at Love N. Books
Editing by C. Marie
Lawrence Editing

Proofreading: Virginia Tesi Carey
Alison Evans-Maxwell

Cover Design: Kandi Steiner
Cover Models: Shailey Collier & Sammy Collier
Paperback Formatting: Elaine York, Allusion Graphics, LLC

# Dedication

*To every soul who has lost themselves.*
*May your favorite lyrics lead you home.*

# Part One

"Music was my refuge.
I could crawl into the space between the notes
and curl my back to loneliness."
— *Maya Angelou*

## Chapter One

# Jasmine

No.

Hearing that word never got easier. It never felt numb or meaningless when someone said it to me. The way their eyes looked me up and down when I walked into a room...the way they judged me for everything I was and everything I wasn't...the way they whispered as I stood still.

*No. No. Sorry. No, thank you. It's a pass this time.*

I'd just turned sixteen, and I'd known rejection more than the average person. I'd been trying to get discovered in the music industry for years, and nothing had ever come from it except rejection.

*No.*

*No.*

*Sorry. No, thank you.*

*It's a pass this time.*

That didn't stop Mama from driving me from meeting to meeting, from audition to audition, from one 'no' to another. That was because I was her star, her shining light. I was going to do everything she'd been unable to accomplish, because that's what kids were supposed to do, she told me.

We were supposed to be better than our parents.

And I would be better, someday. All I needed was for the right person to tell me yes.

I walked out of my third audition that week in New Orleans and I looked at all the other girls who were auditioning for the girl group. I thought I was more of a solo artist, but Mama said I should be happy with any kind of forward movement.

"Girl groups are in right now," she told me. "Pop music sales are big."

I never wanted to do pop music, though. My heart bled for soul but Mama said there was no money in soul music for a girl like me—only disappointment.

All the other girls auditioning each looked like me, but better somehow. Across the way, Mama's eyes were wide with hope as she stared at me. A ball of guilt knotted in my gut as I forced a smile.

"Well? How did it go?" she asked me, standing up from her chair in the waiting room.

"Fine."

She frowned. "Did you fumble your song? I told you to keep rehearsing the lyrics. This school thing is taking too much time from the real work you should be doing," she said disdainfully.

"No, no. That's not it. I didn't forget my lyrics. They were perfect," I lied. I had fumbled the words, but it was only because of the way the casting director looked at me, as if I was the exact opposite of the part they wanted to fill, but I couldn't have Mama knowing I'd messed up because that could've jeopardized me staying at Canon High School.

"You should've tried harder," she scolded. "We're spending so much on singing, acting, and dance classes, Jasmine. You shouldn't be walking out of auditions saying it was 'fine'. You must be the best. Otherwise, you'll be nothing. You need to be a triple threat."

*Triple threat.*

I hated those words. Mama was a singer, but her career had never taken off. She said right before she would have been discovered, she'd gotten knocked up with me, and no one wanted a pregnant superstar.

She believed if she hadn't put all her eggs in one basket, she could've made it in another field. Therefore, she made me a triple threat. I couldn't just be a great singer, I needed to be the best actress and dancer out there, too. More talents meant more opportunities, more opportunities meant more fame, and more fame meant Mama might be proud of me.

That was all I really wanted.

"Well, we better get a move on," she told me. "You have ballet practice across town in forty minutes, then your singing lesson afterward. Then I have to get home and have dinner ready for Ray."

Ray had been Mama's boyfriend for as long as I could remember. There wasn't a memory I had that didn't include his face. For a long time, I'd thought he was my father, but one night when they both came home hammered, I listened to them fighting over how I was being raised, and Mama shouted about how Ray didn't get a say in my life since I wasn't his daughter.

But still, he loved me like I was his own.

He was the reason we moved around so much. He found decent success as a musician and was able to make a living touring around the world. Sure, he wasn't a household name to a lot of people, but he did well enough to support himself, Mama, and me. We were Ray's biggest groupies, and he made it his priority to take care of us.

Mama never worked a real job. She bartended some nights, but not often. She said her job was making me a star, which included her homeschooling me so I wouldn't lose focus. Being homeschooled was my only option, and I never complained. I was certain other kids had it worse.

Yet, for the first time, when we'd stopped traveling for a while, Ray and I had both convinced Mama to let me go to public school. When I learned we'd be in New Orleans for a bit of time due to a gig Ray had gotten offered, I begged Mama to let me start my junior year at an actual high school, with kids my age. *God*, what I wouldn't give to be surrounded by kids my age who weren't just auditioning for the same roles as me.

A chance to make real friends...

I was shocked when she agreed to it, thanks to Ray and his way with words.

It meant the world to me, but to Mama it meant time away from studying the craft of music. To her, high school was child's play, and I was too old to still be playing.

3

"I still don't think public school was a good idea," she said scornfully as we walked toward the city bus stop. "It's distracting."

"I can do it all," I promised, which was probably another lie, but I couldn't give up being in school. It was the first time in such a long time that I felt like I belonged. "I'll work even harder than ever before."

She cocked an eyebrow, unsure. "If you say so, but the minute I think it's too much, I'm pulling you out."

"Okay."

It was six o'clock on Saturday evening when we stepped on the bus, and instead of going home, we headed to my ballet class. Mama handed me a bag of measured out raw nuts to eat beforehand, because otherwise I'd end up feeling faint. I wasn't the best dancer in the class, but I wasn't the worst. There was nothing about my body that read 'ballerina', though. My body was made like Mama's: small waist, thick hips. I had curves in all the right places, except ballet class. In ballet class, I was the oddity.

"Have you been eating clean?" the instructor asked me as she fixed my posture.

"Yes. I had lemon water this morning then Greek yogurt with berries."

"And lunch?"

"Salad with nuts and thin chicken slices."

She raised an eyebrow as if she didn't believe me. "And snacks?"

"I just had nuts on the way over here."

"Ah..." She nodded and placed her hands on my waist to straighten me up. "You look bloated. Maybe skip the afternoon snack."

A few of the other dancers giggled at her comment, and my cheeks heated up. They all looked at me as if I were a fool for even being in the class. If it weren't for Mama, I wouldn't have been, but she thought dance lessons were a very important part of becoming famous.

It just made me feel like a failure.

"Well, that was humiliating," Mama barked after rehearsal, barging out of the studio. "You haven't been practicing."

"I have."

She turned to face me and pointed a stern finger my way. "Jasmine Marie Greene, if you continue to lie, you'll continue to fail, and your failure isn't just yours. It reflects on me, too—remember that. Think of this as strike one of three. Three strikes means no more public school. Now come on, we must get to the studio."

Acme Studios was a tiny place on Frenchmen Street where I could get behind a microphone and record some of my songs. I always wanted to write my own lyrics, but Mama said I wasn't skilled enough with the written word to ever do it on my own.

It was an amazing studio, and most people wouldn't have been able to record there, but Ray had a way of making great connections. I sometimes wondered if that was the only reason Mama stayed with him.

I couldn't understand what they had in common other than loving music.

We made it to Frenchmen Street, and the moment we stepped foot there, I smiled. There was something about the energy of it that made me feel alive. Bourbon Street was famous to many tourists, but Frenchmen Street was where the magic of the locals existed. The music you could stumble onto always shocked me. It was amazing how a street could be filled with so much talent, so much soul.

When Mama's phone started ringing, she stepped aside to take the call, and that's when it happened.

That's when I saw the boy who played the music.

I'd always say I saw him first, but he'd argue that was a lie.

Technically I didn't see him at first—I *felt* him, felt his music crawl along my skin. The chords and bars of his saxophone sent chills down my spine. It sounded magical, the way the notes danced through the air, so hauntingly beautiful.

I turned on my heels to see a skinny boy standing on the corner of Frenchmen and Chartres. He was young, maybe my age, maybe a bit younger, with thin-framed glasses sitting on his face. He held a saxophone in his grip and he played as if he'd die if the music wasn't perfect. Lucky for him, it was more than perfect.

I'd never heard anything like it. I got emotional listening to the sounds he was crafting, and I couldn't help being on the verge of tears.

How had he learned to play that way? How could someone so young possess so much talent? I'd been surrounded by musicians my whole life, but I'd never witnessed anything like this.

He played as if he were bleeding out into the streets of New Orleans. He left nothing on the table and gave his music his all. In that moment, I realized I never gave anything my all—not like him, not like that.

People started surrounding him on the street, tossing change into his open instrument case. They took out their cell phones to record his sounds. It was an experience to watch him stand on that corner. His confidence was high, and his fingers danced across the keys as if he had no fear of failure.

Failure was probably not a part of his vocabulary.

His music was beautiful, and kind of painful, too. I hadn't had a clue that something could be painfully beautiful until that evening.

Once he stopped playing, it was interesting what happened: the confidence he'd exuded completely melted away. His once strong stance dissolved as his shoulders slumped over. People complemented him on his music, and he struggled to make eye contact.

"That was amazing," a woman told him.

"Th-th-thank you," he replied, rubbing his hands together before packing his instrument away. The moment I heard his shaky voice, I realized who he was.

*Elliott.*

I knew him—well, knew of him. He went to my school and was extremely shy. He was nothing like the boy who'd just played the music. It was almost as if he had two distinct personalities—the powerful musician and the bullied teenager.

The two looked nothing alike.

I stepped forward, wanting to speak, but I was uncertain what to say. As my lips parted, and I searched my mind for words, nothing came to me. He deserved something, a compliment, a smile, a touch of congratulations—*anything*—but I couldn't even get him to look my way.

He wouldn't look anyone's way.

"Jasmine," Mama called, breaking my stare away from Elliott. "Will you come on already?"

I glanced over my shoulder one last time, feeling a knot forming in my gut before hurrying over to Mama. "Coming."

After my studio session, we got on another bus to head home. On the way, Mama told me everything I'd done wrong. She informed me of all my missteps and mistakes repeatedly as she cooked dinner. Then, we sat at the dining room table with the food untouched because we wouldn't eat until Ray was home.

Of course, he was late, because Ray never knew how to leave the studio on time, so Mama's temper grew, and she took it out on me. She never took it out on Ray, and I never understood why. Everything he did wrong was taken out on me.

I didn't resent him, though. If anything, I was thankful Ray chose to love Mama, because it meant I was able to love him. He was a safe haven of sorts. When he wasn't around, Mama was dark, lonely, empty, and mean. When Ray walked into a room, her eyes lit up.

"I'm late," Ray said, walking into the house with a cigarette hanging from his lips. It was half smoked, and he put it out in the ashtray by the front door. I hated the smell of cigarettes, so he always did his best not to smoke in the house. Mama said he was a grown man and could smoke anywhere he pleased, but Ray wasn't a jerk like that.

He loved me enough to respect my wishes.

"You're not late," Mama told him. "I just cooked too early, that's all."

"Because I said I would be earlier," he said with a smirk.

Ray was always smiling, and it made everyone around him smile, too. He was the kind of man who looked effortlessly handsome. He was masculine in so many ways, from his build and physique to his mannerisms. He was the first to pull out a chair for a lady, the one who'd hold a door open for forty women to walk through before he stepped foot inside. A very old-school, charming gentleman, he was also soft in many spots, like his eyes and smile. His grin was so beautiful and made everyone feel safe when they looked his way.

His eyes kind of felt like home.

"It's fine." Mama smiled and lied. "We just sat down a few minutes ago."

We'd been sitting for forty-five minutes.

Ray approached us and patted me on the top of my head. "Hey, Snow White." He'd given me that nickname a long time ago when I was just a kid, and I loved it. I still loved it just as much at sixteen.

"Hey, Ray," I replied.

He raised an eyebrow. "You have a good day?" Which was code for 'Did your mother drive you insane today?'

Sometimes, even when she wasn't trying to be, Mama could be a handful.

I nodded. "I had a good day."

He wrinkled his nose, unsure if I was telling the truth, but he didn't press for more information. He'd never ask what was wrong in front of Mama, because he knew how sensitive she got if she felt she was being judged. Ray kissed her forehead. "I'm gonna go wash up quickly and change outta these clothes. Then we can eat."

"Okay," Mama replied.

With that, he left to wash his hands. I sat leaning on the table, watching Mama's eyes follow Ray as he disappeared down the hallway. When she turned back to me, the love she held in her stare faded, and she sat up straighter.

"Elbows off the table, Jasmine, and sit up straight or you'll get a hunched back."

Ray joined us at the table, and we chatted about how recording his album was going. "I love it here in New Orleans because there's an authentic feel to the city. People around the world don't make music the way they do down here. It's not as real, as painful."

When Ray talked about music, it made me want to only focus on that.

"Did you ever reach out to Trevor Su for me?" Mama asked, referring to a producer.

Ray cringed. "No. I told you this already, he's not a good guy. We don't need him for Jasmine's career."

Mama didn't like that answer, based on the way her nose wrinkled. "Trevor Su is one of the top producers in the world, and you have an in with him. I don't see why you would think Jasmine isn't good enough to work with him."

"*No*," Ray barked, shaking his head. "Don't twist my words. That's not what I said at all. He's not good enough for her."

"And why not?"

"Because he's a snake."

8

Mama huffed. "Who cares if he's a snake, as long as he gets the job done?"

Ray disagreed, "No. The way he uses people to climb the ladder is disgusting. I've watched him trample good people just for money. It's disgusting."

"It's business, Ray," Mama groaned. "And maybe if you understood that, you'd be more successful than you actually are."

"Mama," I gasped, shocked by her comment.

Ray didn't even flinch. He'd become used to her harsh words. He was pretty much numb to her judgments.

That didn't make it easier for me to hear them.

He and Mama were completely different when it came to the world of music. Ray led with his heart and Mama with her brain.

"It's called *networking*," she'd say.

*"It's called selling out,"* he'd disagree. "Plus, he's too much. He'd push her to her limits."

"Her limits need to be pushed."

"She's just a kid, Heather."

"And she could be extraordinary if you allowed it."

A few minutes went by with the two of them arguing over if it was disrespectful for Mama to meet with Trevor or not. She was a driven manager when it came to my career, and she never thought any idea was too extreme. She was the momager of all momagers, determined to do whatever it took to make me a success.

Ray was the opposite. He believed in my music, but he also be-lieved in me being a kid, too. Having a life outside of music.

"Maybe we should not talk about work at the dinner table," Ray said, clearing his throat.

"Music is all we talk about," Mama argued.

"Well, maybe that should change. We can talk about anything else," Ray offered, moving his food around on his plate. "When I get home, I just want to unplug."

"You're the one who sat down and started talking about music in the first place!" Mama snapped. "But when I start talking about Jas-mine's career, it's too much?"

"Mama," I whispered, shaking my head.

"Jasmine, hush and eat your salad."

"Why are you only eating salad?" Ray questioned.

I parted my lips to reply, but Mama stepped in before I could. "She's on a new diet."

Ray laughed. "She's sixteen and the size of a stick, Heather. She can eat whatever she wants."

Then, like clockwork, they started arguing about the ins and outs of how Mama was raising me. By the end of the conversation, Mama had told him he didn't have a say because he wasn't my father.

I hated how she threw that in his face whenever she didn't get her way.

I always noticed how sad Ray's eyes grew whenever she said those words.

Maybe on paper he wasn't my father, but there was no doubt in my heart that he was my dad.

"I'm gonna take a breather," Ray said, pushing his chair away from the table. He left the apartment with his pack of cigarettes to clear his head, which meant he was going to watch live music. Music always helped when Mama stressed him out.

It helped when she stressed me out, too.

After dinner, I headed straight to my room and started my home-work. I was so behind on everything, but it was really important for me to seem as if I had my life together. Otherwise, I'd be forced back into being homeschooled, and that couldn't happen, not after getting a taste of what being a true teenager felt like.

"You have a good day, Snow White?" Ray asked, standing in my doorway hours later with his arms behind his back.

I looked up from my math book and shrugged.

"You don't have to lie—your mom's sleeping. Was she hard on you?"

"It's fine. It's my fault, really. I started slacking."

"She puts too much pressure on you," he warned me.

"'Pressure makes diamonds,'" I said, mocking Mama's words. Then, I smiled because Ray was beginning to frown. "I'm okay. Just tired today."

"You want me to try talking to her again?"

I shook my head. If Ray told Mama I was stressed or overwhelmed, she'd be embarrassed, and whenever she felt embarrassed, she took it out on me.

"Why just salad for dinner?" Ray asked.

"Not hungry."

"That's too bad." He grimaced and pulled out a bag of takeout. "Because I just picked up a burger and fries from down the street."

My stomach growled the moment I saw the bag.

"But since you're not hungry, I'll toss it—"

"No!" I shouted, shaking my head back and forth. I cleared my throat and sat up straighter on my bed. "I mean, I'll take it."

He laughed and tossed me the food. "You're perfect the way you are. Don't starve yourself for the dream, Snow White, and don't starve yourself for your mother. Neither are worth it."

"Thanks."

He nodded. "And whenever you want me to talk to your mom, let me know. I got your back."

"Ray?"

"Yeah?"

"Do you love her?" I asked, my voice low. The two of them never acted like they were in love. Not as far back as I could remember, at least. Maybe there was a time they were, but it wasn't something that existed in my memories.

Ray gave me a tight smile. Which was a clear no.

"She's mean to you," I told him.

"I can handle it," he replied.

"Why do you stay with her? Why would you stay with someone you don't even love who treats you the way she does?"

He cleared his throat and stared at me with the gentlest eyes I'd ever seen. Then he shrugged his shoulders. "Come on, Snow," he softly spoke. "You know the answer to that question."

*Because of me.*

He stayed because of me.

"I love her because she gave me you. You may not be my blood, Snow White, but don't for a second think that you are not my family. I stay for you. I'll always stay for you."

My eyes glassed over. "I just want you to be happy, Ray."

He snickered. "You know what makes me happy?"

"What?"

"You being happy. So, just keep being happy—*and eating*—and my heart is full, Snow. That's all I've ever wanted. Your happiness." He walked over to me, kissed my forehead, and stole one of my fries before he headed to bed.

Ray might not have been my biological father, but there was no doubt in my mind that he was my dad.

# Chapter Two

## Jasmine

The happiest moments of my life were spent in a high school build-ing. Most people would've been happy to miss out on going to school, but it was the first time in my life that I felt as if I were exactly where I was supposed to be.

Having a break from Mama was so nice, nicer than I'd ever imag-ined it would be. I loved her, but sometimes I needed a breather, and school gave me that space to breathe. When I walked the hallways, people made me feel included in something. I wasn't surrounded by adults in the music industry, talking about grown-up things. I wasn't auditioning for parts I didn't want. I wasn't making sure Mama was proud of me.

I was just a kid.

But it wasn't always like that for others at school. I was one of the lucky ones. Others often fell victim to the likes of Todd Clause, the typ-ical handsome senior who lived for applause.

"Jasmine, hey!" Todd called after me. He leaned up against a lock-er, wearing a white T-shirt with a gold chain necklace, and nodded me over. He was one of the most popular kids and half the time he was a complete jerk to anyone who wasn't as striking as him.

Me though, he thought I was beautiful—or at least he thought the size of my chest and the fullness of my lips was beautiful.

*Lucky me.*

I flashed him a fake smile and kept walking. "Hey, Todd."

He hurried over to me and placed his arm around my shoulders. "How are you? Where were you this weekend?"

"This weekend?"

He cocked an offended eyebrow. "I had a party at my place. You said you might stop by."

"Oh...right." I bit my bottom lip and wrapped my hands around my backpack straps. "Sorry. I was at an audition, and I had dance rehearsal."

"Miss Hollywood," he joked, slowly sliding his hand down my back.

"No, just me," I replied, quickly sliding his hand up my back.

"Well, I'm having another party this weekend. My parents are always gone on weekends, so there's always a Saturday party going on."

"That's cool," I said, uninterested.

"You should definitely come. I live in the Garden District."

"Oh?" I raised an eyebrow, uncertain what that meant exactly.

"It's one of the richest areas in New Orleans. My family has a shit-ton of money. I only go to this crap school because I got kicked out of private school."

"Oh, cool."

"You can come to my house and see my horses. I'll even let you ride me." He laughed an arrogant laugh. "I mean ride *them*. I'll let you ride a horse."

I didn't have the faintest idea how to reply to that, so I didn't.

"Hey, Boney Bones," Todd said, breaking away from me to push a guy in the hallway.

*Elliott.*

The unlucky one.

I noticed him a lot, or more so I noticed people bullying him a lot. He was a quiet guy and he mostly kept to himself. He was a skinny boy with beautiful caramel skin and hazel eyes. He never in the history of ever bothered anyone. He had braces, glasses, and nervous habits, like the shaky hands I always noticed.

He was the easiest target for Todd: timid, kind, and lonely.

I noticed the loneliness most, because I knew the distinct look. I'd been lonely my whole life, and Elliott's stare mirrored my own.

14

How was it possible? How did a boy as nervous as Elliott create music the way he did?

Todd and a few other guys walked up and started pushing him around in such a mean-spirited way. Elliott cringed and kept his head down as he tried to get away.

"Todd, lay off," I called after him. "Leave him alone."

Todd glanced back and snickered. "I'll leave him alone if you promise to come to my party."

I groaned.

I hated the idea of that.

Todd shoved Elliott, this time pushing him into a metal locker.

I groaned again.

I hated that more than the idea of Todd's party.

My fingers raced through my dark hair, and I bit my bottom lip before speaking. "What time's the party?"

## Chapter Three

### Jasmine

The worst moments of my life were spent in a high school. I couldn't wait until that chapter of my life was over and done with. Waking up each morning knowing I had to go back there was the worst feeling in the world.

"Boney Bones, I see you decided to dress like shit again," a kid called my way.

I didn't know who it was, and I didn't have any drive to look up to try to figure it out.

*Keep your head down and try not to get noticed*, I told myself every single day. *Only five hundred and sixty-two days until graduation.*

I hated school, and that was putting it mildly. If I'd had the choice, I would've never gone back, but Mom had this addiction to the idea of my sister and me getting our high school and college diplomas, because she hadn't been able to get hers. She wanted us to be better than her, do more than her, succeed more in life.

I wasn't really thinking that far ahead, though.

I was just trying not to get a wet willy on the way from math class to history.

"Hey, Elliott," a person said from behind me.

I didn't turn around, though, because if they weren't calling me Boney Bones or Brace-face or Piece-Of-Shit-That-Should-Commit-Suicide, they weren't talking to me.

"Elliott! Hey! I'm talking to you," the voice called after me. It was a girl's voice, and they *definitely* weren't talking to me if it was a girl's voice. "Hey!" A hand landed on my shoulder, making me halt my steps and cringe. I always cringed when someone touched me, because normally touches led to fists in my gut.

"Why are you cringing?" the voice asked as I slowly opened my eyes.

"So-sorry," I whispered, almost certain she didn't hear me.

"Why does everyone bully you?" the girl asked me—and it wasn't just any girl, it was *the* girl. Jasmine Greene.

The prettiest girl I'd ever seen.

I raised an eyebrow at her, uncertain as to why she was talking to me. Jasmine was new and insta-popular. I wasn't the type who ever received attention from the popular kids.

Well, that wasn't completely true. I wasn't the type who ever received *positive* attention from the popular kids.

"What?" I questioned, baffled that she was looking at me.

"I said, why does everyone bully you?"

My eyes darted back and forth, making sure her words had been spoken for me. "I, um, I-I-I—" I cleared my throat and my shoulders slouched. "I su-su-ffer from stuttering?"

"Is that a question?" she asked, walking backward toward the theater so she could look me in the eyes. I hated eye contact, especially with girls like her. Pretty girls were the worst. They always made me sweat through my T-shirts, and there was nothing I hated more than sweat stains—except for my own voice.

Jasmine's hands wrapped around her backpack straps, and she smiled as if we were friends.

We weren't friends, not that I wouldn't want to be her friend, but, well, we just weren't.

"Is what a question?" I responded.

"You just said, 'stuttering?' as if it were a question."

"Oh."

"Yeah, so...?"

"It's not a question. I have a s-stuttering issue, but, like, a mild version. I'm not a freak."

"I didn't say you were."

"Oh."

"People bully you for that?"

I nodded.

"That's a stupid reason to bully someone," she remarked.

"I'm sure they also bully me due to my looks."

"What's wrong with your looks?"

I laughed. "Are you kidding me? Look at me."

She tilted her head slightly and narrowed her eyes. Her lips parted, and she spoke softly. "I am." Her voice was like Princess Leia, and I liked that more than I wanted to admit.

"Yeah, well, you're nicer than other people. Since we're in high school, they don't need much reason to bully me, but I guess I give them plenty."

"Assholes," she murmured.

"It doesn't b-bother me."

"It does bother you."

"You don't know what bothers me."

She smiled knowingly.

I smiled knowingly back.

*Man*, it was hot. The palms of my hands were sweaty, and I couldn't imagine what was happening in my armpits. She was pretty and talking to me in a non-bullying way. People as pretty as Jasmine never talked to people as awkward as me in a non-bullying way. I was really confused, and every person we passed seemed just as baffled as they saw the two of us speaking.

I held my arms out a bit to air out my pits.

"You play the saxophone?" she asked, still walking backward.

"Yes?"

She smirked. "Is that a question?"

I broke my stare away from her and cleared my throat. "No. I mean, y-y—" I blinked my eyes shut and took a breath. "Yes, I play the saxophone. How did you know?"

"I saw you performing on the corner of Frenchmen Street."

"Oh."

"Do you perform down there a lot?"

"I didn't used to, but my Uncle TJ sa-said I should every Saturday. So, now I have to since he's my music instructor."

"Why does he make you do that?"

"Because he said music shouldn't live in a basement. It's meant to be spread around to fix people's scars or something. I hate doing it."

"Well, you're probably alone in that hatred." She paused her steps and looked at me with the sincerest eyes. "You're the best musician I've ever heard."

I didn't have a clue what to say, so I just stood there staring at her like an insane person.

"Elliott?"

"Yes?"

"You're staring at me, and it's a bit weird now," she stated, combing her dark hair behind her ear.

"Oh, sorry, but, well, thank you?" I shook my head a little and moved my stare to the floor. "I mean, thank you...for the compliment. Thank you."

"You're welcome?" She winked before she turned away to talk to someone else, because other than being ridiculously pretty, smart, and kind, Jasmine was popular. I'd never seen someone become so popular as fast as she had.

Jasmine Greene had walked into Canon High School as if she owned it. She'd started a few weeks into first semester, but that hadn't stopped her from acting as if the whole student body deserved to bow down to her, and bow down they did. As a junior, she had the popularity of a senior. She excelled at everything she took part in, from arts and crafts to algebra.

I hadn't even known she knew I existed, even though I knew all about her. I was still wildly confused, though. Why was she being so nice to me?

The moment she started talking to someone else, I let out the heaviest sigh of my life.

"Eli," a familiar voice said, and the nickname indicated that it was a safe voice to hear. I turned around to see my older sister, Katie, standing behind me with a concerned look on her face. Her stare moved down the hallway to Jasmine. "Are you okay?"

"Yes, why?"

"You were talking to that new girl, Jasmine."

"Yeah, so?"

Katie cleared her throat and stood up a bit taller with her books in her hands. "What were you talking about? I just don't understand why she'd be talking to you."

"Wow, thanks," I said wryly.

She rolled her eyes. "I didn't mean it like that, Eli. You're just better than those people."

"Those people?"

"Ya know, the Chanel bag girls—the popular kids."

"You wanted a bag like that last year."

"I know, but that's not that same, and I don't care about things like that anymore. Plus, I saw her talking to Todd Clause, too, ya know, and if he's her type—"

"Maybe I'm her type too," I joked, puffing out my chest. "I am pretty..." I blinked my eyes shut tight. *Muscular—just say it. The word is muscular.* My throat tightened, knowing the word I wanted to escape from my mouth and trying my hardest to say it. "I think I'm pretty..." Nothing. I choked on the air and my mind raced, trying to think of another word, a synonym that could work in place of muscular. Anything...anything would work, but once I started panicking, words were impossible to find. I took deep breaths and tried to push out the word. "I'm pretty..." But it didn't work. It hardly ever did. "I think I'm pretty beefy," I finally choked out, my ears burning from the struggle, my face bright red.

"Beefy?" Katie giggled. "Elliott, you're as beefy as a chicken wing."

I laughed as my face started to cool down from the pressure of trying to pronounce a simple word.

My sister never mentioned my stuttering, never made me feel bad about it. Normally she just whistled or hummed to herself and patiently waited for me to finish. Sometimes she'd stop looking at me, because she knew having someone stare at me made it more difficult. She never tried to guess the word I was trying to say, either, because she could tell how much worse that made the situation.

Katie grimaced and nudged me in the arm. "Look, I know with Jason off in Nebraska for the year, you've been a bit lonelier..."

"I'm not lonely," I lied, and Katie knew it was a lie, too. My best friend Jason had moved to Nebraska for the year, and with him gone, I really had no one to talk to except for my sister.

I hated that.

I hated how hard it was to be alone all the time.

"Just be careful," Katie warned, like the overprotective sister she was. "I don't want you to get hurt, that's all." She gave me a smile before walking off. Katie might've been my sister, but she didn't have the same social struggles as me. She was beautiful, like Mom, and well-spoken like her, too.

Her choice not to hang out with the popular kids was due to an incident that happened the previous year. Before that, she was one of them, the cool ones, but now she kept to herself. She didn't care much. At least I didn't think she did. She always said there were more important things than being popular in high school.

She had better things to do, like focusing on where she'd be going to college next year.

She'd never admit it, but one of her full-time jobs was making sure I was okay. Part of me hated her for watching over me the way she did, but mostly I was thankful to have a sister as caring as her. She and my mom were above and beyond the definition of love. Yeah, high school sucked, but at least I knew when I went home, I'd be okay.

Every night, the three of us ate dinner together at the dining room table. Mom always cooked, too. We never ate takeout. She'd learned to cook from Grandma, and she always went the extra mile. She said comfort-food and conversation were staples of her childhood, and she wanted it to be the same for us, too.

"How was school?" Mom asked, setting a roasted chicken on the table next to all the side dishes she'd prepared. Dinner always felt like a feast. Even though we didn't have much, we always had food on our plates, which was more than some people could say.

"It was good," Katie said, scooping up some mashed potatoes and placing them on her plate. "Brooke has a new boyfriend." Brooke was Katie's old best friend, and after the incident, they never talked. Katie said she didn't mind, but she sure seemed to still know a lot about the ins and outs of Brooke's life.

"Again?" Mom rolled her eyes, sitting down in her seat. "Didn't she just start dating Trey?"

"Travis," Katie corrected. "Trey was three boyfriends back, but now she's with Tyler."

"She sure likes the letter T," I said with a grin.

"She likes all letters if they're attached to a boy's name." Katie laughed. "But ya know, she likes making bad decisions."

"As long as you're not following her bad decisions," Mom said.

"Trust me, Mom, I have no time for high school boys. They are so last year. I'm waiting until college to even consider dating."

"Well, if you ever become friends with Brooke again and she's interested in the le-letter E, keep my name in mind," I joked, biting into my chicken leg.

Mom raised an eyebrow at me. "Someone's in a good mood."

"I had a good day." I witnessed it happen—Mom's eyes watering over. "Don't cry, Ma," I groaned.

"I'm not gonna cry," she lied, wiping her eyes. My mother was an emotional lady. "I just haven't heard you say you had a good day in a long, long time."

"Every day is fine," I told her.

"Yeah, but not *good*. It's just..." She sniffled and kept wiping at her teary eyes. She gave me a smile, the kind that made me feel her love. "I'm just really happy you had a good day."

I shrugged my shoulders and continued to eat.

Mom wasn't over it, though. She crossed her arms and rested them on the table, staring at me with stars in her eyes. "Any reason?" she wondered out loud. "For the good day?"

"Nope," I replied.

"He spoke to a girl," Katie blabbed.

"Katie!" I hissed.

"Eli!" she hissed back.

"A girl?!" Mom hissed with her own excitement. "Tell me more."

"It's nothing," I told her.

"He's right, it's nothing. She's not right for him," Katie agreed.

"Why is that?" I asked, somewhat offended. "Because she's popular and cool and I'm not?"

Katie's eyes grew gloomy. "No, Eli, of course not. It's just that girls like her are a dime a dozen, and you deserve something with more meaning, someone who understands you more."

"Maybe she does understand me."

"Maybe, but there's a much bigger chance she doesn't," Katie argued.

Mom kept smiling at the exchange between my sister and me. She always found it comedic the way Katie and I talked things out. She just stood by as a mediator most times. "Well, you know what I think?"

"What's that?" I replied.

"I think you had a good day today," she told me. "And anything that helps you have a good day is fine by me."

"But, Mom, you don't know what this girl is like. She walks around with her makeup and designer bags and—" Katie started, but Mom shut her down with a calm hand raised in the air.

"I'm sorry, Katie, did you just judge someone based on their possessions?" Mom questioned, her stare growing stern. "Because I'm pretty sure judging someone based on what they have is just as awful as judging someone for what they don't have. How would you like to be judged for your non-designer bags?"

Katie grumbled and lowered her head. "Sorry, Mom."

"Look, I get it. You love your brother and don't want him to get hurt, but you're not always going to be around to protect him. He has to make his own choices, and I think that's all there is to say about it."

Katie apologized again then went back to eating, and I did my best to hold my smile inside.

I loved when Queen Mom overruled Princess Katie.

And I kind of loved having a good day, too.

## Chapter Four

### Jasmine

When Saturday night came around, I dreaded going to Todd's party. I waited until Mama went to bartend to sneak out. She'd told me to practice my vocals, and truthfully, I would've rather done that than go to Todd's.

There was nothing I liked about the idea of going to his house and being surrounded by drunks. Plus, I knew Todd was just trying to get in my pants, and I had no interest in that whatsoever, but I also couldn't stand by and let him keep bullying Elliott.

If all it took was me showing up at his stupid party for him to leave Elliott alone, then I'd make my presence known.

But first, I made a pit stop.

Elliott was already performing on the corner when I arrived. He had a newsboy hat sitting on top of his head, and he wore a white button-down shirt with black suspenders attached to his pants. He looked exactly how a jazz musician should, and he sounded even better. He was so nervous at all points in his life, except for when that saxophone was in his hands. When Elliott had his music, his soul was free. Because of jazz, Elliott was able to breathe.

It was insane what his music did to me, how it made me want to be happy and sad all at once. Some of his songs were upbeat, and sometimes he'd even dance a bit as he played.

Other songs...they cried.

I could feel the sadness in them, and I could see Elliott being affected by them. There were more people standing around watching him this time, more individuals tossing change into his instrument case. It was as if he was building his own little fanbase.

And I was the leader of the pack.

There was no way I could walk away until he finished his last note. When he finished, I just wanted more, and so did everyone else.

"Encore!" a few shouted, and Elliott lowered his brows, appearing to be deep in thought.

"I-I-I can do one more?" he told everyone, earning a round of cheers.

As his fingers danced across the keys on his saxophone and he began to blow, my heart tightened. The sounds, they were familiar, but I didn't recognize them at first. As he played, tears formed in my eyes, and I listened to him, wanting nothing more than to move in closer. I wanted to feel his energy, his heartbeats as he played.

As the tears fell down my cheeks, I prayed for him to never stop playing, but still, eventually he finished.

As he started packing up, he returned to his nervous self, and this time, I wasn't going to miss my opportunity.

"You were perfect again," I said, smiling his way.

When he looked up, his eyes darted, paused, then shifted again before they settled on me. His glasses were sliding down his nose, and he used his index finger to adjust them. "You came to watch me?"

I nodded. "I told you, you're the best musician I've ever heard."

His lips parted to speak, but he didn't say anything.

I shifted around in my shoes, unsure what to say but needing to say something...anything. "You said your uncle taught you to play?"

"Yeah. Well, he's more of a family friend, but he's al-always been an uncle to me. He's beyond talented in everything he does."

"Tell him I said job well done."

Elliott smiled, and I felt it in my own cheeks.

"I better get going," he told me, placing his saxophone in the case and locking it.

"Oh, well, okay." I bit my bottom lip. "Have a good night."

He nodded once. "You too." He lifted his case and started walking off, but then I called after him. "Yeah?"

"What was that last song you played?"

"Oh. Um..." He cleared his throat and nodded once. "It was 'The Rose' by Bette Midler. It's, like, my mom's favorite song. I learned it one year for Mother's Day." He grimaced and shook his head. "That made me sound like the biggest loser in the world."

I laughed. "Or the sweetest son in the world. I really liked it."

He shifted back and forth for a second before rubbing the back of his neck. "Okay, well...bye."

In a flash, he hurried off.

*What a strange boy.*

"Well, look what the cat dragged in," Todd said the moment I showed up at his house. "I thought you were gonna stand me up."

I gave him a forced smile as he walked over and wrapped his arm around my waist. "I told you I'd show up, didn't I?"

"Of course. Come on in. Make yourself at home. Mi casa es su casa." He winked. "Let me give you a tour."

I sighed but agreed as he took me around his house, only really showing me one area—his bedroom.

"This is where the magic happens," he declared.

"Do you pull a rabbit out of a hat?" I joked.

"No, but I do have a solid-sized carrot if you're interested in seeing it," he replied, making my skin crawl.

"Do you think you could get me a drink?" I asked, trying to change the subject.

He nodded and hurried off, leaving me to stand in the living room. There were a ton of people at the party, all wasted and high. I wanted to be neither of those things. I wanted to be at home with my music.

If I had to choose between people or music, music would always win.

"Here you go," Todd said, handing me a beer. I pretended to sip it, and when his hand landed on my butt, I jumped, spilling the drink all over my shirt. "Whoa! Easy there, girl. I know I have a way of getting girls wet, but we can ease into that."

"I'm sorry. I think I'm actually gonna head out," I told him, my nerves building. I was out of my element. I loved high school, but these were not my people.

"You legit just got here. How about we play a game of spin the bottle?" he offered. "A few already have a game going in the kitchen."

"No, sorry. I'm just tired."

"That's too bad," he replied with a frown. "I just hope Boney Bones doesn't have too rough of a Monday."

I stood up straighter. "What's that supposed to mean?"

"I'm not stupid, Jasmine. I know you only agreed to come because you felt bad for that loser. I'll admit, it's sexy as fuck that you care about those in need, but I don't know how much I can leave him alone if you're only gonna hang out for five minutes."

I was taken aback by his comment. "Is that a threat?"

"What? No way." He laughed, moving in closer to whisper near my ear. "It's a promise. A few rounds of spin the bottle, and Boney Bones will make it to see Tuesday."

"And if I don't play?"

"Well, let's just say things could get a whole lot worse for Elliott Adams."

I swallowed hard, fighting the urge to slug Todd right in his privates. I hated him more than words could express. I wanted nothing to do with him and his stupid games, but if kissing a few boys meant Elliott wouldn't be pushed around as much, I'd spin a freaking bottle.

On Monday, my heart dropped when I saw Todd and his followers shoving Elliott around. I rushed over and pushed Todd. "What the heck are you doing?" I barked. I'd stayed at his stupid party on Saturday. I'd done things I didn't want to do just so this wouldn't happen to Elliott.

"You said you would leave him alone," I scowled at Todd.

He licked his lips and combed his hands through his hair. "Did I? I don't remember. Maybe you should've stayed longer, or perhaps next Saturday you'll use tongue."

I wanted to vomit as I watched him and his goons walk off. I hurried over to Elliott and helped him up.

"Are you okay?"

He wiped his forehead and pushed his glasses up his nose. "I'm sorry," he said, leaving me bewildered.

"What? You did nothing wrong. Those guys are jerks."

"Yeah, well, I'm u-used to it."

"Just because you're used to it, that doesn't make it right."

He nodded once, and his embarrassment was clear in his stare. "I be-better get to class." With that, he walked off.

*Poor guy.*

As I went to my locker to get the books for my next class, a girl snapped at me. "What's your angle, huh?" she barked, barging up to my locker.

I raised an eyebrow, at how forward she was being as she crossed her arms and glared my way.

"Excuse me?"

"I said what's your angle? Is it some kind of mean prank where the pretty girl pretends to like the quiet boy and then the popular kids break his heart?"

"What are you talking about?"

"I'm talking about my brother, Elliott."

*Oh...*

"I didn't know he had a sister."

"Yeah, well, now you do. I'm Katie, and you're the girl who's using my brother," she replied.

"What? No. Elliott is my—"

"Don't say friend, you don't know him," she sneered, cutting me off. "People like you don't befriend people like my brother."

"People like me? What's that supposed to mean?"

She nodded to my purse. "You have a Chanel handbag on your arm. You obviously have money and you can have any guy you want looking your way."

I held my bag close to my side and twitched a little. It had been a gift that Ray found at a secondhand shop last Christmas. "You don't know me, and the fact that you're judging me based on a purse shows exactly how much you don't know."

She sighed and chewed on her bottom lip as she narrowed her stare. "Come here."

"Where?"

"Jesus, will you just follow me?" She marched off toward the court-yard. We stepped outside into the hot New Orleans air and she pointed to the flag pole. "Last year, some kids handcuffed Elliott to the flag-pole, sprayed silly string at him, and cracked eggs on his head. Two months before you got here, they cornered him in the locker room and attacked him with water balloons."

"That's awful."

She grimaced. "You have no clue. Some of the balloons were filled with piss."

I gasped, disgusted and shocked by how low some of my class-mates could go. "What fucking assholes!" I hissed, my hand clasped to my chest.

Katie arched an eyebrow. "Why are you talking to him?"

My lips parted and I paused, trying to figure out the best way to an-swer. How could I express to her what I hadn't even realized yet? How could I make her understand the feelings racing through my gut? How could words sum up what Elliott did to my heart and mind?

"Well?" she asked, her foot twitching against the cement.

"Because I heard his music. I heard his music last weekend, and then when I listened to him play…I don't know…" I swallowed hard. "It's like, for the first time in a long time, I didn't feel alone."

Katie's hard glare softened. "My mom was right—you're more than the Chanel bag."

"Wait, you've talked to your mom about me?" *Because that's not weird at all.*

"Not the point. The point is…" Her voice was low and faded away. Everything about her softened. She was the complete opposite of who she'd been when she first approached me. "I don't mean to judge, but I've seen my brother go through more wars than anyone ever deserves to go through. I'm just very protective of him."

"No, I get it. I hate that he's going through so many of his own wars."

"His wars? No. It all started years ago when he went to war for my mom and me. After that, he never really had a chance to stop."

"You love him."

"He's the best little brother in the history of little brothers."

"He's not like most people. He's...innocent."

"I know. It's strange, isn't it? How someone who has been through so much shit can still be so far from jaded. Can you just do me a favor?"

"Sure."

"Keep listening to his music."

"Of course." She started to walk away, and I called after her. "Thank you—for going to war for him."

"We're family," she whispered. "We take care of one another."

*Family. We take care of one another.*

I loved that.

That afternoon as I walked to my science class I found Elliott standing at his locker. The moment I saw him, my heart began pounding against my ribcage. I couldn't get the images out of my head—the water balloons, the silly string, or the handcuffs.

Why would anyone treat someone as kind as him in such an ugly way? It made no sense.

"Elliott!" I hollered, hurrying over to him.

"Hey," he said timidly.

I wanted nothing more than to wrap my arms around him and hold him close to me. I wanted nothing more than to pull him close and let him know that all the jerks that picked on him were nothing more than trash themselves. I wanted to wrap my arms around him and apologize for a world that didn't treat him right for stupid reasons.

But, his space was his, and so, I waited.

"I have a question," I said softly, butterflies swarming in my gut.

"I have an answer?" he replied, but in the form of a question—because he was Elliott, and he answered things with question marks.

"Can I hug you?"

He stood up tall, and cleared his throat. Sweat formed on his forehead. "What?"

"I said, can I hug you?"

He grimaced and stepped backward. "My sister was r-r-right," he murmured.

"What?"

"She said you were mo-mocking me, and she was right."

"No, Elliott, that's not it. I just..."

"Just what?"

My hands started shaking, and I couldn't find the words for what I needed to express. "Because..." I twitched, feeling more nervous. "Well, because...because..." My eyes glassed over, looking at the skinny boy who seemed so fragile. "Because..." My voice trembled, and Elliott narrowed his eyes.

"Jasmine?" he asked.

"Yes?"

"Breathe."

"I-I am."

"You're not. Trust me, I know what it's like not to br-breathe."

I took a deep breath, and Elliott's eyes stayed locked with mine. "I saw your sister, and she told me what the kids did to you before, and I just hate them, you know? And I hate that... I mean, you're just so nice! And you keep to yourself and...and...and—"

"Jasmine?"

"Yes, Elliott?" I asked, my eyes filling up as I became shakier.

"Can I hug you?"

I laughed shyly and wiped away the few tears that fell from my eyes. "But why?"

He gave me a smile that felt so huge, so warm, like a home I'd never known existed. "Because I don't want you to cry."

He wrapped his arms around me and held on tight. It was funny how it had worked out. When I'd approached him, I'd been determined to comfort him for his past pain, but somehow the situation had been reversed. As Elliott held me, he was healing the parts of me I always pretended weren't broken. When his skin touched mine, we melted together and all my cracks were covered with temporary bandages.

And then he whispered, "You'll be okay."

How had he known?

How had he known my biggest fear was that I wouldn't be okay?

"You know what?" he whispered, his mouth close to my ear as he held me tight.

"What?"

"You never have to ask me for a hug, okay?"

I sighed and fell a little more into him. "Okay."

"Jasmine?" he whispered one more time.

"Yes, Elliott?"

"Does this mean we're friends?"

I laughed and nodded against his shoulder. "This means we're friends."

# Chapter Five

## Elliott

Every Saturday night, Jasmine showed up to listen to my performance. Knowing she was there made me want to be better, to put on the best show I could, and every time I finished, she'd tell me it was the best show I'd ever had.

She didn't know how much that meant to me.

Afterward, she always hurried off and she never really said where she was heading, which was fine. I already knew, since every Monday morning I'd overhear the popular kids talking about the party at Todd's house.

I didn't care, though, because at least she showed up to hear me.

"Hey, Jasmine," I called out at the end of my performance one night. My adrenaline was still racing through my body from my best show to date, and I felt more confident than I ever had in my entire life. If I was ever going to ask her the question I'd wanted to ask for weeks, this was the time. It was now or never.

She turned around with a big smile on her face. "Yes, Elliott?"

"Do you..." I cleared my throat. "I mean, maybe next week, be-before my show...do you want to like, meet at my house and come down here together?" I asked, one hundred percent prepared for rejection. "We can get food?"

She kept smiling. "Is that a question?"

I snickered. "Maybe?"

She walked over to me and held her hand out. "Give me your cell phone."

I complied, and she typed in her phone number then handed it back to me. "I've always wanted to go to Dat Dog."

"Okay. Cool. So, it's a date." I panicked at my own words. "I mean, like, a friends date—like, friends. Just two friends eating wieners." *Nope. Just stop talking.* "Okay, well...bye."

She laughed. "I'll see you at school, Elliott."

And she did see me at school. She didn't only see me, she talked to me in the hallways, almost as if she wasn't embarrassed to be seen with me. She laughed with me too, which was nice, because laughing alone at things kind of took away the fun. The closer the weekend got, the more the nerves built up in my gut, and I was regretting asking her to hang out with me before my show. What would we talk about? How would I control my sweating? Was I supposed to buy her friendship flowers?

Were friendship flowers a thing?

"You're telling me you have a girlfriend?" my friend Jason said into his headset as we played video games on Saturday afternoon. We'd been best friends since elementary school, and I missed him pretty much every day. His mom had moved to Nebraska after Jason's dad cheated on her and he'd gone with her because he always chose his mom over his dad. He hated his dad more than words could say—we had that in common. Jason and I always played games over the weekend, since Mom didn't let me play too many games during the school week, and it was a good way to catch up.

"No, a girl friend. She's a girl who's a friend."

"Oh God," he groaned. "I left you alone for a minute and you went and became cooler than me."

"Not quite."

"Is she hot?"

"Like, real hot."

He groaned again. "That makes no sense, because you're so ugly," he joked.

I laughed. "So ugly, which is why she's just a girl friend, not a girl-friend."

"Well, it sounds like you like her. So, here's what you do: when you see her tonight, tell her she looks hot. Chicks love being told they look hot. Oh, and order her a salad—chicks love lettuce."

That was exactly what I wouldn't do.

Jason knew less about girls than I did, which wasn't much to begin with anyway. Everything I knew about girls, I'd learned from Katie, the biggest feminist in the world. She told me I had to respect women, because they deserved respect. She always told me Dad had never re-spected Mom, and that was why Mom had left him.

*"Just be better than him, Eli. You don't have to be the best man in the world, you just gotta do better than Dad."*

That wasn't asking for too much.

"Does she have a chubby best friend for your chubby best friend?" Jason asked.

I rolled my eyes. "I'm not even gonna answer that."

"I'd like you to know that since I moved away, I'm down two pounds and four ounces. I'm getting slim as hell. I think hanging out with you and your mom's cooking was making me fat."

That was a possibility—Mom certainly liked butter.

"Anyway," Jason said, changing the subject, because his mind was floaty. "after you tell her she's hot, make sure you have condoms. You'll need condoms."

"What? No, I won't. Anyway, I wouldn't even know where to get condoms."

"Just check your sister's tampon box. That's where my sister keeps hers," he said matter-of-factly.

I cocked an eyebrow. "Why were you in your sister's tampon box?"

"Safe sex first, questions later," Jason told me, as if he were a sex professional. If there was anything I knew for certain, it was that Jason and I were both the last two virgins in the history of virgins. Him mov-ing to Nebraska hadn't changed that fact.

"We aren't having sex!" I told him again. "She d-doesn't like me like that."

"Fine, but if you do want her to like you like that, you gotta smooth your way into her life. Oh! You know what you should do? Take her to your spot!"

"My spot?"

"You know, your spot, behind the bars, where you listen to the music."

"What? No way. It's dirty back there."

"Or romantic, if you do it the right way. I'm just saying, buddy, it's not every day a hot girl talks to guys like us. You gotta carpee damum the moment."

"You mean carpe diem?"

"God, Elliott, I'm glad to see you stopped being such a nerd since I left."

I heard Jason's mom call him and he hurried away, saying he had to get dinner. I shut off my game and went to shower to get ready for my show and non-date.

When I finished my shower and got dressed, Mom smiled my way. "If I'd known you'd up your hygiene for a girl, I would've had you dating a long time ago."

"We aren't dating," I groaned. "She's just a friend. And I always showered before."

"Always is a stretch," she joked. "Soon enough you'll be wanting cologne to impress her."

*Cologne...*

*Interesting.*

I hurried to my neighbor's house and started pounding on the door. When it opened, I looked at Uncle TJ, who was cleaning a trumpet. "Hey, Elliott, what's up? Ready for your show tonight?"

"Cologne!" I barked at him, glancing at my watch, realizing I was running behind. Jasmine was probably getting on the bus any time now to head over to my house, and I wasn't ready—physically or mentally.

"What?"

"I need cologne for tonight."

Uncle TJ gave me a sheepish grin. "What's her name?"

"What?"

"The girl?"

"There's no girl," I lied.

He just kept grinning.

"I'm seventy-five years old, son. I have lived many lifetimes, so trust me when I say, there's always a girl."

I shifted my feet around, not wanting to miss Jasmine arriving at my house. "So...?"

Uncle TJ laughed and stepped aside, letting me rush into his house. "First floor bathroom, second shelf. Take your pick."

I sprayed a few different ones into the air to see what smelled best, but they all grossed me out, so I just picked one. If girls were into that stuff, I'd suffer the pain of the bad smells.

When I walked out, Uncle TJ fanned his hand in front of his nose. "You weren't supposed to spray that much. Jesus! Come here, we gotta air you out." He stood me in front of a fan and had me flap my arms up and down to try to take off some of the scent. "What's her name?"

"There's no—" I started, but then I noticed Uncle TJ's raised eyebrow. He didn't believe me. "Jasmine."

"Jasmine." He smirked. "Do you call her Jazz?"

"No."

"You should."

*Maybe.*

"So what's the situation? Are you dating?"

"No."

"Do you want to?"

*Maybe.*

"We're just friends."

"Has she heard you play your music?"

"Yeah, she comes out every Saturday to listen."

His interest piqued. "Really? Oh, she likes you."

I shook my head. "She just li-likes the music."

Uncle TJ lowered his eyebrows, not believing me. "No woman can only fall in love with the music of jazz. She always quietly yearns for the musician behind the bars."

I gave him a you're-full-of-it stare, and he shrugged.

"Just saying. Do this: find out her favorite song, okay? Then bring it back to me, and we'll take it from there."

"What for?"

"You'll see." He shut off the fan and patted me on the back. "I think you're all good to go now. Have a great show tonight."

"Thanks."

"And, buddy?" he called after me as I was almost outside the front door. "Take it slow. There's no need to rush it. Let the harmony fall together the way it's meant to. There's nothing worse than a rushed note that could've been so perfect. Then, when you're ready, call her beautiful, not hot, not sexy, but beautiful. They love to be called beautiful."

Now that was the type of advice I was okay with receiving. Uncle TJ always knew what to say, even when I didn't know I needed to hear it.

I waited on my front porch for Jasmine to show up. When she walked up to the house, I almost jumped out of my skin upon hearing a voice from inside.

"She's cute!" Mom called from the living room window, peering out.

"Mom! Go away!" I whisper-shouted, and she shook her head.

"Okay, okay, but she's so cute, Eli!" Mom replied before disappearing—at least she disappeared far enough to keep me from seeing her. If I knew my mom, she was finding some way to creep on the current situation.

"Hi," I said to Jasmine as she walked up to me. She looked perfect, because she always looked perfect.

"Hey," she replied, sliding her hands into the back pockets of her jeans. We stood there for a second, just staring at one another with the sun beating down on us. When she smiled, I smiled. When I smiled, she smiled.

And that's about all we did.

"Um, we should get to the b-bus stop," I stuttered, nodding in the direction of the bus. She smiled and nodded in agreement. We stood on the corner, waiting for the city bus to pull up, and we had no words to exchange. The discomfort may have been in my head, but I hated the silence. Then again, I didn't have a clue what to say.

As the bus finally pulled up, I stepped to the side and nodded once, parting my lips, but no words came out. *After you. After you.*

*Say after you!*

Nothing.

My ears started burning, and my mind went searching for the words that seemed to be missing from my tongue. "Go!" I finally said, except I didn't say it—I shouted it. I shouted the word at her, and I hated it the second it left my mouth. It sounded aggressive, but it wasn't supposed to. The aggression came from my own problems, but the word flew out as if I were snapping at her.

She gave me a smile that looked like a frown, and walked onto the bus. I took a deep breath and slapped my hand against my forehead before walking on, too. I slid into the seat beside her. My eyes blinked closed and I squeezed them tight, filling my lungs with air.

"I didn't mean to yell," I said softly. "I'm sorry." I hated myself in that moment, because I'd seen the flash of panic race across her face when I shouted.

"Was it because of your stuttering?" she asked.

I nodded. "I knew what I wanted to say, but it just wouldn't come out right. So, I just blurted that out. I'm sorry."

"Can I ask you a question?"

"Sure."

"What does it feel like in your head when that happens?"

"It feels like standing in front of a freight train, unable to move."

She turned away from me and stared out the window for a second before looking back my way. "I think your voice is beautiful."

I chuckled. "There's nothing b-bbe—" No, not again. *Beautiful.* That was always a hard one. I couldn't remember a time I was actually able to get that word out. There were many words I avoided altogether, and beautiful was at the top of the list. I shut my eyes, embarrassment building up in my gut as I tried to spit out a word that wasn't going to work. Sweat gathered on my forehead, and I clawed my fingernails into the palms of my hands.

Jasmine's hand landed on my leg, making me open my eyes, and there she was, smiling my way. "Your voice is beautiful, Elliott," she repeated.

I just smiled back, half convinced I was having a weird hallucination.

The past few weeks felt like a dream I was afraid to wake up from. Things like Jasmine didn't happen to guys like me, not in reality.

Once we arrived, we grabbed a few hot dogs from Dat Dog and sat on one of the balconies, looking down on Frenchmen Street. The later it grew, the more the street came to life with people and music. I was shocked to see how fast and how much Jasmine ate.

"This is the best thing I've ever eaten," she moaned, stuffing fries into her mouth. "My mom would murder me if she knew I was eating this. How many calories do you think is in all this food?" I parted my lips, but she held up a finger to silence me. "Don't ever tell a girl how many calories are in the food she's already eaten."

"Even if she asks?"

"Especially if she asks." She tossed the last fry into her mouth.

"Jasmine?"

"Yeah?"

"Why do you hang out with me? I mean, I'm pretty much a loser."

"Don't worry, I am too."

I rolled my eyes and rubbed my hand up and down my arm. "You're not a loser, Jasmine. Everyone loves you."

She frowned and shook her head. "How can everyone love me if they don't even know who I am?"

I wasn't certain what to say to that, so I just sat there studying her. That's when I saw it in her eyes—the same kind of loneliness I felt daily. How could someone as beautiful as Jasmine ever feel alone?

"I know you look at me and probably think I have it easy, but I don't. There's a lot to me that people don't know."

"Sorry, I didn't mean—"

"It's fine, Elliott. No apologies needed. Now come on, I want to hear your music."

We went down to the street, and as I began playing, she sat on the curb and never took her eyes off me. Whenever I paused, I saw her chin was resting in her hands and she was grinning. I wondered if she knew how nervous and happy she made me, how she made me confident and fearful all at once.

I wondered if she knew I'd dreamed of someone like her, and I wondered if she'd dreamed of someone like me, too.

After I finished, she stood up and clapped, shouting, "Encore!" over and over again. Then, she rushed over and pulled me into a hug.

I loved when she hugged me because she knew she didn't have to ask permission.

"So good," she said earnestly. "So, so good."

I glanced at my watch, checking the time before looking back at her. "Do you have to go ri-right now?"

She shrugged. "Why do you ask?"

"I just wanted to show you something I think you might like."

"Lead the way."

I led, and she followed. Every now and then I'd pinch myself, just to make sure I was awake. I took her down the alleyway, and I could see her getting nervous. "I promise you're safe," I told her. She walked closer to me, wrapping her arm around mine.

I didn't complain.

We reached my spot, right in front of a dumpster that was closed, and I held my hands out. "Tada!" I said jokingly.

"What am I looking at exactly?" she questioned.

"No, it's not something you see. It's something you hear...something you feel." I rubbed my hand on the back of my neck. *Man, this is weird. I should not have listened to Jason's terrible advice.* "Normally I hop on top of the dumpster and sit, but I doubt a girl—" I didn't finish my sentence because Jasmine leaped on top of the dumpster. I followed right after her. "I can't get into the bars to listen to the music, but here, I'm able to hear everything." We sat in the alleyway behind the bars, and I asked her to close her eyes. "Tell me what you hear."

"Country music," she whispered, making me smile.

"That's from Mikey's Tavern. What else?"

"Um, is that...Billie Holiday?"

"That's coming from the rhythm and blues bar, Jo's Catz." I raised an eyebrow. "You can pick out Billie Holiday music?"

"My mom's boyfriend is a musician, so my brain is pretty much a sea of music knowledge."

"But you didn't know 'The Rose' by Bette Midler?"

Her cheeks blushed over as she started swaying her feet back and forth on the edge of the dumpster. "I might have known that."

"Why did you ask then?"

"Because...I wanted to talk to you and I didn't know what to say. I get tongue-tied with you sometimes."

"With me?"

She nodded. "You make me nervous."

"Why?"

"Because when you look at me, you actually look me in the eyes. A lot of boys at school never look me in the eyes."

"Sucks for them," I told her. "Your eyes are really pretty."

She blushed some more. "Thanks, Elliott."

"Tell me something I don't know about you."

"I sing."

I raised an eyebrow. "You do?"

"Yeah. I love soul music, but my mom thinks pop is the way for me to get famous. So, pop music it is."

"I don't get it?"

She laughed. "Is that a question?"

"Yes, kind of. I mean, i-if you like soul, why wouldn't you sing soul music?"

She shifted around in her seat and shrugged. "My mom says soul music is for a certain type of person with a certain type of skin tone, and my skin doesn't fit that description."

"Tell that to Adele," I told her.

She smiled. "Mama says Adele is one in a million, and I'm not. I can't break down the same barriers Adele did."

"No offense to your mom, but that's the st-stupidest thing I've ever heard. You don't *see* music, you *feel* it. Music doesn't see color. Music transcends all stereotypes. You'll be the greatest soul singer known to mankind."

She laughed. "You haven't even heard me sing."

"Then go ahead." I waved my hand in front of us. "Sing."

"Right now?" she asked, swallowing hard.

"Right now."

"I'm nervous," she whispered. "I don't want you to watch me."

"I'll close my eyes." That was the best way to feel music anyway.

"Promise you won't peek?"

"I promise."

I shut my eyes and waited for her to sing. When she began, it took everything inside of me to keep my eyes shut, but I kept my promise to her. She sang "Mercy Mercy Me" by Marvin Gaye, and I felt every word of it. Her voice was deep and smoky, powerful. She sounded even more beautiful than she looked. As my eyes stayed shut, I knew Jasmine was going to be a star. There were no ifs, ands, or buts about it. Some people wanted to sing, but others were destined to do it. Jasmine Greene was designed to be a star. There was no reason she shouldn't have been inside any of those bars performing her music.

There was no reason her music shouldn't have been on the radio.

As she sang, all the other sounds around us were drowned out. Her voice made everything around us disappear.

Once she finished, I opened my eyes and saw her reddened cheeks. "How bad was I?" she asked, chewing on her thumbnail.

"I'm gonna hear you on the radio and be watching you on TV someday."

She giggled and nudged me in the leg. "If I end up on TV, I want you to be in my band."

"Deal."

"What is jazz music to you?" she asked, crossing her arms. "What does it mean to you?"

"Jazz is...um, jazz is the reminder that when I'm alone, I'm not really alone."

"That's what soul music is to me," she agreed. "It's my best friend when everything else in the world is just an acquaintance."

She glanced at her watch, and then shifted around. I could tell her mind was wandering away as unease built up in her movements.

"So...are you going to Todd's party tonight?" I asked.

She sat up straight. "How did you know I was going to Todd's?"

"I hear everyone talking about his parties on Mondays."

"What do they say about me?" she asked, her voice more aggressive now.

"Uh, nothing, really. Just th-that you're there and wasted."

She shifted around in her seat, and embarrassment seeped into her eyes. "That's all they say?"

"Yeah."

"I don't drink a lot," I told him.

"It's okay if you do."

"Yeah, but I don't. It's just…at those parties, I just need…" Her fingers combed through her hair, and she glanced back my way. "Do they still mess with you, Elliott? I noticed in the hallways they don't seem to mess with you as much."

I gave her a fake smile, and she saw right through it. "It's fine," I told her. "I don't mind."

She twisted her body more my way and shook her head. "They're still messing with you?"

"Yeah, but I think they noticed it bothers you when they bother me, so…they do it when you're not around. I can handle it."

"No. *No.* God, I hate them. How bad has it been?"

"Just a few br-bruises."

"Show me."

I cringed. "But—"

Her hand landed on my forearm, and there was a sense of despair in her voice. "Please, Eli?"

She called me Eli; only Katie and Mom called me that.

I knew pulling up my shirt was going to shock her. I knew she'd have a hard time seeing what the guys did to me, but I knew it would bother her more not knowing. I untucked my shirt from my slacks and pulled it up, displaying the black and blue skin that was the result of Todd and his friends using me as a punching bag in the locker room after gym class.

"Elliott!" Jasmine cried, her hands flying to my side. She lightly touched the bruises, and I cringed a bit. "Oh my gosh. I can't believe those lying assholes!" She jumped off the dumpster and started pacing. "You have to come with me tonight."

"What?"

"You have to…I-I don't know! You have to stand up to these jerks! I get it, you don't want to fight back, but they aren't going to stop because they think you won't stand up to them."

"I-I d-don't think that's a good idea."

"No, we have to." She grew more and more emotional as she paced. "There is nothing I can do to stop them from hurting you. I've tried everything, but maybe if you stand up to them—if *we* stand up to them, we can win. I know we can. You and I can be, like...the two musketeers. All for one and one for all, ya know?"

"I..."

"Please. I just...please."

I didn't know how to say no to her eyes. I didn't know why the bullying bothered her more than it bothered me, but it did. There was no way I could say no to her as she sat on the verge of tears. I hopped off the dumpster and nodded once. "Okay. Let's go."

# Chapter Six

## Elliott

"**Y**ou should go in without me," I told Jasmine, my throat tightening as nerves swelled in my gut.

"What? No way!" she replied, pulling me by my forearm. "The only reason I'm even a little okay with being here is because you're with me. I hate everything about these parties."

"Then why have you been coming every weekend?"

She lowered her stare for a moment before glancing my way. Her eyes were filled with guilt, and I realized exactly why she was standing there on Todd's porch, about to enter his house.

*Because of me.*

"They said they'd stop bullying you if I came to parties."

I grimaced and stuffed my hands into my pockets. "Because that's not embarrassing at all."

"Elliott..."

"You don't have to stick up for me, you know. I can handle them."

She shook her head. "But you shouldn't have to."

"But I do. I've dealt with people like them my whole life. It's not your j-job to protect me, and trust me, having a girl stand up for me isn't going to help any. My sister has been doing the same thing for years now and nothing has changed. Coming here was a bad idea."

"Just come with me," she begged, clasping her hands together. "We can have fun and mock them for mocking us, and then you can stand up for yourself, and I'll stand up for you. It'll be perfect."

I bit the inside of my cheek and stared at the flickering porch light.

"Please, Elliott?" she begged. "Think of it this way: you going into this party isn't me protecting you, it's *you* protecting *me*."

"You're lying."

"I'm not."

I stood still, unable to look away from the flickering light. *Please, stop with the flickers.*

"Eli," Jasmine said softly, her voice low and filled with care. "Please."

Her hand landed on my forearm, and my stare moved from the lights to her fingers. My chest...it tightened even more. My heart...it sped up. Jasmine Greene was touching me, begging me to be her plus-one to a house party I hadn't been invited to and never would be invited to, and I couldn't even build up the courage to walk her inside.

"Just five minutes," I told her with a hitch in my voice. "I just need five minutes before I can walk inside."

"I'll wait with you."

"No," I snapped. She frowned, and I felt awful. I just didn't need her to be there to watch my panic attack take place. I didn't need to give her any more reasons to feel sorry for me. I was already embarrassed enough. "I mean, I need five minutes to breathe a little. I need a moment by myself." I added a smile at the end to make her smile too.

"Promise you'll come in?"

"I promise."

She nodded in understanding, even though I was one of the hardest people to ever understand. "Okay. I'll get us some drinks."

"Okay."

Her hand finally left my forearm and she reached for the door. But before she stepped foot inside, she turned back to me. "Elliott?"

"Yes?"

"I don't feel sorry for you. Sometimes you look at me like you think I feel sorry for you, and I just want you to know that I don't. I think you're great the way you are."

"I'm a little messed up," I told her, placing my hands on the back of my neck.

"I know—that's why I like you." She smiled. It was the kind of smile that made my armpits sweat. "Because I'm a little messed up, too."

The second she walked inside, I hurried off the porch. I reached into my pocket and pulled out my iPod. Music always helped me before anything terrifying. Whenever I forgot to breathe, I'd put my earbuds in and lose myself in my favorite sounds: jazz music.

Duke Ellington.

Charlie Parker.

Ella Fitzgerald.

So many great legends lived inside of my iPod, so many mind-blowing talents.

My uncle TJ had taught my sister and me all about the greatest jazz musicians in the world. I was almost certain 'Miles' and 'Davis' had been my first two words, and they'd be the last two words I'd say on my way out.

Music was my therapy, and after a few songs, I always felt stronger. It was crazy how jazz fixed the broken pieces of me every time, how the sounds always took me back to a safe place in my soul.

Life was hard sometimes, but maybe God gave us music as his apology.

I looked around Todd's home. He came from money, and the acres and acres of land were signs of his wealth. We obviously lived very different lives. To the left were orchard fields, and to the right, horse stables. Todd often tried to impress the girls at school by telling them about all the horses his family had. The thing Todd did best was show off—he was a professional at doing so.

I walked toward the stables, because animals often brought me more peace of mind than any human ever could. As I opened the stable door, I froze. Todd and three of his idiot friends were sitting there drinking beers with lighters and whips in their hands. They were standing in one of the stalls with a horse, cussing and hitting her with the whips, making her whimper in pain.

"What a dumb bitch," Ted Jones said, laughing as he flickered the lighter by the horse's face. "I should set part of her tail on fire," he mocked.

"Dude, I'll give you fifty bucks if you do it," Keaton said, egging him on.

"Shit, I'll give you fifty, too," Todd said with a laugh.

As Ted grew closer and closer to the horse's tail, panic built more and more in my chest. I knew these guys were assholes, but I hadn't realized just how much until I listened to the horse whimper and cry in pain.

"S-s-s-stop!" I hollered, my voice trembling as I stared wide-eyed at the guys.

It happened immediately—the attention shifting from the horse to me.

My stomach dropped.

My armpits sweated.

But I didn't regret speaking up, not if it meant helping the defenseless animal.

"Who invited fucking Bones?" Todd hissed.

My chest tightened, and I tried my best to avoid all eye contact. *Be invisible.* I hated anyone's attention on me. I hated how I felt them judging, staring, belittling me for the simple fact that I looked the way I did.

"Leave that horse alone," I said timidly. I was always so timid; I hated it.

They hurried over to me and started shoving me around, just like they always did.

"Who said that you could come to my place, freak? Huh?" Todd barked.

"J-J-Jasmine said I could come with her?" I answered, unintentionally saying it as a question.

"Jasmine?" Ted questioned. "That bitch isn't your friend. She probably brought you here for us to have a good laugh."

"No. She's my friend," I argued.

"Oh?" Todd started walking toward me and cocked an eyebrow. "What, do you have a crush on her or something, Bones?" He laughed, and all the others joined in with him. "Dude, you think you have a shot with someone as hot as her? Come on, man. You couldn't even get any ugly pussy if you tried, let alone a hot one like her."

I swallowed hard.

*Pussy.*

I hated that word.

I hated how they talked about girls. My sister would've hated how they talked about girls, too. My father, he wouldn't have cared. They reminded me of him sometimes—most times, really, so heartless, cold, and angry for no real reason.

I hated my father.

I hated them, too.

"Listen, Bones, let me do you a favor." Todd wrapped his arm around me and gave me a sheepish grin. "I'm gonna go inside and fuck the living hell out of Jasmine Greene. I'm going to screw her until she can't walk straight. I'm going to screw her until she stutters like your dumb ass. Shit, we've all been screwing her for weeks now, the damn whore. Then I'm going to let her tell you to your face how you're so far from her type. It will be a great lesson in teaching you to stay on your level and not try to hang out with the big dogs on campus. I'm going to make the bitch my bitch."

My hands formed fists and I stood up a bit taller. "She's not a b-b-*bitch*!" I hollered.

I didn't realize what had happened until the stinging set in. I didn't notice my reaction until my fist came back down and I saw the blood on my knuckles. I hadn't known I had it in me.

"Motherfucker!" Todd shouted, stumbling backward, holding his hand over his nose. "He fucking broke my nose! I'm going to ruin you," he barked.

"Get him!" Ted hollered, and three of the guys grabbed me by the arms and started dragging me across the stable. I tried my best to get out of their grips, but I wasn't strong enough.

They were stronger. They were always stronger.

*I'm not strong enough.*

*I'm not strong enough.*

"Toss him into one of the stalls!" Todd ordered, blood gushing down his face. "Your life is about to be a living hell, Bones!"

Ted pushed me into a stall and I slammed against the ground, terrifying the horse that was in it. *I'm sorry.* I stumbled to my feet, but before I could get my footing, they locked me inside.

*No.*

I hated being locked in places. I hated having no way out. I couldn't breathe. I couldn't, I couldn't...

"Let m-me out!" I yelled.

"No fucking way," Todd snapped. "You did this shit to yourself." He stood tall for a moment and dropped his hands down, revealing a wicked grin. "Speaking of shit..." *Oh no.* "Boys, get those shovels and come over here."

"Wait," I cried, the adrenaline I'd had coursing through me seconds before completely gone. "Don't," I begged.

They didn't listen and were quick to grab the shovels.

"Now go into the other horse stalls and collect all the shit," he ordered his followers.

They did as he said, and I backed into the corner of the stable, knowing what was coming next. They collected so much horse crap and began slinging it over at me, hitting me with shit continually. They laughed as I covered my face with the palms of my hands. It only went on for a few minutes, but I swore it felt like years.

It was everywhere. I felt it. I tasted it. I gagged repeatedly, unable to breathe. Wet, mushy, and disgusting...in my hair, in my shoes, down my shirt. I curled myself into a ball and tried my best not to breathe in the disgusting smells that engulfed me.

Todd slammed his hands against the locked door and shouted, "That will tuh-tuh-teach you to not get in my way ever again, you little prick. Now, I'm going to go fuck Jasmine, but don't worry—I'll let her know you had to leave and get back to being a nobody."

They left me there alone after shutting off the lights.

I tried to stand up, but I slipped in the horse poop.

I couldn't breathe.

I couldn't move.

I couldn't do anything at all.

So, I just sat there, quiet, alone, and broken.

## Chapter Seven

### Jasmine

"You're finally here," Todd said, walking up to me on his front porch. I'd been standing there for a few minutes, waiting for any signs of Elliott. Todd gave me his smug smirk and wrapped his arm around my shoulders. "How about I give you a good reason to stay a bit longer?"

"What happened to your nose?" I asked, stunned by his bloody face.

"Don't worry about it. How about we go inside and get situated?"

I rolled my eyes. "I'm actually waiting for a friend," I replied, sliding his hand off me.

"Boney Bones?" he asked.

"Elliott," I corrected. "What happened to your face?" I asked again.

He ignored my question. "You're joking, right? About Bones?" Todd laughed, tossing his hands up in confusion. He narrowed his eyes and said, "That dude's a fucking joke, so you must be kidding."

My eyes moved over to his group of friends coming out of the stable, and I stood up a bit taller. "Elliott's my friend."

"Then you're stupid. I'll be your friend," he said suggestively, wrapping his arms around me. I took a breath, feeling the unease caused by Todd's touch on my body, feeling uncomfortable due to his proximity, feeling a little dash of fear.

"Don't," I whispered, pushing him away.

"Stop acting like you don't want it. I know girls like you."

"Girls like me?" I huffed, still trying to claw his hands off my skin. The moment I could rip myself away, I hurried down the steps as his followers laughed.

"Yeah, girls like you—easy whores," Todd hollered, making my skin crawl. "Remember last week when your lips were wrapped around my cock?" he asked. "Easy."

*I'm not a whore, I'm not a whore...*

My mind was fogged, and one of Todd's followers looked my way. "Everyone knows you love screwing around with guys, Hollywood."

"Leave me alone." I started walking away, unsure where I was heading, unsure what had happened to Elliott.

"You just committed social suicide," Todd barked. "You might as well go hang out with that fucking loser in the stable."

I paused. "What did you do to him?"

The guys started laughing, and Todd raced his blood-tinted hands through his hair. "Let's just say he got himself into a shitty situation."

My hands balled into fists, and I started back in Todd's direction. "If you hurt him—"

"He hurt himself by being a little bitch. Come on, guys. Let's go find some chicks without herpes."

*Assholes.*

I darted toward the stable, unsure what I would find when I entered. As I opened the door, my stomach formed knots and I hurried inside, checking each area in search of Elliott. The smell of horse poop was strong, and I covered my nose with my T-shirt, trying not to gag.

"Eli?" I whispered, my voice low as I saw him balled up in the corner. He hadn't looked up once and was rocking back and forth with his head tucked between his knees. I hurried over to the gate and unlocked it. "Oh my God..." I started in his direction, and he stood quickly, completely thrown off. As he turned around, he flinched, as if he was terrified it was someone else coming into the space. His eyes were wide, and I noted his earbuds were in.

When he realized I wasn't one of the jerks, his shoulders sagged. Then, the embarrassment set in.

"It's okay," I told him, taking a step in his direction.

"No!" he ordered, holding both hands up. "Don't."

I stood still and watched him gag, spitting up. When he was done, he blinked hard and walked past me, hurrying outside. I followed after him.

"Elliott!" I called.

He paced back and forth. "I sh-sh-shouldn't have come! I shouldn't h-have come!" he stuttered over and over, his hands shaking.

"We just need to get you cleaned up," I said calmly, my hands up in an attempt to comfort him. "It's okay..."

"There's *shit* in my *mouth*!" he shouted, his anger strong. Then, he took a breath and turned my way. His eyes were filled with sadness and apologies. "I'm s-sorry I c-cussed at you."

*Oh, Elliott.*

It was my fault. I should've never forced him to come to the party. I should've never pushed him into a situation like this, but I hadn't had a clue anything like this would happen. I mostly figured he'd have a chance to stand up to the bullies and I'd be there to back him up, but I wasn't. I wasn't there for him when he needed me the most. He had trusted me, and I'd let him down.

"I c-can't go home, not like this. I can't go home. I can't. My sister, my mom...I told them it was better. I told them the bullying stopped. I-I-I told..." His voice shook and shook as my gut twisted in knots.

"Come to my place," I told him.

He paused his pacing. "What?"

"You can come to my place and shower. I can give you some of my mom's boyfriend's clothes. Your family won't even know what happened, I promise."

"But your family will."

I shook my head. "No. Ray took my mom to a concert and then to network afterward. They'll be out all night. No one's home."

He grimaced. "You'll have to smell me the whole way there."

I gave him a tiny smile. "I'd rather walk next to a poop-smelling Elliott than ever look at a poop-looking Todd again."

He gave me a small grin back. I walked over to him, took the sleeve of my shirt to wipe his face clean.

"Now you're covered in it, too," he told me.

"All for one and one for all, right?" I joked, shrugging.

"Yeah." He nodded. "All for one, and one for all," he agreed.

We started walking beside each other, and for a few blocks, we stayed quiet. I was surprised once we hit the bus stop that the bus driver even let us get on, but in a city like New Orleans, I was almost certain he'd seen and smelled stranger things.

"By the way, what happened to Todd's nose?"

"I broke it," Elliott said matter-of-factly.

"What? How? Why?"

He shrugged before turning to look out the window. "He called you a bad name."

"What was it?"

"It doesn't matter."

"Eli," I started.

He turned my way and locked his hazel eyes with my browns. "Jazz..." He shook his head. "It wasn't true."

I swallowed hard, a big part of me certain Todd's words held some form of truth.

Elliott saw it in me—my fear. He kept shaking his head and whispered, "I don't feel sorry for you. Sometimes you look at me like you think I feel sorry for you, and I want you to know I don't. I think you're perfect the way you are."

I quietly laughed at him repeating the words I'd told him earlier. A few tears rolled down my cheeks. "I'm a little messed up."

"I know." He nodded. "That's why I like you."

He went back to staring out the window, and I kept staring at him. And there it was.

So small, so tiny, so real.

*Love.*

It wasn't love, but it was the beginning of it.

I knew I was young, and I knew it was stupid, but in that moment, I began to fall in love with the quiet boy who quietly cared for me. The boy who was scared and still strong. The boy who stood up for me when he was surrounded by reasons not to do such a thing. I hadn't known much about love. I hadn't known how it looked, felt, or tasted. I hadn't known how it moved, how it flowed, but I knew my heart was tight and currently skipping a few beats. I understood the goose bumps covering my arms. I knew this stuttering boy who was sometimes so scared was someone worth loving. He was worth being the first one I gave my heart to.

I knew Elliott Adams was love.

And I was falling into him so fast.

I hadn't felt safe in a very long time, and Elliott gave me that comfort.

I lay my head on his poop-covered shoulder, and a tear rolled down my cheek. "No one's ever stood up for me like that," I told him.

"I'll always stand up for you like that," he replied, making my heart twist and butterflies form. "Because you aren't the things people say you are, Jasmine."

I sniffled and snuggled in closer to him. "And neither are you."

"Hey, question."

"Answer."

"What's your favorite song?"

My lips turned up. "'Make You Feel My Love', by Adele. Why?"

"Oh." He shrugged. "No reason."

We walked into my apartment building, leaving a trail of horse poop in our wake, but I didn't care. My only concern was getting Elliott cleaned up. Once I unlocked the door, he stood in the foyer of the apartment, not moving an inch. I went to my mom's room and grabbed some clothes I was certain would be five times too big for him, but it was better than nothing.

"Come on," I told him, walking back into the living room area. He was still in the same spot.

"No. I don't want to track this all over your place. It's bad enough that it smells so bad."

"Elliott, don't worry. We'll clean it up. Trust me. Come on."

I walked him to the bathroom, but he stood outside the door. "You can shower first," he said. "I can wait."

I smiled. Besides Ray, I had thought the idea of a gentleman was an urban legend. "It's okay, I'll use my mom's shower in her bedroom."

"Oh, okay."

He walked in and closed the door behind him. I went into my room, grabbed a pair of pajamas, and then headed to the other shower. As the water hit my body, I couldn't let go of the feeling Elliott left me with. He was exactly what I needed when I hadn't even known I needed it, the light that lit the darkness I'd been walking in for so long.

Traveling so much meant I never had time to know what it felt like to belong. Elliott gave me that feeling, and I'd never be able to thank him enough for it.

After getting dressed, I walked into the living room to see Elliott in his oversized clothes, scrubbing the floor. "You don't have to do that," I told him.

He looked at me and rolled his eyes. "I'm pretty sure I do."

I got down on my knees and started cleaning up the mess with him. "I'm really sorry about tonight. It was perfect, until it wasn't."

"Yeah. It's okay."

"It's not," I stated sternly. "It's not okay what they did to you."

He shrugged. "I'm used to it."

"Just because you're used to it, that doesn't mean it's okay."

"In life, you have the nobodies and the somebodies," he explained. "It just so happens I'm a nobody and Todd is a somebody, and somebodies are able to get away with treating the nobodies any way they want. It just is what it is."

"You're not a nobody," I told him.

He smirked. "Says the somebody."

If only he knew how many times I'd been told differently.

When we finished cleaning, we tossed the dirty clothes in the washer and sat on the sofa together. I grabbed two glasses of water, and we talked—about nothing and about everything, about each other, and about everyone else.

Talking was great when both people listened. I listened closely to each and every word Elliott said, and he did the same with me.

"Why jazz music?" I asked as we both lay facing opposite directions on the sofa, our heads beside one another and our legs hanging off each end.

"Because it tells stories in such a unique way, and there are no mistakes in jazz, not really, only chances to make a misstep shine."

"I like that."

He nodded. "Chet Atkins once said, 'Do it again on the next verse, and people will think you meant it.' And Miles Davis said, 'When you hit a wrong note, it's the next note that makes it good or bad.' That's my favorite thing. You get the chance to make bad moments seem perfect. I like that about it."

"I've never listened to jazz," I confessed. "I mean, not really."

He lifted his head a bit. "You mean you're a normal teenager who doesn't listen to old-school jazz? Shocking," he joked.

I laughed. "Can you play something?"

"Sure." He pulled out his iPod and handed me an earbud. "Don't worry, I cleaned them."

I placed it in my ear and closed my eyes.

As the music started, chills raced down my spine. The trumpets, the saxophones, the pain, the joy...it lit me up inside, but what warmed me the most was turning my head to face Elliott. His eyes were shut, and his lips were turned up into the happiest of grins. This was his happy place. His safe haven was in jazz. It was as if the awful moments of the night faded away as he took in the sounds.

I loved how music saved him.

"Listen to her voice," he told me, his eyes still shut. "Listen to how she cries as she sings. It's painful, right?"

"Yes." It hurt to listen to the woman's voice. It hurt to hear her suffering behind the bars she sang, but still...it was beautiful. Tears fell down my cheeks, my emotions falling out of me. "But it's so beautiful."

He opened his eyes and turned his head to face mine. Our eyes locked. "Exactly."

"Who knew things could be painfully beautiful?"

"Yeah." He wiped away my tears and shrugged. "Who knew?"

We grew closer, my heart racing, my chest tight, my butterflies still strong. We were so close, and his lips were hovering near mine. *He's going to kiss me*, I thought to myself. The moment was there, and I knew he was going to seize it.

"Eli," I whispered, my lips hovering near his.

"Jazz," he whispered back.

But I couldn't continue speaking. My eyes closed, and I waited. I was going to have my first real kiss with the first boy I'd ever really cared for, and right before it happened, Elliott spoke. "Why did you hook up with those boys?"

My eyes sprang open, and I saw the sincerest gaze staring back at me. "What?"

"Was it because of me?" he asked nervously. "Did they say they'd stop bullying me if you hooked up with them?"

"It doesn't matter."

"It matters a lot."

My lips parted, and my voice cracked. "It's just sex, Elliott."

He sat up on his elbows, confusion in his stare. "What?"

"I said it's just sex."

He stood up from the sofa and kept shaking his head back and forth. "Who told you that?"

I chuckled lightly, confused by his sudden change of mood. "The first guy I ever slept with told me that. I told him I loved him, and he told me it was just sex, nothing else. Which is fine. It's not a big deal."

"No," Elliott argued, still shaking his head. "*No*," he said once more, sternly.

"What's wrong with you?"

"That's not true. It is a big deal." He paused his movements, and his hazel eyes locked with mine. His tone was so adamant, so sure his words hit me hard in my chest. "It's not just sex."

Before I could reply, I heard keys jingling outside the door.

"Oh crap!" I hissed, falling off the sofa and hurrying to my feet. Elliott froze, and as the door opened, I felt a stabbing in my gut when I saw Ray and Mama standing there.

Mama's face went white when her eyes landed on Elliott, and then her gaze turned livid. "What the hell is going on?" she barked.

"Jesus," Ray murmured, rubbing the back of his neck.

"Wh-what are you doing home?" I asked, my mind scrambling, trying to catch my breath. Elliott hadn't moved an inch, and all the color had drained from his skin.

"Is that really the question you want to ask me, Jasmine?" Mama said, her voice solid and stern. "Tell your friend he has five seconds to get out of my house."

"We weren't—" I started.

"FIVE!" Mama shouted.

Elliott scattered. I'd never seen a person move as quickly as he did as he left. The moment the door slammed shut, I felt a knot in my stomach as both Mama's and Ray's eyes peered into me.

"Snow White, what were you thinking? Bringing a boy here alone?" Ray asked calmly, because Ray never raised his voice at me. "Do you know how dangerous that could've been?"

"We weren't doing anything," I told him, my voice shaky. Mama's stare was terrifying me. "He's just a friend."

"You said you were sick," Mama scolded. She tossed her purse onto the sofa and placed her hands on her hips. "The only reason I went out with Ray tonight was because you told me you were sick and couldn't make it to dance class or the studio to work."

"I know, but—"

"And instead, here you are, messing around with a boy like a little hussy," she remarked, making my skin crawl.

"Come on, now, that's harsh," Ray scolded her as I lowered my head.

"Stay out of this, Ray," Mama snapped. He parted his lips to stand up to her for me, but I shook my head slightly. He shouldn't have to fight with her over me. "You are so childish and you're missing out on all of your opportunities because you're running around with some boy. This wouldn't have been an issue if you were homeschooled. So, from here on out, I forbid you to see him, or any other boy for that matter."

"But, Mama!" I cried. "He's just a friend."

"No, Jasmine, he's a distraction, and tonight you proved that you are not capable of dealing with distractions and your career. You know the rules: three strikes and you're out of public school. This is strike two. Now go to bed."

I started to argue, but she wasn't having any of it. As I lay down in my bed, I listened to Ray fight with Mama as he tried to stand up for me.

"She's a teenage kid, Heather, and you're treating her like a grown adult."

"She needs to focus. The last thing she needs is some boy knocking her off her path to success. While she was running around with that boy, she was missing meetings, opportunities, her life."

"Her life can't be spent in music studios, dance studios, acting studios. You're suffocating her."

"I'm saving her life! I'm giving her more than I ever had, and if you have a problem with that, you can leave at any time," Mama said, her voice so cold.

*No...*

*Don't go, Ray.*

The argument ended with a slamming door and Mama remaining in the apartment. I reached for my iPod and put my earbuds into my ears to listen to music. It was the only thing left in the apartment that understood me.

Through the music, I could hear Mama's footsteps coming toward my room, and as she entered, I pretended to be sleeping.

"I know you're awake," she told me. "Tomorrow you owe me four hours of vocals and three hours in the gym. You're going to make up for every single second of time wasted this evening, and if you ever pull something like that again, you will bear the consequences. Do you understand me?"

I remained quiet as a tear rolled down my face.

She walked over to my bed and sat down, nudging me in the arm. "I said, do you understand me?"

"Yes, Mama," I said with a slight tremble in my voice as I nodded slowly.

"Good. Maybe now you'll think about your future instead of being a little whore for a boy who can't provide you anything in life."

She stood up and walked away, closing my bedroom door behind her.

As she left, I turned my music up high and silently repeated four words to myself.

*I'm not a whore, I'm not a whore, I'm not a whore...*

# Chapter Eight

## Jasmine

Monday morning, I walked into the hallway, and it felt different. The whole environment of the place that gave me the happiest moments in life wasn't as fun. People were whispering as I walked through the hallways. I held my backpack straps and started walking faster, trying to get the idea out of my head that it was me they were laughing at, but I couldn't. My skin crawled as I rushed to my locker to get my books, and then I stood still in my shoes when I saw why everyone was laughing.

WHORE. SLUT. TRAMP.

It was written in bright red spray paint across my locker. A janitor stood with a sponge and a bucket of soapy water, scrubbing away.

"Oh, shit," Todd said, sliding behind me and placing his hands on my shoulders. His nose was taped up, and the skin underneath his eyes was black and blue from when Elliott punched him. "Isn't that your locker?"

"Why would you do this?" I asked, feeling sick to my stomach.

"Me? What makes you think it was me? Trust me, everyone knows you have a million guys on your roster. It could've been anyone. As for me"—he moved in closer to my ear and whispered—"I wouldn't touch your STD ass with a ten-foot pole. I told you, you committed social suicide, Hollywood. Now deal with it."

He walked off, and I stood shaking as a crowd stood around me. Some girls mocked me, laughing, calling me "disgusting", repeating the rumors they'd heard about me and Todd's parties. I didn't know what was worse—the rumors being spread or the fact that most of them were true.

"Come on," someone said, grabbing my arm and pulling me down the hallway. When my eyes focused enough to realize who was yanking me, a bit of relief hit me.

*Katie.*

She led me through the hall, and we walked down a set of spiral stairs until we hit the basement floor. No classes were held down there except for auto shop, which was mostly taken by guys, which meant the girls' bathroom on that floor was almost always abandoned.

We walked in, and she hopped up on the countertop by the mirror. "You okay?" she asked.

"Define okay," I joked.

She frowned. "I'm sorry that happened."

"It doesn't matter."

"Yeah, but it does. What they did to your locker is crap. They're jerks because they struggle with the fact that this is it for them. High school is where they'll shine before going out into the real world and realizing they are nothing more than just assholes who belittle girls because they're terrified of being lesser than us."

"Are you always so passionate?" I asked.

"Only when it comes to guys treating girls like crap. Yeah, I'm always passionate about that."

My hands raced over my face. "What if they aren't wrong, though? What if the words are true?"

"True or not, what they did is still disgusting. You didn't deserve that. No one deserves that."

I swallowed hard and hopped up onto the counter beside her. "Elliott's going to see it," I whispered, nerves writhing in my gut.

"He won't care."

"It's just...embarrassing, him seeing that."

"He won't care," she repeated.

"But—"

"Jasmine." Katie placed a comforting hand on my shaky leg, and gave me a stern look. "He won't care." I listened to her words, but still, they were hard to believe. I wasn't sure how I could face him, especially after seeing how he reacted at my place when he found out I was screwing around with guys to keep him from getting beat up. I saw it in his eyes when he told me it wasn't just sex—I saw how I had let him down.

"He's too good for me," I told her.

"He's Elliott." She laughed. "He's too good for everyone."

"Why did you pull me away up there? Why did you help me?"

"Because I know how it feels." Katie ran her hands through her dark curly hair and shrugged her shoulders. She looked just like her brother in many ways, from her caramel skin to her hazel eyes. The only difference between the two was how she carried herself. She held her head high while Elliott's confidence shook. "Last year, I was you. I was the one the guys talked about. I was a junior getting attention from senior guys and I felt unstoppable. All the girls hated me, but I didn't care. They were just jealous, I told myself. They just wished they could be me. Then, one night I made a mistake at a party. I got wasted and..." She swallowed hard. "There was a video of me doing things with a group of guys, and it got around. Needless to say, I wasn't as unstoppable as I imagined. Come Monday morning, my locker was painted red, and the video was viewed by just about everyone at school. I was humiliated. I mean, Jesus, even my little brother saw it."

"Oh my God," I muttered, stunned. "I can't even imagine."

She nodded. "It was bad. I spent a lot of nights crying in my room. My mom didn't know how to help me, because I couldn't bring myself to tell her what had happened. I was too ashamed. Then one night as I was crying, Elliott came into my room, and he sat on the edge of my bed and said, 'It's not true, what they wrote about you.' I laughed, because it was comedic, ya know? I knew it was true. I told him that, too. He'd seen the video, so there was no real way to deny what had happened, but still, he said, 'It's not true.' I asked him how it wasn't true, and he said, 'Because they don't get to label you. Those guys don't get to tell you who you are.'"

*Oh, Elliott.*

"When he overheard the guys talking about me at school, he got into a fist fight with them, and obviously, he lost. That's the reason he gets beat up so bad now. He beat up Todd's older brother, who graduated last year. So now, because of me, he's bullied every day."

"It's not your fault those guys are jerks. They would've found a reason to hurt someone regardless."

"I know, but I just wish it wasn't Elliott. He'll never admit that it bothers him, you know? He just takes the bullying," she told me. "Which is why I worry about him, because he'd rather get himself hurt than his loved ones. He's been that way all our lives."

"I can see that."

"When my mom was with my dad, he used to shout at her all the time. Then, one day the shouting turned into shoving. The next time, hitting. He normally hid it well from us kids, but one night, Dad got so upset that he went to slap Mom in front of us. Elliott leaped up and shoved Dad into a wall." She snickered and shook her head. "He was seven years old and stood up to our dad, to protect Mom. I don't know if you've noticed, but Elliott is a stick—there's no part of my brother that should be fighting."

"But still, he gets up and goes to war," I said, my chest feeling tight.

"Yup. Every day. Every day he goes to war for the ones he loves, and he'll make sure to go out of his way so you know it wasn't your fault. So, I get you feeling embarrassed about him seeing what they wrote on your locker, but don't, because he won't care. He'll just want to make sure you're all right."

When I finally built up the courage to leave the bathroom, I headed back to the world of high school. I didn't see Elliott, though. I was both happy and sad about that fact; I was afraid of what he'd think of me, but I also craved being in his presence.

At the end of the day, I walked toward my locker, and when I saw Elliott standing next to it, butterflies formed in my stomach. He gave me a half-grin, and I gave him one right back. My locker was scrubbed clean, but still, the memories persisted.

"Hi," he said.

"Hi.

"Are you okay?"

"I'm okay." I shifted my weight around on my feet, unable to stand still. "Did you see my locker earlier?"

"Yes."

"Oh."

I looked down at my hands and started to fiddle with my fingers. My nerves were building more and more as I waited for his reaction, but he didn't give me one.

"I should get going so I don't miss the bus home." He rubbed his hand on the back of his neck. "Are you okay?"

"Yes."

He parted his lips as if he wanted to say something, but no words came out.

I smiled. "Are *you* okay, Eli?"

His smile was laced with nerves. "Yes. Sorry. Okay, well, I'll see you later." He started to walk away, but then he paused, turning back to face me. "Can I t-t-take you out?"

"What?"

"I just...I was wondering if I could take you out on a date, and not like a friend-date, but like a *date* date." As he spoke, the butterflies in my stomach kept swirling around. "You can say no!" he added quickly.

"I want to say yes, it's just..." I bit my bottom lip. "Is it because you feel bad about what happened to my locker? Is it a pity date?"

He laughed. "Trust me. It's not a pity date."

"I've never been on a date before."

"It's okay." He shrugged his left shoulder. "Neither have I. So, Saturday?"

"What about your show?"

"I'll skip it for you."

My heart stopped beating and beat faster all at once. "Okay."

He smiled so wide and anxiously raced his hand over his head. "Okay. Good. Um, I'll see you t-t-tomorrow at school."

"Bye." As he walked away, I turned back to my locker and opened it. I started collecting the books from the shelves, and I jumped a little when I heard my name.

"Sorry, it's just me again," Elliott said. "I just forgot to say something."

"Oh, what?"

"First, can I..." He stepped toward me, but then stepped back again. "Can I hug you?"

I laughed, always so amused by everything about his movements. "Please."

He wrapped me in a hug, and I breathed him in.

I relaxed a bit as he held me.

"I forgot to tell you that none of it is true. The words they put on your locker—none of it's true. I'm going to hug you right now until you believe me, and don't say you believe me, because I know you don't."

"It may take a while." I shut my eyes as he held me closer. "You're going to miss your bus."

"It's okay," he replied, so matter-of-fact. "I'll walk home."

"Are you seriously asking me to do this, Snow?" Ray wondered, standing in the doorway of my bedroom that afternoon. He had a look of disbelief in his stare as he crossed his arms. "The answer is obviously no."

I groaned. "But it's just a small lie," I promised.

"Just to be clear"—he narrowed his eyes—"you're asking me to set up a fake meeting between a music producer and your mother this Saturday so you can go out on a date with a boy who was randomly in my house this past weekend wearing my clothes?"

"Yes."

"Jasmine." He sighed heavily. Whenever he used my real name, I knew he was annoyed. "Normally I'd agree that your mom is over-the-top and out of line, but this time she was right. You lied to her and you snuck around."

"It's the only way I can have a life!" I argued.

"That still doesn't make it right," he replied. "Listen, Snow, I'll go to bat for you with your mother, okay? I'll stand up for you and fight for you to have some freedom as a kid, but we can't win the war if you go into battles lying."

"I'm sorry I lied, okay? I knew she wouldn't have let me go, but this Saturday...this is important. I promise I'll never ask you for anything ever again if you help me out with this. Plus, if you actually set up a meeting with someone, it's not a lie at all."

"No, the lie is me telling her I'm taking you to the studio to work."

"You can take me to the studio afterward—then it's not a lie. Pleeease?" I begged like a five-year-old. I gave Ray my best ever puppy-dog eyes, and he cringed.

"Don't do that."

"Do what?" I asked innocently.

"Look at me with those stupid Snow White doe eyes." He groaned. "Fine, fine, but if we do this, I have a few rules of my own, like one: we will go to the studio after this date thing."

"Okay, deal." My grin spread from ear to ear.

"Wait, I'm not done, and you'll also let me meet this boy. I drive and drop you two off."

I grimaced. "You're not going to harass him, are you?"

He laughed. "Oh, I'm going to harass him. I'm going to inform him that I'm going to make his life a living hell if he ever tries anything or breaks your heart." He held his hand out toward me. "Deal or no deal?"

I grumbled, stood up, and shook his hand. "Deal."

# Chapter Nine

## Elliott

Uncle TJ kept frowning during my music lesson Friday afternoon. "No, no, no. That's not right," he said, cutting me off as I played the saxophone. He marched back and forth in his living room, waving his arms around. "There's nothing there."

"What?"

"The way you're playing, it's boring. There's nothing there—no heart, no meaning."

"I played e-exactly what you wanted," I stuttered, growing irritated by his criticism. We'd been working on the same opening bars for over two hours. We'd spent the past week working on the same section over and over. I was tired of hearing myself play.

"Yes, you played the chords, you hit the notes, blah, blah, blah." He grimaced, still waving his arms around. "But where's the voice?"

"What?"

"Where's. Your. Voice?" he asked again, this time more emphatically.

"I don't k-know what that m-means," I barked back.

He locked his eyes with mine, and sat down on his sofa. "You don't know what that means?"

"No."

"It means, Elliott"—he lifted his cup of coffee from the side table—"that you sound like shit."

69

"There's no way to make it better," I argued. "It just is what it is."

"Play it again."

I groaned. "But—"

"Play it again."

Sometimes working with Uncle TJ drove me insane. He always pushed me to give him something I could never deliver, but still, I kept showing up to our lessons, because at the end of the day, he was always right.

I picked up the saxophone and began to play. My fingers moved against the keys and I performed the exact number he wanted me to, and still, it wasn't good enough.

When I finished, he didn't make a peep. He didn't criticize me. He didn't hold the same annoyance in his stare. All he did was stand up, walk over to his own saxophone, and start to play.

He played the same piece as I did.

But man...it wasn't the same.

Uncle TJ performed in a way where his whole existence infused into the music. It wasn't simply the saxophone that created sounds, but his soul bled out through each note. TJ made music that could fix any broken person. He made sounds that were meant to heal the world.

When he finished, I sat looking like a fool. He took his seat and went back to sipping on his coffee.

"Okay." I sighed. "I'll try again."

He didn't allow me to leave his house until I got it right. We worked long into the night, missing dinner but not caring. That was when the magic started happening. It came after the struggle, after the exhaustion, after the pain.

TJ was a unique kind of music professor. He didn't teach people how to play an instrument or how to sing; he took those who already knew and taught them soul. He showed them how to dig deeper and discover more within themselves.

Once TJ could get you to a place where nothing existed in the world except for the music, that's when you'd find it—your truth, your voice.

If it weren't for TJ, I wouldn't have even known I had a voice.

Sure, his belief in me drove me up the wall sometimes, but I wouldn't trade it for anything.

He believed in my gift when I didn't believe in myself.

"There!" He clapped his hands together and nodded. "There it is!" he remarked after I took the song I had thought I'd already perfected and made it magic. "See? You see what I mean, son? That was it! That's why we keep going."

I smiled, because I knew he was right.

"Now go home. I'm sick of looking at you."

I laughed and gathered my things.

"Wait, I got you something," TJ called after me. He walked into the back room and came back out with a box. "Your mom said you were going on your first ever date."

"Mom talks too much."

"Only because she loves you. Here, this is for you. Figured you might want it."

I took the box and grinned. "Cologne?"

"Only two sprays, buddy. No need to drown yourself. Be subtle about it."

"I will."

"And, Elliott? Have the best time of your life. You deserve this. You deserve all of this." I left before he got too emotional, because TJ was very much like Mom in many ways; he loved me so much, it often made him cry whenever something good happened.

And Jasmine Greene was my something good.

Saturday morning, I stood in front of the mirror, staring at myself. *Today's the day—my first date.* Mom had already cried about three times that morning, and Katie couldn't help giving me tips on how to treat Jasmine like a lady.

I didn't really need too many ideas, though. When a guy lived with two girls all his life, he learned what to say and what not to say pretty well.

I stared in the mirror, my face bright red as I tried to say the only thing I really wanted to say to Jasmine. "You're b-be—" I grimaced. *Beautiful. Beautiful. The word is beautiful.* "You're b-b-b...God!" I groaned, slapping my hands against my face. Sometimes I hated my-self more than I could describe. I took a deep breath and stared myself in the eyes. "You. Are. B-Be—"

"You don't have to say it," Katie said, walking past the bathroom. "The way a guy looks at a girl already tells her he thinks she's beautiful."

"How am I supposed to look at her to let her know she's b-b-be...?"

"Trust me, you already are looking at her that way. Get out of your head, Eli, and just have fun."

I took my sister's advice. I let go of overthinking everything and got out of my own way.

"And here. Let me fix your tie." She walked over to me and started retying my poorly put together tie. "I like that you're wearing a tie. I'd never been on a date where a guy wore a tie."

I tensed up. "Is it too much? Is it st-stupid?"

She shook her head. "It's charming. Trust me, girls like charming. And, I know I was mean to her because I thought she was one of them, but she's not, Eli. She's nothing like the popular kids. Jasmine is a good thing. You deserve a good thing."

I gave her a halfway smile as she fixed my tie. "Thanks, sister."

"Anytime, brother."

I waited on the front porch for Jasmine to pull up. She'd told me earlier that week that her dad-who-wasn't-really-her-dad, Ray, was going to be dropping us off and picking us up. That added a whole new level of nerves to the idea of my first date.

As the car pulled up and parked, I walked down the steps toward the sidewalk. A man climbed out of the driver's seat and approached me.

Jasmine hurried out of the car, shouting, "Be nice, Ray!"

"I'm always nice," he replied, his voice stone cold. As he walked up to me, my shoulders slumped and my nerves built up more and more. Ray took off his sunglasses, and I lost my mind.

"Holy crap, you're Ray Gable!" I shouted, my mind exploding.

Ray's harsh stare softened. "You know me?"

"You know him?" Jasmine echoed.

"Know you? You're only the amazing guitarist and lead vocalist for Peter's Peak. Not to be dramatic, but I'm your b-b-biggest fan. Can I just say one thing?"

"Sure." Ray smirked, appearing somewhat excited to be recognized.

"Please don't go mainstream."

He cocked an eyebrow. "What?"

"Well..." I cleared my throat, the knot in my stomach tightening. "When indie artists go mainstream, the world of music loses true talent because the music industry turns you into money-hungry demons that lose all sense of self and start sounding more like bubble gum and less like music. It has happened to a lot of the greatest artists out there, and I would hate for it to happen to you because your music is raw and real, too great to sacrifice for money—not that I'm saying I don't want you to succeed and make money, because I mean, I'm sure that's the goal, and more people should know Peter's Peak exists, but, it's just that I would hate for you to lose what you have."

After I finished speaking, I let out a deep sigh.

"Whoa," Jasmine murmured, stunned. "You just went into full fanboy mode, and you didn't even stutter once."

"Snow White"—Ray tilted his head toward her—"why didn't you tell me your friend had the best taste in music?"

"Oh God," Jasmine moaned, slapping her hand against her face.

"Come on, Elliott. Let's get a move on," Ray said, wrapping his arm around my shoulders. "Your cologne smells great."

I could've died a happy man right then and there.

The whole ride over to Bourbon Street, Ray and I talked about all things music. He gave me songs to listen to, and I gave him some of my favorites to check out. Jasmine sat in the back of the car, and she was lucky enough to take part in the forming of a true bromance.

"You'll have to wear bowties, dude. Your tie is great, but chicks dig bowties," Ray told me, and I took his notes to heart. As he pulled up to the French Quarter, Jasmine was quick to jump out of the car. I thanked Ray for the ride, and my hand went to open the door, but when I pulled, it wouldn't budge.

"Sorry buddy, you're locked in," Ray said, sliding his sunglasses back on.

"Oh?" I went to unlock it, and he was quick to lock it back. "Um..." I swallowed hard and turned to look at him. The cool musician was gone, replaced by the overprotective dad-who-wasn't-really-her-dad.

"She's a great girl," he told me.

"Yes, sir."

"She's the most important thing in my life. If you hurt her, I will find you, take your saxophone, and shove it down your throat. Do you understand me?"

"Yes, sir?" I said with a shaky voice.

"Is that a question?"

"No! It's the answer, Ray. Jeez, back off. He answers things with question marks, it's no big deal. Now let him out," Jasmine shouted.

The second the door was unlocked, I hurried out of the car.

"Call me when it's time to pick you up, okay, Snow White? And, Elliott?"

I swallowed hard. "Yes?"

He gave me a bright smile. "I'll check out those songs you sent me." Then his face turned to a scowl. "And keep your hands out of your pants, and off Jasmine, or else I'll murder you. Okay, bye!"

As he drove off, I stood there, a bit terrified of Ray's final words, but still starstruck too. It was an odd moment to say the least.

"Ignore him," Jasmine told me. "He's all talk."

"Yeah, but just to be safe, don't be surprised if I don't touch you, like, ever. Come on, we're gonna be late to the steamboat."

"A steamboat?" Jasmine asked as we walked down Bourbon Street.

"Yeah, it's called the Steamboat Natchez. It kind of t-takes you around New Orleans and you see all the sights."

"Oh, how cool."

"Yeah. They do live jazz music and stuff on the boat too. I think you'll like it."

"I'll love it." She nudged me in the arm and grinned. "I know what Ray said about bowties, but I like your regular tie."

My face heated up, and I looked at her the way Katie said I always looked at her. "Thanks. I like your, uh, everything."

She laughed and linked her arm with mine. "Thanks, Eli."

I wasn't sure if she noticed, but I definitely stopped breathing—partly because we were linked together, mostly because I feared Ray was somehow watching us.

Once it came time to board the ship, we sat in the dining hall as the crew served us a late lunch.

"I've never done anything this cool," she told me. "It's pretty sad, though, seeing how Hurricane Katrina ruined so much."

"Yeah, but it's a strong city. Rebuilding was the only choice."

"Was your family affected by the storm?"

"No, but a lot of our neighbors were. We were some of the lucky ones. Others in the neighborhood, not so much."

"I can't imagine." She pushed her food around on her plate and shook her head. "But it must be nice, ya know, to have a city you call home."

"Maybe this can be your new home," I told her. "Maybe a home isn't where you begin, but where you end up."

"I like that." She grinned. "Maybe." She shifted around in her seat and I watched her frown. "Elliott? Can I ask you something? Why would you want to take me out on a date after...everything you found out about Todd's parties?"

"The only things I want to find out about you are things you tell me. I couldn't care less what other people think or say."

"But I told you what I did with those boys."

"For me," I argued. "You did that to try to protect me—and by the way, no offense, but please never stand up for me in that way ever, ever again. I'd rather get beat up for the rest of my life than ever have you put in that situation."

She nodded and agreed.

Before we could talk more, one of the musicians in the jazz band came and tapped me on the shoulder.

"It's time," he said.

"What's happening?" Jasmine asked.

I just smiled. "My uncle said I couldn't miss a Saturday performance, so I hope it's okay if I perform a song?"

Her smile spread wide. "Yes, yes, yes!"

"But, well, you have to sing with me."

"What?"

"I, um, my uncle's friends said they'd help me perform a song if you'd sing it. I've been practicing all week."

"What? I can't. I can't just sing. What if I don't know the words?" She rubbed her hands up and down her arms. "There are a lot of people here, too. I can't do it. What if I don't know the words to the song you're singing?"

"How would you not know the words?" I asked, grabbing the microphone and holding it out to her. "It's your favorite song."

I walked up to the small stage set up in the dining hall and spoke a few words to the other musicians who were going to help me out with the performance. As I started playing, I saw Jasmine's eyes well up as she heard, "Make You Feel My Love" by Adele filling the space.

Uncle TJ had been having me perfect the song over the past week, and seeing the way her eyes lit up made every moment more than worth it. I nodded her over, and she slowly walked up on the stage then closed her eyes and began to sing. I closed my eyes, too, and gave myself to the song, for her.

It was all for her.

Once we finished, the audience applauded like crazy, making tears roll down Jasmine's cheeks. I walked over and stood beside her. "You hear that? Th-those are your fans. That's for you. That's for your soul music."

"It's amazing. You're amazing."

"Happy tears?" I asked.

"The happiest tears," she replied.

After our meal, we grabbed two ice cream cones and walked outside to sit and watch the views as we cruised down the Mississippi River. We talked about everything and nothing, and it was all perfect. There wasn't a second that felt uncomfortable. It just felt...good. It felt good to feel good.

"I saw you first!" She laughed, lightly shoving me in the arm. "I noticed you first."

I laughed and shook my head back and forth. "No, you didn't."

"Yes, I did, Eli! I did."

"There's no possible way that's true."

"Why do you say that?"

I shrugged. "You were st-standing in the principal's office. You wore a y-yellow sundress and you were smiling like crazy, and I remember thinking, 'Wow, she's the prettiest girl I've ever seen.'"

She sank down in her chair a bit. "Eli..."

"I also thought you were on drugs, because no one should look that happy about being at school," I joked, making her laugh and shove me again.

The way she laughed so freely made me want to make her laugh forever.

"Have you ever heard of the artist Banksy?" I asked as we coasted down the river.

She shook her head.

"He does graffiti art, and on this building coming up, it's rumored that he created this piece. I, um, I've b-been trying to say something to you each day for a long time, but...my words..." I started fumbling with my fingers. "I just can't say what I've been trying to say, but I can show you."

She sat up straight, and as the steamboat glided forward, tears formed in her eyes as I gestured toward the building to show her the words.

*YOU ARE BEAUTIFUL.*

"Eli," she whispered, her voice low.

"You are, you know. One hundred percent, you are."

After the cruise was over, we went to Frenchmen Street and sat on top of the dumpster to listen to more music behind the bars.

"This is the best day of my life," Jasmine said as her feet swayed back and forth, and she stared up at the stars.

"Yeah. Same here."

"Elliott?"

"Yes?"

"Are you going to kiss me tonight?"

"No."

"Why not?"

"Because I like you too much to do that."

I wasn't sure if she knew what I meant, but it was true. I couldn't kiss Jasmine—not yet. She'd had a lot of guys use her in ways that weren't good, and I didn't want to be one of those guys. I wanted to prove to her that I wanted her for more than her body. Just being close to her was enough for me.

"Oh," she replied, with a hint of disappointment.

I took her hand into mine. "I like you a lot, Jazz...more than music."

She nervously laughed. "Don't lie."

"I'm not."

"But you *really* like music."

"Yeah, and I *really* like you."

She smiled and combed her hair behind her ears. It was always cute when she blushed. "I really like you too, Elliott."

"You wanna perform with me every Saturday?" I asked without a second thought as I looked at the stars.

"What?" She gaped at me.

"Do you wanna perform with me regularly?" I asked again.

"Yes." She leaned in and placed her forehead against mine. "I do."

When it came time to meet Ray, we walked down Frenchmen Street, stopping whenever random music caught our attention. We took it all in, and the way Jasmine smiled made me feel like a million bucks. She was having a great time, and she was having a great time with *me*.

I hadn't known a girl like her could have a great time with a boy like me.

# Chapter Ten

## Jasmine

"I had a great time tonight," I told Elliott through the car window after Ray dropped him off at his house. I tried to get out of the car, but Ray locked me inside to keep me from hugging Elliott.

"I did too," Elliott said, shifting around on the sidewalk with his hands stuffed in his pants. "Th-thanks, Ray, for driving us."

"Elliott, no need to be so informal—go ahead and call me Mr. Gable," Ray joked, making me roll my eyes. "Say good night, Snow White."

"Night, Eli. I'll see you at school on Monday."

"Night, Jazz."

As Ray pulled away from the curb, he smiled over at me. "He's a good kid. I hate him because he likes you, but he's a good kid."

I nodded. "He asked me to perform with him when he does his Saturday shows on Frenchmen Street."

"Pop music or soul?"

"Soul."

"Well, shit, Snow White." Ray pinched the bridge of his nose. "Now we're gonna have to keep lying to your mom and setting up meetings for her to go to."

My smile spread wide. "You'd do that for me?"

"Does soul music make you happy?"

"Yes."

"Then it's your duty to share that happiness with the world."

"Mama might be really mad at you if she finds out the truth."

He huffed. "Yeah, well, when isn't your mother mad at me nowadays? Besides, I think once she sees how good you are and how happy it makes you, she'll be happy too."

Ray picked Elliott and me up each Saturday, and he always stayed to watch our performances. He recorded every single one, too. I'd never seen him look excited when I sang pop songs, but when it came to the soul music, he always praised me. He didn't know how much it meant to me, him showing up to watch me perform.

It was as if he was looking at me and saying I was good enough, no matter what.

"I've never seen you like this before, ya know." Ray nudged me one night as we were driving home.

"Like what?"

"Happy."

Ray and I made sure to make it home each night in time for dinner with Mama. She'd tell me how she was making connections with the most important players in the industry, going on and on about how I'd be discovered in no time, all thanks to her hard work.

"This could've happened sooner if you weren't so selfish with your contacts, Ray. Luckily, I found my own."

"My apologies," Ray replied, and he gave me a smile. "Snow White has been amazing in the studio. I think you'd be proud of her."

Mama scrolled through her emails on her cell phone. "Yes, well, I'll hear soon enough."

"I actually have some video of her," he replied, taking out his cell phone.

"I don't need to see it," Mama said, cutting into her chicken. "I was there."

"What?" I asked.

She stabbed the meat with her fork and placed it in her mouth. "I said I saw it. I had a feeling you two were lying, so I followed you this afternoon. I saw Jasmine performing on the corner with that strange boy."

"He's not strange," I whispered.

She raised an eyebrow before cutting more chicken. "He's strange."

"Okay, so..." Ray sat up straight and cleared his throat. "I know you're probably upset, but...you saw her. Her music is amazing, Heather. She was meant to perform soul music, ya know? And I think—"

"Nothing," she cut in.

"Huh?"

"You think nothing," she told him. She placed her silverware down on the plate and gave Ray a cold stare. "You had no right to take her there, to get her hopes up on this silly music. She's nowhere near as good as she is with her pop music."

"That's a lie," Ray argued.

"It's not, and anyway, you have no right to decide what's best for her. You are not her father."

"Mama!" I cried. "Stop it."

"I really wish you would stop that," Ray said, his hands forming fists. "I've been by both of your sides for fifteen years, Heather. I watched that little girl grow up from a toddler to the teenager she is today. I gave my all to make a life for you both, so will you stop with that bullshit? Yeah, I might not be her biological father, but I am her dad, and I'm tired of you trying to take that away from me. She's my daughter—our daughter—and maybe you'd realize she's been so damn unhappy with the life you're trying to force her into if you thought about someone other than yourself for one minute."

"Force her into? She loves her life!"

"She hates it!" Ray barked. I closed my eyes and took a deep breath. "She hates it all, and admit it—you saw her on that corner performing, saw that for the first time in a long time, she's actually happy, and it kills you inside that you had nothing to do with that success. It drives you insane that you couldn't control this aspect of her life."

"Go to hell," Mama hissed.

"I'm already there!" he fired right back.

Mama pushed herself away from the dining room table and stood up. "You're not welcome here anymore. You need to leave."

"What?" I asked, bewildered. "Mama, this is his apartment."

"Not anymore." She crossed her arms. "Go, Ray."

"I'm not leaving. We aren't going to sit here and have you act dramatically and—"

"I slept with someone else," Mama said, so matter-of-fact.

My mouth dropped open, as did Ray's, and we just stared at her, stunned.

His voice dropped low. "Excuse me?"

"It doesn't matter. I just, I don't want to be with you anymore. You're weak."

Ray took a deep inhale. "Who was it?"

"It doesn't—"

"Who?" he shouted. I'd never seen him look so angered and heart-broken in all my life. Sure, Mama wasn't the easiest person to love, but still, Ray was Ray. He was a good man, and good men always hurt a little more than others.

"Trevor," she answered softly. "I've spent over fifteen years with you, and you've never done anything for me. Trevor is different. He's promised me so many great things."

"Trevor Su?" he asked.

"Yes, Trevor Su. You know—the one you refused to have meet with me."

"Because he's a snake!"

"He's a mogul!" She stood tall, proud. "And he's going to change our lives."

"You can't work with him, Heather. You can't have Jasmine around that asshole."

"I can, and I will."

"I'm serious. He's dangerous. He's a wildfire, and I swear to God he'll burn you."

Mama pursed her lips together and shrugged her shoulders. "I'd rather play with a wildfire than a weak spark like you."

Ray's eyes grew heavy as sadness hit him hard. It was as if the ulti-mate betrayal destroyed his heart. Sure, he wasn't madly in love with Mama, but he'd never step out on their relationship. He was loyal to a fault. He rubbed his hands against his face and then blinked hard. "Fine. You win. I'm leaving." He pushed himself away from the table. His hands clenched and his face was red from anger, but he didn't say another word.

He just stood up and left, gently closing the door behind him.

I hadn't known how painful a broken heart could look until I stared into Ray's eyes that night. I hadn't known how quickly my heart could shatter until I watched the closest thing I had to a father walk out the front door.

"How could you, Mama?" I asked, in shock. "How could you do that to him?" *To me…*

"He was nothing, a wannabe star who was holding you down. So, I found new opportunities. Life is about opportunities that move you forward, and Ray was getting us nowhere." She went back to eating her chicken, and I couldn't let go of the confusion in my chest. I knew Mama was hard sometimes, but I didn't know she was heartless.

"But he loved you."

"Love?" Mama asked. "Love doesn't get you anywhere in this world, child. Don't be ridiculous."

"You didn't love him?"

"I loved what he could've done for this family, but he didn't follow through. Like I said, love makes people weak, and I have no time for weakness."

"Do you love me?" I asked, terrified to hear her answer.

Her brows knitted together, and she placed her fork down. "I'll love you the day you stop letting me down."

I'd never known true loneliness until that very moment.

## Chapter Eleven

### Jasmine

Weeks passed, and Ray didn't come back. Like the true man he was, he still paid all the bills without a moment of hesitation. *For me.* Everything that man ever did was for me.

Each day that went by was more painful, and Mama was more aggressive and mean. She was obsessed with working me all day and night whenever I wasn't at school. Seeing Elliott was out of the question, and the only time we were really able to talk was in the hallways before and after classes.

I was tired. I missed Elliott, I missed Ray, and I missed soul music.

At school one Monday afternoon, a knot formed in my gut as I walked past the office and saw Mama shaking hands with the principal. I hurried over just as she was walking out of the office.

"What are you doing here?" I asked.

"It's good to see you too, Jasmine," she replied dryly.

"What are you doing here?"

She glanced around the hallways. "I don't understand why you were so desperate to go to public school. I hated school."

"I love it here."

"Yes, well, now you can say you've had the experience. We're leaving tomorrow morning."

"What?"

"Unlike Ray, Trevor set up some great opportunities for you over in Europe. He even booked the trip for us and found us a place to stay in London."

"What?" My heart flew to my throat. "No..."

"Yes. It's going to be great. We're meeting with the best studio known to mankind over there. They are known for making superstars."

"I'm not going."

"Yes, you are. I just finished the paperwork with your principal."

*What?* "How long have you known this was going to happen?" I asked her. "When did you know we were going to be moving?"

Mama rolled her eyes. "Stop being dramatic, Jasmine."

"How long?"

"A few weeks, almost a month."

My heart fractured. "You weren't going to tell me, were you? Until tomorrow when we were boarding a plane? If I hadn't run into you just now, you wouldn't have told me we were leaving until it was actually happening."

"What does it matter?" she asked, appearing confused by my anger. "It's what we do—we move, we chase the dream."

"I don't want your stupid dream!" I cried, running away from her. I hurried down the spiral staircase toward the bathroom in the basement. I slammed my hands against the door and hurried inside, taking deep breaths. Pulling out my cell phone, I dialed Ray's number, and a sigh of relief hit me when he answered.

"Snow? What's up?" he asked. "Shouldn't you be in school? What's wrong?"

"She's making us move," I told him, swallowing hard. "She said we're going to London to work with Trevor, and I don't want to. I don't want to go, and she's trying to make me. Please, Ray, don't let her take me. Please ask her to let us stay."

"I was hoping it wasn't true..."

"You knew?"

"Yeah. I just thought she wouldn't go through with it. I'm so sorry, Snow White."

Tears flooded my eyes as I shook my head back and forth. "I want to stay here. I want to stay with you. Just let me stay with you. Mama can go on her own for all I care. I want to stay here. This is the closest thing I've ever had to a home, and you're the closest thing I have to a dad, Ray. Please, let me stay with you."

There was a long pause. Each second that passed made me cry even more.

"There's nothing I'd love more than that, Snow White."

*Yes...*

"But..." he started.

*No...*

"At the end of the day, I don't really have a say in that choice. I don't get a say, because I'm not your father."

I wondered if those words hurt him as much as they stung my soul.

I hung up the phone and left the bathroom. As I was walking the hallways, still on the verge of more tears, Elliott was standing up after being pushed around by Todd and his friends. Ever since Elliott had punched Todd, he'd been getting harassed more and more.

He never mentioned it to me, and whenever I brought it up, he'd say he was fine and change the subject.

"Jazz? What is it?" Elliott asked, walking over.

"I...I..." Tears started falling down my cheeks, and I shook my head. There were still three hours left of the school day, but I knew I couldn't make it. I was too heartbroken to keep going to class that afternoon. "Run away with me?" I asked him. "Just for the rest of the day?"

"What's wrong?" he asked again.

"Everything."

He glanced down the hallway and then held his hand out. "Okay. Let's go."

I sniffled nonstop as Elliott and I sat on top of the closed dumpster in the alleyway of Frenchmen Street, listening to the music playing in the bars we weren't allowed to step foot inside. We'd been there for hours, watching the sun start to fade into night.

"You're really leaving?" Elliott asked, his voice low as he fiddled with his fingers. His round, thin-framed glasses sat on his face, hiding the hazel eyes I loved, and his lips were turned down.

I nodded, unable to stop looking at him, even though he couldn't bring himself to turn my way. "Yes."

We hardly knew each other, but we knew enough.

My year in New Orleans had come and gone too fast. Each hour felt like minutes, and each minute felt like seconds. *Time*—that was all we wanted. We both craved a little more time, and there was never enough of it.

We'd spent so much time behind those bars, listening to different types of music and making promises we couldn't keep—promises of futures and dreams, of us keeping in touch, of forever.

We were only sixteen years old, but our hearts felt older whenever we were together. Before I met Elliott, I thought loneliness was a thing I'd always feel. Then he found me with his music and everything changed. If I'd had it my way, I would've stayed with him, but, as life taught me, sixteen-year-olds didn't get to make those decisions.

We were simply supposed to follow wherever the adults led us.

"Where are you guys going this time?" he asked.

I hated the feeling in my gut. I hated how I felt so unimportant to Mama. I'd been homeschooled my whole life, and it wasn't until Ray got the contract in New Orleans that I got a glimpse of what a true life could feel like...what it felt like to have a bed in the same place, to go to an actual school...what a best friend looked like, what home meant— and now I was losing it all.

"London. We'll be over there for a while."

He turned toward me, searching for a bit of hope in my eyes. "And then you'll come back here?"

I frowned. We never went back.

I shrugged. "Maybe."

He frowned too, because he didn't believe me. "How much does it cost to call overseas?"

"Probably a lot."

"This is good, though. It's going to help your career."

"I don't want a career," I told him, speaking honestly. "I just want to stay with you."

"I want you to stay, but if it's good for you, I want you to go."

"Don't make logical sense," I stated softly. "I hate when you make logical sense."

"Just think, if you make enough m-money, you can move back h-here and buy a big house with big trees, and you can sit on the porch drinking iced tea. Your own place... a home of your own..."

I sighed. "Yes." I lowered my voice and looked down at my hands. "But I don't want to leave you. You're my only friend. And Ray is my only family." The only family that cared, at least.

Elliott took note of how my body reacted, how my hands shook a bit, how my voice slightly cracked. He sat up straighter. "Do you think this will really help your career?"

"My mom does."

He inched a bit closer to me and kicked his feet back and forth. "That's not what I asked."

"Yeah, I know." I raced my hands through my thick, black hair that matched Mama's. "But that's all that matters."

Elliott looked at me and smiled, though his eyes appeared so heavy and sad. "You want to run away with me tonight?"

*Yes.*

*Please.*

*Anywhere.*

*Let's go.*

"I wish," I whispered.

He turned away from me and went back to fiddling with his fingers. "Me too."

"Will you tell your sister I said bye?"

"Of course."

"Thank you." For a few minutes, we sat on that dumpster, pretending our lives weren't about to change forever. We sat and listened to the music blaring in The Jazz Lounge. We listened to the rhythm and blues over at Jo's Catz. We smiled at the sound of the bluegrass at Mikey's Tavern. For a few minutes, we lived in the moment.

"You're my favorite person, Jazz," Elliott told me in such a low voice, I wondered if I'd heard him right. I loved that he called me Jazz, because it was his favorite kind of music to play. Yes, Ray was a great musician, but no one could play a saxophone like Elliott could.

"You're my favorite person, too. I'm going to miss your music."

"I'm going to miss your voice."

My lips parted to speak, but no words came. What else could I say?

It was crazy how much my heart hurt that night. I hadn't known Elliott for long at all, only a few months that felt like forever. We were complete opposites in so many ways. I was the popular new girl, and he, the bullied shy boy. Where I was outgoing, he was tame. Where I was lost, he was the roadmap home.

And now, we had to say goodbye.

"Jazz?"

"Yes?"

"Make me a promise?"

"Okay."

Elliott scooted closer and moved his hands to my cheeks, making me turn to face him. "If she ever makes you feel like you're not yourself..." I closed my eyes at those words, and tears started to fall down my cheeks. Elliott's thumbs wiped them away each time they fell as he kept talking. "If she ever hurts you and you need to run, run back here. Run back to me and I'll take care of you forever. I'll always take care of you, okay?"

"Okay, I promise."

He reached into his back pocket and pulled out a set of keys. He took one off his keychain and handed it to me. "This is a spare key to my family's house. You should keep it."

"Why?"

"In my family, whenever we go through good times or bad, we give each other a key. It stands for a reminder that you always have a place called home, no matter what. Plus, whenever you're having a bad day, you can hold the key and remember that you aren't alone, not really. It's your st-strength on the hard days. It's a reminder so you know you always have a home to come back to."

I held the key tight in my fist. "Thank you, Eli."

"Always, Jazz."

We sat behind the bars that night until the music faded away. After the sounds were gone, we sat a bit longer, wanting to stay in the same place until the music grew loud the next day.

Then, when we ran out of time, we both stood up.

Elliott wrapped his arms around me, and I pressed myself against him.

He pulled away slightly and combed my hair behind my ears. Our eyes locked—his zoomed in on my brown eyes, and I studied his hazel stare. I loved his face. I loved every part of him, really, but my gosh did I love his face.

We didn't say it, but we felt it that night.

*Love.*

He was so skinny and fragile, and I swore I weighed three times as much as him, but he loved me just as much as I loved him. He was all bones, and I was all meat. His skin was painted caramel, and mine was white as cream. We were polar opposites. We weren't meant to fall for one another, but when we blended together, we were some kind of beautiful.

If it weren't for Elliott, I would've always thought love was supposed to be jaded. If it weren't for him, I wouldn't have ever learned what it meant to be young and free. All my life, I'd been caged, and Elliott opened my door and allowed me to fly.

"We'll email each other," he swore. "All the time, we'll email each other."

"Okay."

"Jazz?"

"Yes, Eli?"

"I'm going to k-kiss you now?"

I snickered, a chill running down my spine. "Is that a question?"

He shook his head. "No."

Tears rolled down my cheeks and I closed my eyes. "I've never been kissed."

He raised an eyebrow. "But..."

I nodded. "I know. It turns out all the guys before you weren't interested in kisses," I said with shame in my voice.

"It's okay," he promised. "I've never been kissed either."

I nodded, my stomach filled with nerves. "I hate that our first kiss is also going to be our last."

"No. This won't be the last time. The next time we see each other the first thing I'm going to do is kiss you for everything we missed. The next time I kiss you, it's going to mean forever."

"Promise?"

"Promise."

And I felt his promise, too. I gasped lightly as his lips brushed against mine. He kissed me so gently, yet I felt it from the top of my head to the tips of my toes. It was sweet, and sad, and happy, and real.

So, so real.

*So that's what it's supposed to feel like. That's how my heart is supposed to beat.*

*This is love.*

Even though I was leaving the next day, I believed I'd be okay. I'd be okay because Elliott had shown me what true love was meant to feel like and taste like, and nothing could ever steal that feeling away from me. Even when life got dark, that feeling would sit in the back of my mind.

Elliott Adams, his love, and his gentle kisses that promised me forever.

## Chapter Twelve

### Elliott

For the past week, Mom had been frowning at me over dinner. She could see my sadness, but I tried to hide it so she wouldn't be so sad.

"I'm fine," I told her, twirling around the pasta on my plate with my fork.

"It's okay if you aren't," she told me. Katie had a grimace on her face, too. They both felt so bad for me. "It's okay to not be okay all the time."

I shrugged. "Can I go to my room? I'm not that hungry."

"Of course. Let me know if you need anything, and I know it's a school night, but if you want to play video games with Jason, that's fine by me," Mom said, hoping to make me smile.

I smiled for her. "Okay."

"I love you, Eli."

"I love you, too, Mom."

I lay in my bed and put in my earbuds to listen to music. The saddest part of jazz music was how each song affected you differently based on your own mood. Some of my favorite songs made me want to cry, while others made me want to throw my iPod against a wall.

I missed her.

She'd been gone for six days, and I missed her more than I'd known I could miss a person. We'd emailed each other, but we were never really able to talk. When she was sleeping, I was awake; when she was going about her day, I was in bed. It was tough, learning about what was happening in her life after it had already happened.

School wasn't any easier with Jasmine gone. If anything, it was worse. Katie did her best to watch my back, but Todd and his gang were back to harassing me full steam ahead.

A new semester meant a new class schedule, and I was lucky enough to have Todd or one of his friends in five out of seven of my classes.

The worst one was fifth period gym class, where I had three of them at once.

"You think you can just get away with breaking my nose, freak?" Todd hissed behind me as I sat in the locker room while two of his followers held me down. "Now that your whore girlfriend is gone, you don't have any kind of pussy to protect you," he said, spitting at me.

I didn't say anything back to him, because words never worked.

"Just wait for it, sunshine. You're going to get what's coming to you. But, it's kind of sad now. Now that I can't fuck your whore any-more, I'm gonna need someone new." He smirked. "I mean, your sister has a great rack, and let's be honest, everyone's already seen those tit-ties, so I might as well see what they taste like, too."

My hands formed fists, and I leaped up, wanting to slug him, but his friends held me down.

*I'm not strong enough.*

*I'm not strong enough.*

"If yo-you t-touch her!" I warned, and they all laughed.

"I-I-If I to-to-touch her *what*?" Todd mocked me. "I'm gonna touch her all right. I'm gonna touch every inch of her, and then I'm going to kick your ass for my nose, loser. You'll never see it coming. Your life is officially a ticking time bomb, and I'm going to destroy you."

I tried again to get loose from the jerks' grips, but I couldn't.

*I'm not strong enough.*

*I'm not strong enough.*

"Let him go, guys," Todd ordered, and the two pushed me back-ward on the bench, making my head slam against the lockers.

My mind was spinning, and I didn't have a clue what to do, how to protect my sister, how to make sure nothing happened to her. If anything happened to her, I'd never forgive myself. If anyone touched her...

I couldn't stop my skin from crawling as I paced and pushed my glasses up my nose. There was only one thing I could do, and I didn't care if it made me a loser, didn't care if it made me look weak. The only thing I cared about was protecting my sister, which meant going straight to my mom.

If there was anyone who could fix this, it was her, and it didn't take long for her to swoop right in.

A few days later, Mom, Katie, and I sat in the principal's office with Todd and his parents beside us. Katie hadn't looked up once, and my hands fiddled in my lap.

"You do know that this is a big allegation, Mrs. Adams," Principal Williams warned, sitting back in his chair. "Saying Todd would do something like this—"

"I wouldn't!" Todd insisted, looking innocent as ever. "I would never do anything like that to a girl."

*Jesus.* He should've really considered becoming an actor. If I hadn't known he was the devil, I would've believed the jerk.

Katie huffed, rolling her eyes. Mom was livid. Her fingers tapped against the arms of the chair. "There has to be something that can be done about this, some kind of action that can be taken against him. I don't feel comfortable having my daughter walking the same halls as this boy, and you shouldn't either. Frankly, you should be concerned about all of your female students' safety!" she barked.

"This is absurd," Mr. Clause groaned, rolling his eyes. "I can't believe I was pulled out of work for something so pointless. Todd hasn't even done anything."

"He threatened to rape my daughter!" Mom shouted, ten seconds past pissed off. "If you think that's absurd and not worthy of some form of discipline, then that's terrifying, to say the least."

"Oh, come on. Are we not going to address the elephant in the room?" Mrs. Clause said, gesturing toward Katie. "Can we really take anything to heart when it's about this girl?"

"What's that supposed to mean?" Mom asked.

My stomach twisted in knots, and Katie's eyes widened with fear.

"Mom, forget it. I want to go," Katie whispered, tugging at her arm. "This is stupid."

"No," Mom stated sternly, still looking at Mrs. Clause. "What is that supposed to mean?"

"It means that your daughter was the girl of the year last year for screwing multiple boys at a house party. The video went viral. I'm surprised you didn't see it."

"I beg your pardon?" Mom asked.

"I just think it's ridiculous. My son wouldn't want to go anywhere near a girl like her," Mrs. Clause barked.

"A girl like her?" Mom was red in the face and seconds away from exploding.

"You know—easy."

"*How dare you!*" Mom shouted. "Your son's a little shithead who deserves punishment for his actions."

"Even if he said it, they're just words, not actions," Mr. Clause corrected.

"Really," Mom hissed, flabbergasted. "Is that how you raise your son?"

Principal Williams tried to cut in to stop the arguing, but that ship had sailed.

"It's better than how you raise yours! One child is running around the school as a little slut, and the other can't even articulate a whole sentence. I guess that's what happens when you don't have a father figure for them to take after," Mrs. Clause said with revulsion.

Mom leaped from her chair and marched toward Mrs. Clause, and I was quick to grab her arm to stop her. When she looked at me, her eyes were wild, as if she were moments away from killing for her cubs.

"It's o-okay, Mom," I told her.

"Yeah, Mom. Let's go," Katie begged.

Mom's eyes watered. She looked at Principal Williams and harshly said, "I don't know how much they are paying you, or giving to this school in order to control your damn mind, but these are my children. This is your job. *Do something,*" before she turned and marched out of the office, ordering Katie and me to follow her.

We hurried our way to the car. She flung the driver's door open and quickly sat inside, slamming it shut behind her. I slid into the back seat, and Katie took shotgun. Mom's hands wrapped tightly around the steering wheel, and her breaths were uneven.

"I'm so sorry, Mom," Katie finally choked out, tears falling down her face. "I…"

"Is that why you stopped hanging out with those friends?" Mom asked.

Katie nodded. "It was a stupid party, and, and I was too scared to tell you and embarrassed and…I'm sorry," Katie cried.

Mom turned to her and locked eyes with my sister. She placed her hands on her shoulders. "Katlyn Rae Adams, you never, ever have to be ashamed of yourself or too embarrassed to talk to me. Do you understand?"

Katie nodded. "Yes, Mom."

"We are going to talk about this at some point, okay? But right now, I just need to know you're okay. Are you okay?"

"Yes."

"And those, those—*monsters* in that office today? Those adults who talked so disgustingly about a child like that? They are the problem. This world is the problem, not you."

Mom pulled Katie into a hug, and they both cried against one another for a long time. We stayed in the school parking lot until both could catch their breath. Mom wiped Katie's eyes, and Katie wiped Mom's.

"Let's get home for dinner," Mom declared, putting the car into drive. "And then we are going to look into transferring schools."

"Mom?" I called out.

"Yes, Elliott?"

"Did you, um, d-did you call Todd a sh-shithead?"

She smirked in the rearview mirror and shrugged. "I think I did."

I smiled my biggest grin as she started drove us home.

*Coolest. Mom. Ever.*

# Chapter Thirteen

## Jasmine

"Mickey Rice is one of the best producers in the whole wide world, Jasmine. This could be life-changing if we get him to work with you. He has connections with the best of the best, and he's pairing us up with T.K. Reid, the mixing engineer. You really couldn't be luckier," Trevor exclaimed as we took a taxi to the studio in London.

Mama was staring out the window taking pictures of all the buildings as we drove by. We'd been in England for a few weeks now, and it's been nonstop work for me. When I wasn't in a studio or meeting with potential producers, I was with Mama being homeschooled.

Whenever I got a free minute, I'd email Elliott. It was the only way we had to communicate, and with the time difference, there were so many times I'd wake up to a new message from him and go to sleep wishing I had more words from him.

"When we get up to the meeting, let me lead it, okay?" Trevor told me, fixing his tie. His attire told me it must've been a very important meeting.

Trevor was the complete opposite of Ray. He looked and acted like a snake. There was no softness to him at all.

"Can I come into the meeting?" Mama asked.

Trevor cringed a bit. "I don't know, Heather. I think it might just be best to, ya know, keep it to the professionals." He winked her way.

"I want her in there," I said, staring out the window as we drove past Elizabeth Tower.

"But—" Trevor started, and I glared his way.

"If Mama doesn't come with me, I'm not going in there."

"No, it's fine, Jasmine. I'd probably just get in the way and step on people's toes," Mama joked, smiling at me. "Trevor will be there with you. It will be fine."

I argued with her, but I could tell she wasn't going to go against Trevor. Unlike Ray, Trevor didn't put up with Mama's sharp tongue. When she bit him, he bit her back—harder.

I reloaded my email, hoping a new letter from Elliott had arrived since I'd checked five seconds before, but still nothing. Even though it was only three in the morning back in New Orleans, I really wished he were awake to talk to me.

"How long has she been performing?" Mickey Rice asked Trevor as he leaned against his desk. He spun a pencil between his fingers, eyeing me up and down.

"Six years," Trevor answered for me. "She's been performing professionally for six years."

"And how old is she?" he asked, his stare locked with mine though he spoke to Trevor.

"Sixteen."

Mickey cocked an eyebrow. "She could pass as nineteen."

"It's the makeup. We can always tame it if need be," Trevor told him.

Mickey's eyes traveled up and down my body once again. I crossed my legs and arms as discomfort washed over me. I hated how they spoke about me as if I wasn't in the room. I hated how I wasn't allowed to speak for myself. I hated how Trevor—a complete stranger—was my voice.

"No, no. We want her to pass as older. More attention." Mickey gave a sly grin. "How much does she weigh?"

"Why don't you just ask me?" I snapped. Trevor pinched my arm and gave me a stern look.

"She's one hundred and thirty pounds."

"Get her to drop fifteen."

"But I'm five eight," I argued.

"You're right—get her to drop twenty."

"What does any of this have to do with my career?" I asked, annoyed.

"This is the music industry, sweetheart—it has everything to do with your career." Mickey pulled out a pack of cigarettes and placed one between his lips. He offered Trevor one, and he took it. *God*, I hated cigarette smoke.

"So, describe her genre for me," Mickey continued.

This went on and on. The two talked about my flaws and my talent, the direction they each believed I could take, etc. I grew tired of it all, and every now and then I'd steal a glance at my cell phone to see if I had a new email from Elliott.

*Of course not.*

*He's still sleeping.*

"And she dances?" Mickey questioned.

"Don't you want to hear me sing?" I cut in, growing tired of their talk. Mickey gave me a hard look.

"Excuse me, missy. Two grown men are having a conversation here."

"About me," I argued.

Trevor gave me a shut-up-right-now look, but I didn't care.

"You're talking about me and my career and my this and that, but you haven't even asked me to sing for you."

"What does your voice have to do with anything?"

"That's the whole reason I'm here—for my singing."

Mickey laughed. "This is the music industry—that has nothing to do with your career."

Trevor leaned toward me and slightly shook his head. "Just let me handle this, kid. I got your back."

I didn't believe him.

They went back to their conversation, and I went back to refreshing my email. My heart jumped when I saw EAdams pop up in my inbox.

## Subject: Three A.M.

Jazz,
I woke up to go to the bathroom and 3:33AM was flashing on my alarm clock, and then I thought of you. What time does that make it there? Nine in the morning? You have that meeting with the big producer, right? It's going to go perfect. They'd be crazy not to sign you.

I miss you.

-Eli

---

## Subject: Re: Three A.M.

Eli,

I'm in the meeting now. It's almost ten in the morning here. The guy doesn't care about me as a person at all, he's only interested in how to sell my brand.
I didn't know I had a brand.
I just wanted to sing soul music.
Trevor seems to be in his happy place.
I miss you more. Go to sleep.

-Jazz

**Subject: Re: Re: Three A.M.**

I can't go back to sleep.
Tell them you only sing soul music.
Tell them pop music sucks.
Tell them your truth.
Are you happy?

-Eli

---

**Subject: Happy?**

Happy? Yeah, I am.

-Jazz

---

**Subject: Re: Happy?**

Liar.

-Eli

**Subject: Re: Re: Happy?**

Good night, Elliott.

-Jazz

P.S. Listen to Ella James—she always helps me get to sleep.

---

**Subject: Re: Re: Re: Happy?**

Good morning, Jasmine.

-Eli

P.S. Listen to Tupac—he always helps me tell the world to piss off.

---

**Subject: P.S.**

Jasmine?

-Eli

---

**Subject: Re: P.S.**

Yes, Elliott?

-Jazz

—

**Subject: Re: Re: P.S.**

I think you're beautiful.
I think you're so freaking beautiful.
Inside and out.

-Eli

Oh, also, I love you.

---

**Subject: First time**

That's the first time you've ever said that to me.

-Jazz

---

**Subject: Re: First time**

I know.

-Eli

---

**Subject: Re: Re: First time**

Elliott?

-Jazz

**Subject: Re: Re: Re: First time**

Yes, Jasmine?

-Eli

---

**Subject: Re: Re: Re: Re: First time**

I think your voice is beautiful.
Even when it shakes.

-Jazz

Also, I love you, too.

## Chapter Fourteen

**Elliott**

"You know what happens to snitches?" Todd whispered as he walked past me, bumping into my shoulder just slightly. He'd been harassing me each day, but his harassments were much quieter now, almost as if he was afraid to get caught. It was the same with his friends, and the only thing they really called me was a snitch, because I'd gone to Mom about Katie.

I didn't care, though. As long as my sister was okay, I'd take being called a snitch.

I reloaded my emails, checking to see if there was anything from Jasmine. Whenever I reloaded the page, a big knot sat in my stomach as I waited to see if she'd written me back.

When she hadn't, I just reread her old emails.

That was good enough for me.

On Saturday, Uncle TJ still made me go to the corner to play my music, even though I didn't want to without Jasmine there. "Music must live on right beside the broken hearts, Elliott. If it didn't, how would people ever heal?"

I played on the corner, and everyone cheered me on as they always did, but the cheers seemed a bit quieter without her there, a bit lonelier.

Uncle TJ was right, though—music did help me. What helped even more was Mom, TJ, or Katie showing up each night for my performance. That night my sister came and cheered me on.

"You don't have to come here, ya know," I said as Katie kept applauding for me.

"I'm not gonna have you out here without any support, brother, and since Mom has to work and TJ is teaching tonight, I'm here. Plus, I love seeing you perform. You're amazing, Eli." I awkwardly smiled. Compliments were hard for me to accept sometimes. "Are you going to sit in the alleyway to listen to music?" she asked.

"Yeah, just for a little while."

"Want me to grab some hot dogs from Dat Dog and join you?"

I raised an eyebrow. "Even if I say no, are you going to come?"

"Yep, pretty much."

"Then I'll take an alligator sausage and Coca-Cola, please."

"On it! I'll meet you back there in a few." She hurried off to the restaurant, and I wandered toward the alley.

Sitting on top of the dumpster behind the bars was a way for me to unplug from the world. Listening to the music playing was more than enough peace. During my time spent back there, I imagined what it would be like to see Jasmine again, what it would be like to hold her.

Jasmine Greene was the girl I was never supposed to get, and if I ever had the chance to see her again, I knew I wouldn't let her go.

I heard a voice as I was staring up at the darkened sky, but it wasn't Katie's.

"You know what happens to snitches?"

Todd and his guys walked down the alleyway toward me. I tensed up, jumping off the dumpster to run, but one of them grabbed me by my arm.

"Where are you off to so fast?" Todd barked. "We've been asking for weeks now, and I think it's time you answered us, Boney Bones. What happens to snitches?" he hissed as two guys pinned me with my back against the dumpster. Todd slammed his fist into my gut, pushing all the air out of my lungs. "Snitches get stitches and buried in ditches."

"N-no, p-please," I begged, but they didn't care. They were obviously drunk or high—or both.

"I saw you talking to your sister on the street. Is she meeting you back here?" Todd asked as I kept moving, trying to get out of their hold.

"No," I lied, swallowing hard.

"Well maybe I should call her real fast and tell her to hurry back over. Grab his cell phone," Todd ordered.

"Leave her alone!" I shouted. The guys slammed me against the dumpster, making me groan in pain.

They snatched my phone, and Todd flipped it open. He tried to get into the phone and he grimaced. "What's your passcode, freak?" I kept my mouth shut. He huffed as he walked over to me and locked his eyes with mine. "I said"—he slammed his fist into my gut—"what's..." *Fist.* "Your..." *Fist.* "Passcode?"

Vomit began to rise from my stomach, but I didn't say a word. I couldn't. I had to protect my sister. He could beat me as long as he wanted to, as long as she was safe.

"What the hell are you doing?" a voice shouted at the end of the alley. I turned to see my sister dropping the food to the ground.

*Oh no, Katie...*

"Well, aren't you a liar?" Todd scolded me, slapping my face.

"No, Katie! Run!" I hollered, but she didn't listen to me at all. She started running toward us. "No!"

"Goddammit, shut him up, will you?" Todd groaned. "Toss him into the dumpster while I deal with this bitch." He flipped open the lid, and the guys started to lift me. One grabbed me by the ankles, and the other wrapped his hands tight around my wrists. They lifted me into the air and then swung me in. As I tried to hurry to my feet to leap out, they shut the lid and jumped on top of it.

I pressed my hands against the lid, trying to push it up, but I couldn't.

*I'm not strong enough.*

*I'm not strong enough.*

I listened to them snicker and laugh. The smell of the rotting foods made me want to gag, but I did my best to keep it down. My first and only concern was making sure Katie was okay.

"Well if it isn't the biggest whore in town," Todd huffed.

"Let him go, Todd," Katie said stern. "Stop being an asshole."

*Katie, no...leave.*

"Don't worry about him. He was just feeling down in the dumps," Todd joked before someone pounded their hand against the dumpster.

"Eli." Though her voice was steady, I could tell Katie was terrified. I didn't want her to worry about me.

"Run, Katie!" I shouted, my voice burning as I kept pounded against the cage I was trapped inside.

"I'm not leaving," she replied. "Don't worry. I'm calling the cops."

"No, hold up. I think we should talk first," Todd said.

"Give me my phone back, jerk!" she hissed.

Todd laughed. "Do you know my parents took away my car privileges after that stunt your shit brother pulled?"

"Well, maybe if you weren't a complete pig, you wouldn't have gotten in trouble," Katie barked, not a tremble in her voice. I loved that about her—she wasn't afraid of anything. At least not on the outside. Even with everything she'd been through, she always held her head up high in the face of conflict.

"You got a slick mouth, don't ya? What else can that mouth do?" Todd said ever so slyly.

I pounded against the lid as I shouted. My veins popped out of my neck as my hands bled from hitting the lid repeatedly. I kicked, clawed, and punched the lid. The skin on my knuckles ripped and tore. My body was beat and bruised as I tried to escape the cage I was locked inside, but nothing worked. I used everything I had, I used every inch of my body to try to escape, but still, I couldn't.

*I'm not strong enough.*

*I'm not strong enough.*

"Let me go!" Katie yelled. The fact that his hands were on her made me livid, but still, I couldn't budge the lid.

"How about you use those lips for something other than talking, huh? I know my brother loved your mouth," Todd hissed before I heard him shout in panic. "What the fuck?!"

"What happened?" one of his friends asked, leaping down off the dumpster. I took the chance to push on the lid once more, but I still couldn't move it.

"The bitch sprayed me with pepper spray!" he hollered. "You're going to fucking pay, you slut. Get her, Tim! And, Ryan, don't you dare get off that dumpster!"

There was a loud commotion, and I listened to Katie try her best to get out of their grips.

"Let me go! Let me go!" She fought, trying to get to me as I tried to get to her, but nothing was working. Nothing I tried worked. "No," she cried. "No, please," she begged.

Then, Katie's voice disappeared.

"Dude, Todd, you're choking her," one of the guys muttered.

"Shut up, Ryan! I got this!" he said.

"What the fuck are you doing, man?" Tim said, his voice sounding shocked.

"She's a fucking whore," Todd hissed.

"She's not breathing!" Ryan hollered, and I felt him leap off the dumpster.

I shoved on the lid, and finally it opened. I saw Tim and Ryan trying their best to pull Todd off my sister. One of his hands was wrapped tightly around her neck, and she gasped for air while his other hand was down her pants.

*No...*

Todd slammed her body against the concrete wall repeatedly as Katie clawed at his hands.

I hurried out of the dumpster right as the guys forced Todd to let go. I watched my sister's body fall to the ground, saw the blood from where her head had pounded against the wall. I saw the panic in the guys' eyes as they stared at her motionless body.

"Dude!" Ryan cried, terror in his stare. "What the fuck did you do?"

I tackled Todd the moment my feet hit solid ground. I knocked him to the ground, shouting at him, screaming, crying, beyond logic. He was bigger than me, they all were, but I didn't care. My hands flew into his face continually as I punched him. His blood covered my hands as I kept swinging. I hadn't a clue what I was doing, but I needed him to suffer, needed him to stop breathing, needed him to hurt the way he'd hurt my sister. Tim and Ryan took off running, and Todd shoved me hard. The moment I went flying, he took off down the alleyway.

I stumbled to my feet and rushed over to Katie. Her breaths were swallow and her eyes widened, panicked.

"Eli," she murmured, and I wrapped my arms around her.

"It's okay," I told her, panicking when I noticed the blood on my fingers from where I'd touched the back of her head. "You're okay, you're okay."

She started to shut her eyes, and I shook her.

*No...*

"St-stay here, Katie. Stay h-here." I reached into her purse and searched for her cell phone, but then remembered Todd had taken it. My eyes darted around, and I found my cell phone on the ground where the guys had tossed it. I hurried over and dialed 9-1-1, and then I was back to Katie. I held her in my lap, and I didn't let go of her again. She stayed still as her breaths grew lighter and lighter, and my panic grew louder and louder.

I didn't remember what I said to the dispatcher.

The person on the phone asked me questions, and I didn't remember responding. I didn't remember anything. Every inch of me was numb. Every part of me dying from the pain.

"No," I begged, holding her, pulling her motionless body close to mine. "No, no, no, pl-please. Katie, please," I cried into her as the dispatcher told me they were sending someone our way. An ambulance was on the way. *An ambulance... An ambulance is on the way...*

I began to sob into my sister, because I knew she wasn't going to make it. I knew when the ambulance pulled around the block, they'd be too late to help.

I held my sister as she took her last breaths in my arms.

"Katie, no," I yelled as I sobbed uncontrollably.

When they arrived, they pushed me to the side, tried CPR, and then loaded her onto a stretcher. They took me in the truck with them. As they pulled away, they pronounced her dead.

Every part of me died right there beside her—my sister, my family, my very best friend.

I was forever ruined when Todd Clause stole the life of the best human I'd ever known.

And nothing would ever be the same again.

---

**Subject: Making her proud**

I feel like I haven't been myself in so long. Whenever I sing soul music, it's at night, and it's almost a whisper so Trevor and my mom won't hear me.

I'm sorry I haven't emailed you much. Mom has been yelling at me to stay off my cell phone.

I hate that you're so far away. I hate that I can't see you.

There's this superstar producer I'm supposed to meet with. He's known for making megastars for pop music.

I'd gone over and over about how I could tell everyone no. I'd thought about how I could run away and just not come back.

Run back to you. To us. To soul.

But then, I think about my mother.

This might be the what I've been looking for this whole time. Maybe if I do this, maybe if I have a pop career, then she'll be proud of me.

That's all I want.

That's all I ever wanted.

Sometimes she smiles now, ya know. When I sing what she wants me to sing, she smiles.

Don't worry. I'm still singing soul music. It's just a little quieter than before.

How are you?

-Jazz

Also, still love you.

# Chapter Fifteen

## Elliott

I stumbled to my feet and rushed over to Katie. Her breaths were low, and her eyes widened, panicked. *"Eli,"* she murmured, and I wrapped my arms around her.

*"It's okay,"* I told her, panicked when I noticed the blood on my fingers as I touched the back of her head. *"You're okay, you're okay."*

She started to shut her eyes, and I shook her.

"Son," was barked my way, forcing me from my thoughts. My recent memories were on replay in my tangled mind.

*"Son, focus!"*

I shot my eyes open.

Two officers stood across from me as I sat on a bench in the hospital hallway. One was mute with a notepad, and the other talkative with no notetaking. He was the one who kept calling me son, even though I wasn't his son.

"Son, I need you to understand, we need all the information that you can give us. We need every detail about what happened. What you saw. Do you understand, son?"

*I'm not your son.*

I stared forward at the wall, blinking every now and then. A light kept flickering down the hallway, and each time it flickered, I twitched. *Please stop flickering.* My hands were shaky, my throat dry. Each time I swallowed it felt like cuts against my windpipes.

"Son, please. The sooner we get this information, the sooner we can move forward with this accident."

"It it it i..." I murmured, blinking my eyes shut. "It wa-wasn't wasn't..."

"Come on, then. Spit it out," he urged me. "What were they wearing? How many of them were there? Did you have any relation with them? Do you know their names?"

My body started to rock back and forth, and when my eyes opened, I was staring down at my ripped, bloody knuckles. Covered in both my blood and my sister's.

I blinked my eyes shut once more.

*No.*

*No.*

*No...*

Tears streamed down my face as acid rose from my stomach and landed in my throat.

I wasn't strong enough. She was dead because of me.

"Maybe we should take a break, Kenny," the mute cop spoke. "Wait till his mom gets here. He's in shock."

"But," Officer Kenny started.

"Just a break," the other said, cutting in. "I think he needs it."

When they walked away, I went back to staring at the wall as the light continued to flicker above me.

*Please stop flickering.*

"Elliott," Mom cried, rushing into the hospital waiting room toward me. I'd been staring intensely at my bloody hands, shaky as I waited for her to arrive. The moment I saw her, I stood from my seat. TJ wasn't many steps behind her.

"I-I-I-I-" My lips parted as my shaking grew. No words could form in my head, or my heart as I tried to apologize to my mom. I tried to craft words to beg her to forgive me, to understand my mistake. "I-I-I..."

*No.*

*No.*

*No...*

I needed words, but I couldn't grasp them. I needed air, but no breath was there.

I was dizzy. I was nauseous. I was broken. I was lost.

My legs shook beneath me, and my vision began to blur. The second I was about to collapse, Mom wrapped me against her body and held me. Still, that didn't stop either of us from falling to the floor as heartache attacked us intensely.

"No, no, no," Mom cried against me. "Not my baby, not my baby," she sobbed uncontrollably.

TJ tried to help us, but he couldn't. There was no way we could be put back together.

Mom couldn't catch her breath as she began to realize she was suffering from a parent's worst nightmare. She lost herself on the hospital floor and was unable to be fixed, because once a parent lost their child, they lost themselves. There was no way to fix a broken heart that beat for a child. There was no way to console a person whose world had just been stolen away from them.

There was no way to make any of this okay.

As Mom tried her best to comfort me, I tried my best to hold her tight. Neither one of us would ever be okay again. Something inside of each of us snapped, and it was beyond repair. That something would be damaged forever, unable to know what it felt like to be alive ever again.

That something was our hearts.

My heart stopped beating the moment Katie died because of me.

Mom's stopped beating the moment she realized the truth.

I'd never forgive myself.

I'd never expect Mom to forgive me, either.

As we sat there on the floor, broken and damaged, I managed to push out the only words that kept flying through my mind. As tears fell down my cheeks and my throat burned, I finally spoke the four words that would never mean enough, the four words that would haunt me each day moving forward.

"I'm so sorry, Mom. I'm so sorry, Mom. I'm so sorry, Mom."

I kept repeating it over and over again, and still, it felt empty.

**Subject: 4,624 mi**

Eli,

Hey, you. I haven't heard from you, but I'm guessing you're busy. I've been a bit busy, too. But I just wanted you to know I'm still thinking of you.

London is four thousand, six hundred, and twenty-four miles away from New Orleans.

Today I thought about walking each and every one to get back to you.

-Jazz

Also, still love you.

## Chapter Sixteen

### Elliott

The day of the funeral, I stood in front of my bedroom mirror, staring at myself in the black suit. My eyes were puffy, and I couldn't tie my tie. I kept looping it repeatedly, but no matter what, I couldn't do it. Katie always did it.

She always fixed my ties.

"Let me?" TJ asked.

I knew he was standing behind me in the doorframe, but I didn't speak to him. I hadn't really spoken to anyone. Words seemed pointless. Tying ties seemed pointless.

Everything was pointless.

I dropped my hands to my sides, defeated, and TJ stepped into the room. He picked up the two ends of the tie, and as he did it, he cleared his throat.

"You can talk to me, you know. About anything. About everything. About nothing."

I remained quiet.

Mom walked past my bedroom and peered inside. She paused for a moment and parted her lips as if she were going to speak, but nothing came out. She hadn't spoken much to anyone, either.

Especially not to me.

I'd never known eyes could look so sad until I stared into my mother's. She was my Wonder Woman, and watching her walk around so unbelievably broken was beyond heartbreaking. I'd caused her that pain, that suffering.

"She do-doesn't look at me the same," I whispered to TJ. "She hates me."

He frowned, shaking his head. "Elliott Adams, no one could ever hate you."

"She doesn't talk to me."

"Not because she hates you. It's just that she doesn't know how to communicate right now."

I glanced down at my shiny black shoes. "Because I kil-killed Katie?"

TJ shook his head back and forth and gripped my chin in his hand, forcing me to look at him. "Boy, if I ever hear you speak those lies again, I will rip out your tongue." My body started shaking in his grip, and he stared me hard in the eyes. "Do you understand me?" he ordered as tears cascaded down my cheeks. "Do you understand that what happened wasn't because of you?"

"Yes, sir," I lied, and he knew it was a lie.

TJ's eyes filled with tears, and he pulled me into a tight hug as I shook against his hold. "You didn't do this, Elliott. You didn't do this at all. Never say that again. Never say that," he said over and over again, shaking himself. As he held me tight, I could feel it happening to him, too.

His heart breaking.

Many people showed up at the funeral service, and that pissed me off. All of the 'friends' Katie once held walked into the church building as if they hadn't disowned her for the past year. A lot of them even had the nerve to bring tears along with them.

"They sho-shouldn't be here," I angrily barked, my hands forming fists from their level of disrespect. How dare they show up for her now, when in reality they should've stood by her side last year during the darkest times of her life?

How dare they want to speak their apologies?

How dare they pretend to care only because it was too late to change anything?

"Let them be," TJ told me, squeezing my shoulder. "Guilt has a way of swallowing individuals whole, and now they are remorseful."

"They hurt her," I told him.

"And they know that. And that guilt they are feeling? That's not between you and them. That's between God and them."

I hadn't the nerve to tell TJ there wasn't a God. At least not one I'd stand behind after he took my sister.

"Those people made bad choices, Eli. There's no getting around that. They made their beds. Now they have the rest of their lives to sleep in them. But for today...just let them be."

I hated TJ in that moment, because he always did what was right.

At the burial, we gathered around the casket, and I watched them lower my big sister into the ground. It was all so surreal. It blew my mind how one day everything could be fine, and then the next, your loved one was gone.

"Elliott," a voice said behind me. I turned around to see a chubby red-haired guy walking toward me with his hands stuffed in his pockets.

"Jason." I narrowed my eyes, confused that my best friend was standing there in front of me. "Wh-what are you doing here?" I asked.

He was still supposed to be in Nebraska with his mom.

He shrugged. "I wanted to come back to stay with my dad for a while."

"You hate your dad."

"Yeah, but you're my best friend," he said, somberly. "So, I'm going to stay with my dad for a while."

He'd never know how much that meant to me. Whenever I'd start to cry, he'd pat me on the back and turn his head away so I wouldn't see his own tears. Katie was Jason's first crush, the girl he thought he'd someday end up with after life lined up for the two of them. She was the first girl to ever tell him he was good enough the way he was, and she was the first girl to ever call him handsome. He loved her, and I wasn't surprised.

How could anyone not love her? She was everything good in a bad world.

"They are, um, the lawyer Mom got wants to charge the guys as adults inst-instead of minors," I told Jason.

He grimaced. "That's still not enough."

"No," I agreed. "Not enough at all."

Letting someone sit in a prison cell didn't seem like justice to me, not when it was supposed to be the justice for taking my sister's life.

For the remainder of my life I'd be trapped in the prison of my guilt. I'd be trapped behind the bars of my mind, unable to break free from the damage that had been done to my heart and soul.

Yet still, that wasn't enough.

*Not enough at all.*

We stood in the cemetery for a long time until Mom was ready to say goodbye to Katie...until I was ready to say goodbye.

"When my grandpa died, I remember being really sad that I never got to say goodbye. So, my mom turned to me and said, 'Never goodbye, always goodnight until we wake again.'" He knitted his eyebrows and he shrugged. "I never understood what that really meant until now. You're not saying goodbye forever, Eli. Just good night for now."

I lowered my head. "That doesn't make it easier."

"No," he agreed. "It doesn't. But maybe someday it will."

Death was such a foreign creature. You knew it was a sad thing for people, but you never truly understood the grief until it washed up against your shore. Then, once you saw the strange being, you wished you could go back in time to all the others who'd lost someone close and apologize for not giving them any extra comfort. I wasn't sure who death hurt more—the ones who left, or the ones who had to stay behind.

As each day passed, I realized how impossible it was to ever really get over missing someone. There were always the small reminders that brought the loved one rushing back to the forefront. Maybe it was the way someone laughed in a supermarket or danced poorly. Perhaps it was the way you could be sitting alone in a dark room, missing the warmth of your loved one, so you'd cry alone in the darkness. Or it was the way you could be standing at a party with a lot of people, surrounded by love and happiness, and out of nowhere you fell apart because the celebration cake was purple and *purple was their favorite color.*

In a way, it was as if our loved ones never truly left. They were within everything, within everyone.

I wasn't sure yet if that was a blessing or a curse.

It took seven days for Mom to be able to stand in front of me and not cry. One night, she came into my doorway and crossed her arms.

"I'm sorry," she told me.

"I'm sorry," I replied.

Her eyes glassed over, but she didn't cry. "It's not because of you, Eli. I just need you to know that. But when I look at you..." She took a deep inhale and released it as a heavy sigh. "Your beautiful eyes. You have your sister's beautiful eyes. And I guess that's hard for me. But I'm working on it. Okay? I just want you to know, I'm working on being better. For you. Always for you."

She walked over to me and kissed my forehead. "You are my world. Do you know that?"

I nodded. "Yes."

After that talk, each night, Mom would come check on me. She'd smile my way and be the bravest woman I'd ever known. She'd tell me none of it was my fault. She'd say she loved me fully. She'd beg for me not to blame myself for something the devil had laid on our doorstep. She'd say it without a single tear falling from her eyes as the sadness poured out of me.

Then, she'd stand up, kiss my forehead, and tell me to try to get some rest.

Later, I'd hear her.

She kept her tears locked away from me, but I always heard her crying in her bedroom.

So, I'd check on her.

I'd smile her way and be the bravest man I could be. I'd tell her none of it was her fault. I'd say I loved her fully. I'd beg for her not to blame herself for something the devil had laid on our doorstep. I'd say it without a single tear falling from my eyes as the sadness poured out of her.

I'd stay with her until I knew she was sleeping.

Then, I'd fall asleep right there beside her, because I selfishly didn't want to be alone.

---

**Subject: Hey**

Eli,

I haven't heard from you. Are you okay? My mom is making me perform in places I'd never want to perform. I'm trying to do what you said and follow my heart, but it's like she can't hear how it beats. Why haven't you written? I miss you, and I'm starting to worry.

-Jazz

Also, I love you.

## Chapter Seventeen

### Elliott

School was different than before. No one bullied me anymore. Principal Williams stepped down from his position. Mom said it was because of his guilty conscience for not doing anything to stop what had happened.

When I walked down the hallways, everyone's eyes darted away from me. Even teachers had a hard time looking my way. It was as if I were finally invisible, the way I'd always dreamed of being. The only person who could see me was Jason, and he wouldn't leave me alone even when I asked him to go away.

He took his best friend duties seriously and checked in on me every second of every day.

"You okay, Elliott?" he'd ask.

"I'm okay," I'd reply.

"Lying?" he'd ask.

"Lying," I'd reply.

The truth was, I'd never be okay. I'd never be the same person I'd been, because I hadn't been strong enough to save my sister.

Mom forced me to see the guidance counselor, which I hated more than words could express. Mr. Yang sat in front of me, giving me the same kind of broken smiles everyone had been giving me.

"What you went through must have been tough, Elliott," he told me.

"Not really. Death is sh-shockingly easy to deal with," I replied sarcastically. In my mind, I knew I should apologize, but in my heart, I just didn't care anymore. I didn't care about anything anymore. My sister was dead, and it was all because of me. She wouldn't have been in that alleyway if it wasn't for me. She wouldn't have been choked to death if I wasn't a loser. It was pretty much my hands that had been wrapped around her neck, and I'd spend the rest of my life imprisoned by that guilt.

"I got you some pamphlets," Mr. Yang said, handing me some folded sheets of paper.

*Letting Go and Holding onto Memories*

*The Facts about Death*

*How to Deal with the Unthinkable*

*The Seven Stages of Grief*

"I think those will help," he told me.

Right, because mourning was resolved with pamphlets.

"Mr. Yang?"

"Yes, Elliott?"

"Can I leave now?"

"Yes, Elliott."

I sat in the courtroom the day Todd was found guilty. I sat in the courtroom as his mother howled out in anguish. I sat in the courtroom as Todd burst into tears. I sat in the courtroom as his brother's face went pale. I sat in the courtroom as his father stayed completely still.

The sentence: life in prison with no chance for parole.

Todd Clause would spend his life behind bars for the murder of my sister, and the world called it justice.

*There's no such thing as justice.*

There was no justice in that courtroom, because as Todd walked away to rot in a cell, Katie was still gone. As Todd's lungs rose and fell, Katlyn Rae Adams had no more inhales to meet or exhales to release.

I studied their pain and their suffering, but it meant nothing to me.

That case wasn't a victory, it wasn't a win.

There was no such thing as justice when it came to the murder of an innocent person. There was simply a hollowness that lived within each person who had to say goodbye too soon.

Yes, Todd Clause would spend his life locked away, but that didn't bring me any peace of mind. There would never be peace, because my sister was still dead, and it was all because of me.

---

**Subject: Where are you?**

Eli,

I'm worried.
Where are you?

---

**Subject: I don't know.**

Eli,

I don't know what happened. Are you busy? Are you mad at me? Did something go wrong? I just cannot imagine anything that would make you stop talking to me. I just want to know if you're okay, and if you're not, let me help. I'll do anything. I miss you, Eli. I miss you so much, and not hearing from you is making me sick. I don't know what to do.

If I don't hear from you, I'll leave you alone after this. If I don't hear from you, I'll go away.

Please let me hear from you.

-Jazz

Also, I still love you.
No matter what.

## Chapter Eighteen

*Elliott*

Each day I stared at Jasmine's emails, unable to reply. The cursor blinked and blinked, but I couldn't bring myself to type out the words to tell her Katie was gone. I also couldn't bring myself to a place where I would open myself up to being comforted by Jasmine.

Even from four thousand, six hundred, and twenty-four miles away, I knew she'd make me feel better, and I didn't want that.

There was a burning that had been weighing in my gut since Katie had passed away, and I wanted it to stay there as a reminder that I was responsible for her death.

I never mentioned the weight, the burn to anyone, because I knew they'd all tell me it wasn't my fault. In my mind, in my heart, and in my soul, I knew the truth, and I'd feel that suffering each and every day.

Over time, I became annoyed with Jasmine's notes, her thoughtfulness, her care...her heart, her hope.

I didn't want anything to do with hope. I didn't want anything to do with feeling a split second of happiness, because I deserved the sadness.

I read the stupid pamphlets, too—each one, about twenty times.

The one I read the most was *The Seven Stages of Grief*.

I found it interesting, the way they laid it out so clearly.

First, there was shock and denial.

I'd felt that one head-on, but it had quickly moved on to stage two: pain and guilt. The pain never really disappeared, though. It just shifted to stage three: anger.

Anger had hit me hard. I was angry at the world, angry at myself for not being strong enough to help Katie, for not being man enough to save her.

Then, I hit loneliness, and that's where I failed with the seven stages of grief.

I hovered back and forth between anger and loneliness.

I didn't move on to the upward turn, reconstruction, or acceptance.

I just simmered in the darkness of my aching pain. I separated myself from the world. Each day, I grew darker. Each day, I lost myself more.

Instead of playing music, I started doing push-ups.

Instead of going to Frenchmen Street, I started lifting weights.

*I'll be strong enough.*

*I'll be strong enough...*

Over the years, my body began to change. I became obsessed with being strong. Each day, heavier weights—each night, fewer feelings. I took part in anything and everything that would make me gain weight and muscle. I worked hard each day to become stronger.

I grew.

I shifted.

I worked hard.

I changed.

And somehow, someway, I lost everything that made me...me.

I kept to myself, because if no one was near me, how could they get hurt? I became a ghost of a man, once who existed in the world but was no longer part of it.

The music in me had died the day my sister left this earth, and the melody of my heart was officially mute.

# Chapter Nineteen

## Jasmine

I never heard from Elliott again.

I never again kissed the lips of the boy who loved me. I never again saw those hazel eyes. I never again received an email from him, telling me he missed me.

As time went on, life became harder...tougher...*darker*.

Darker than I'd ever thought possible. The only drops of light were when Ray would call and email me over the years. Two times each week we'd FaceTime each other, and he'd ask me the same thing at the beginning and end of our conversations.

"You have a good day, Snow White?"

Some days those words were enough to bring me to tears, but I never let him hear me sniffling. "Yes," I'd always tell him. "Everything's fine."

I'd lie every time, and he knew it was a lie every time, too, but he never pushed it. He knew how hard I was trying to make it work for Mama.

He knew how important it was for me to make her proud. He didn't understand my need to make her proud, but he respected it.

While my music career was coming together, everything else around me was falling apart. I hated waking up knowing I was going to go into the studio and lose myself to an industry that wasn't shaped to love me for me.

Trevor didn't make it easier, either.

He loved to remind me of my flaws, and then he'd order Mama to have me fix them.

Ray was right about him—he was a snake. Everything about him made my skin crawl, from his wicked smirk to the way he sometimes touched my lower back when he introduced me to people.

When I told Mama how uncomfortable he made me, she scolded me.

"Everything he's doing is for you, Jasmine. How dare you speak about him in that way?"

It was different with Trevor than with Ray for her. I noticed it every day. She always backed him up, no matter how wrong he'd been. She looked at Trevor with admiration. To her, he was everything she'd ever wished for. He was the opposite of Ray—which was why I hated him, and Mama loved him. She loved him so much, even though his love for her was mediocre at best.

All I wanted to do was get that same kind of attention from her.

That's all I ever wanted.

Each day that passed, it grew easier to forget the good things, to forget the love, to forget warmth, to forget Elliott. When I was young, I thought I'd endured the hardest parts of my life. As I grew older, I would've given anything to return to my youth, to the days when a young, broken boy loved a young, damaged girl.

But life didn't work like that. The world was determined to shatter every piece of me until my body became a monument of the scars life left behind.

I stayed in London for six years, and it was six years too long.

I'd given myself to pop music, even though my spirit yearned for soul. Every choice I'd ever made was for my mother. I allowed demeaning comments because she told me they were just words. I let grown men lay their hands on my shoulders, on my back, on my curves, because she said that was just part of the industry.

"Know your place, Jasmine," she told me one night after I cried myself to sleep because one of the producers had squeezed my ass. "You knew what you were getting into."

That was a lie, but she believed it.

I wasn't a person anymore, at least not in her mind.

Sometimes I'd catch Mama smiling at me when I performed, but I knew it wasn't really me she saw. It was the brand.

Mama loved the brand, yet she never really loved me.

I often wondered if she saw the men around us and the way they looked at me. I wondered if she noticed their long embraces, their wandering hands, their low whistles. I wondered if she ignored them because she had her eyes on the prize...because she wanted success more than anything in the world...because she didn't want to bite the hands that were feeding her.

She'd known her place.

She'd known what she was getting into.

I wondered if she cared that my skin crawled and how my throat burned, that I took long showers to wash away the day and cried myself to sleep each night. I wondered if she cared about me at all.

She was a business woman who ignored the shadows behind closed doors. Her focus was on my talents and increasing them each day. More talents meant more opportunities, more opportunities meant more fame, and more fame meant Mama might be proud of me.

Each day that passed, I stopped caring a little more about her pride. Each day that passed, I kept saying my new favorite word.

*No.*

It never got easier, saying that word. It never became numb or meaningless when I said it to someone who gave himself permission to place his hands on me. The way eyes looked me up and down when I walked into a room...the way they'd judge me on everything I was and everything I wasn't...the way they'd whisper as I stood still in the room.

*She's sexy. She's hot. I bet singing ain't all her mouth can do.*

I'd just turned twenty-two, and I knew mortification more than the average person. I knew what it felt like to stand in a room, fully clothed, and still be told that I called the attention to myself. To be called a tease when I did absolutely nothing at all. I knew what it felt like to be told I'd find more success if I showed more tits and ass during shows.

I always showed up and did my job—nothing more, nothing less. I kept my clothes on, I kept my voice low, and I kept saying it.

*No.*

*No.*

*Stop it.*

*Don't.*

But that didn't stop them from belittling me. That didn't stop them from taking me from show to show, meeting to meeting, and presenting me as if my body was a bargaining chip. As if I were a prized possession, not a human being. Mama allowed it all, too. I was her star, her shining light. I was going to do everything she'd been unable to ever accomplish, because that's what kids are supposed to do, as she'd told me numerous times.

We're supposed to be better than our parents.

*I am already better than my parent.*

If I had children, I'd never treat them that way. I'd love them. I'd protect them. No matter what.

I hadn't signed up for this.

I hadn't known what I was getting myself into when I entered the music industry.

I signed up for Mama, for her love. Her respect. Her heart. Over time, I'd realized it was never going to come my way. No matter how hard I tried.

In every story ever told, a person reached a limit. Everyone had a breaking point, and I reached mine July 30th.

On July 30th, the voices in my head became too loud. On July 30th, I packed my bags in the middle of the night. On July 30th, my heart screamed at me to run, so I ran.

I ran as fast as my legs allowed.

I ran as far as I could go.

Then I ran some more.

I bought a one-way ticket.

I sat on an airplane.

On July 31st, 2017, with pain in my chest and scars on my soul, I finally went home.

# Part Two

"The things we truly love stay with us always,
locked in our hearts as long as life remains."
— *Josephine Baker*

# Chapter Twenty

## Jasmine

Whenever I thought of home, I didn't think of a place. I thought of people. I thought of the ones who'd shaped me into the woman I'd become, the ones who'd loved me with my scars and told me those scars were beautiful, the ones who'd allowed me to make mistakes and still loved me.

That was home to me.

It wasn't a large gathering of individuals. My home was small, compact. Others would probably look at my home and think I was one of the unlucky ones, but I wasn't. I was far from unlucky, because I always had that small home to return to if I ever needed a place to run. So many people in the world were homeless, with no one in their lives to turn to in a time of need.

If you had one person who'd catch you when you were crashing through life, you were blessed beyond measure.

After years of freefalling, I finally got too close to the ground. When I was terrified of crashing, there it was, waiting right there to catch me.

My home was there, ready to take me in with arms wide-open.

I walked out of Louis Armstrong New Orleans International Airport with nerves in my stomach and a racing heart that wouldn't slow down. Each step was a step closer to the happiest times of my life. Each moment was a chance to start over.

I'd spent the past six years trying to make my mother happy, trying to achieve the dream she believed in, trying to make her proud. Each day I had failed, no matter how hard I tried, though I'd tried with every fiber of my being.

With time and heartache, I learned the hardest truth of life: you can't force love to happen, no matter how hard you try. You can't force someone to love you, to be proud of you, to care. The only thing you're in control of is your own soul and discovering what makes your heart beat.

It was now time for me to start putting myself first, even though that broke my heart because I still loved Mama so much. That was another hard life lesson: you can't will love to go away. It stays as long as it pleases, with or without your permission.

As I stared across the way, I saw a face filled with love, one I'd been dying to see for the longest time. I dropped my bags on the sidewalk, took off running in his direction, and leaped into his arms, pulling him into the tightest hug.

He hugged me back tighter and whispered against my ear, "Hey, Snow White."

I tried to fight the tears that fell from my eyes as I held him even closer. "Hey, Ray."

He drove me to his apartment, which was triple the size of the one we'd stayed in before Mama and I left. It was beautiful, with three bedrooms, two bathrooms, a kitchen as big as Texas, high ceilings, modern art, and expensive furniture.

Ray carried my bags inside for me, and I couldn't stop smiling.

"So, it pays to go mainstream, huh?" I grinned. Over the years, Ray's band had taken off, and they were doing amazing things with their music career.

He smirked. "*Semi*-mainstream. There's a difference. I'm not Adam Levine, but I'm a midlist success story."

"This looks more than midlist, Ray."

He smiled. "It pays off when you connect with the right record company who doesn't want to morph you into something you're not and they still give you enough to buy a decent apartment. Come on, you can have the master bedroom."

I rolled my eyes. "I'm not taking the master bedroom."

"Snow, come on, I was just..." His words faded away as he turned to look at me. He crossed his arms and gave me a goofy grin.

"What is it?"

His eyes glassed over, and he placed his hands behind his neck. "You're just so grown up, that's all."

I shifted around in my shoes and shook my head. "Ray, don't make me cry. I've done way too much crying lately."

He nodded and sniffled a little. "It's just...I'm so fucking happy you're here."

I agreed. "Me too."

He grabbed the handles of my luggage and started back down the hallway. "But you're taking the master bedroom—no ifs, ands, or buts."

I tried to disagree, but he wouldn't have it any other way. The moment we walked into the room, I couldn't even fight the tears. On the bed were six cards and six gift boxes wrapped in gold paper with silver bows.

"What's this?" I asked him.

He nudged me in the arm. "I missed six birthdays, so those are your six gifts."

"Oh, Ray," I murmured, pulling him into another hug, and this time, crying into his T-shirt. "Thank you, for everything—for the gifts, the room, for taking me in."

He smirked and kissed my forehead. "Welcome home, Snow. I'll let you get some rest."

*Home.*

It'd been so long since I'd seen home.

I sat down on the bed and opened each card first, my heart swelling as I read the words. Each card had a picture of Snow White on it, and inside were words he'd written to me over the past six years, wishing me a happy birthday, telling me how he wished he could be there to celebrate with me.

As I opened the gifts, I realized they all went together. The first box held a charm bracelet, and the following five held the charms—a microphone, a heart, a music note, a snowflake, and the letter J. I put all the charms on the bracelet and then placed it on my wrist.

Ray was always there for me, even when he wasn't physically there. During my years with Mama, he told me I'd always be able to call on him when I needed him the most, and when I reached my breaking point, when I needed a place to run to, I ran to him and the only city that had ever felt like home.

I didn't unpack a single thing from my suitcases. All I did was open them up, grab pajamas, and crawl straight into bed. As I closed my eyes, I allowed my battered heart to rest for the first time in a long time. I didn't overthink my life, my current situation, or anything. I gave myself a much-needed break. I climbed into bed, closed my eyes, and went to sleep.

I'd forgotten how good it felt, allowing my mind to rest.

I awakened the next morning with sunbeams dancing through the windows, warming my arms. I jumped up, feeling on edge for a moment in the unfamiliar surroundings. I rubbed the sleepiness from my eyes then let out a sigh of relief.

*I'm okay. I'm home.*

My stomach growled the moment my nose smelled burnt bacon. I pulled myself from the bed and wandered into the kitchen, where Ray was failing at making breakfast.

"What are you doing?" I laughed, watching him flip already ruined pancakes.

He turned around to see me, his face covered in pancake batter, and I couldn't stop giggling.

"You look awful. This *smells* awful."

He snickered. "I just wanted to cook you a 'welcome home' breakfast."

I walked over and picked up the burnt bacon. "And you sure did cook the hell out of it." I bit into the bacon and grimaced. "How about welcome home beignets at Café Du Monde?" I offered.

The sigh of relief that escaped his mouth was so entertaining. "Yes! Beignets are a much better welcome home, anyway, but before we dive deeper into this celebration..." He nudged me over to the living room and we went to sit down. "Has your mom called you?"

I shook my head. "No."

"Emailed?"

"No…"

He sighed. "What happened exactly?"

"Well, I told her I couldn't take it anymore. I told her I couldn't take the way I was being treated and said I wanted to come back here."

"What did she say?"

"She said I couldn't go. She told me we were so close to the breakthrough. Then I begged her." I closed my eyes and took a deep breath. "I begged her to come back with me, to leave Trevor. I told her we could start all over and build a life for ourselves."

"What did she say?"

I nervously snickered and bit my bottom lip. "She said I was the greatest disappointment of her life and if she could…" I let out a breath. *If I could go back in time, I would've never had you.* Her words echoed in the back of my mind as I tried my best to shake them off. "She told me to have a good life," I lied. "And I told her to do the same."

"Jesus," he muttered. "I'm so sorry."

"It's okay. It's better this way."

"But I know how much you wanted her to…be something she's not. I know how hard you tried to build that relationship."

I gave him a bright smile, trying to ease his sadness over mine. "It's really okay. Yeah, I wanted to build that relationship, and I tried. I gave it my all, but it wasn't enough. I've come to terms with it. I'm okay."

"Are you sure?" he asked with hesitation.

"One hundred percent certain."

"Well, just know you got me, and I'm in it for the long run. Always and forever."

"Always and forever," I murmured, at him. "I cannot thank you enough, ya know, for everything you've done for me throughout my whole life. It takes a special kind of person to take on another man's kid."

"Being related by blood doesn't make someone family, Snow White. Love does that."

"I love you, Dad," I whispered, my heart pounding in my chest.

His eyes glassed over, and he pinched the bridge of his nose. "You called me Dad."

"That's who you are."

"I love you, too, Daughter. One more thing..." He grimaced as his eyebrows knit, and he clasped his hands together. "I gotta ask you something that's hard for me, Snow, and I need you to tell me the truth. Okay?"

"Okay."

"Did anyone ever hurt you? Did anyone in the industry ever take advantage of you?"

"Ray, come on."

"I'm serious, Jasmine. Did anyone ever...?" His eyes were filled with fear as he asked me the question.

I reached out and squeezed his hand. "Only with their words. Sometimes they'd touch my lower back or try to put me in demeaning clothes, but nothing worse than that."

"Promise?"

"Promise."

The relief that left his body was intense. "Good, but I swear to God, if I ever come near anyone who made you feel lesser or touched you in any way...I'll murder them."

"My hero." I laughed. "But really, Ray, I'm okay," I swore. "I'm home now."

We headed over to Café Du Monde down in the French Quarter, and as we sat down, we just kept staring at one another, smiling. "I'm real proud of you, ya know," Ray told me as a plate of beignets was delivered to our table. Powdered sugar went everywhere as we dived in. "For taking care of yourself, finally, for walking away when you needed to."

"I should've walked years ago."

He shrugged. "The timing's only right when the timing's right."

*Oh, Dad, how I missed you.*

"So," he said, shoving more beignets into his mouth. "Tell me everything about you that I've missed."

I chuckled. "We talk all the time."

"I know, but it's different having you here, in person. It's just..." He leaned back in his chair in awe. "You're just so grown up. It's crazy how much I've missed."

He didn't know the half of it.

We sat talking and talking over the beignets and coffee. The conversation came effortlessly, and words just rolled off our tongues. Ray was one of those people who made you feel loved just by the way he spoke to you, as if you were the only person he cared about. What I missed most was the way he talked about music, the way his eyes glowed bright when it came to discussing the studio, the fans, and the lyrics of his songs, the way it lit him up inside. Ray's lover was music, and when he spoke of it, he spoke in the sweetest melodies.

"Oh, by the way, you have a job."

I raised an eyebrow. "What?"

"I got you a job at Eve, the rhythm and blues club. You can work as a waitress, and whenever you're up for it, you have the stage to sing."

I shook my head. "Why would they hire me without knowing me? They don't even know if I can sing."

"Yeah, but they trust me. I used to perform there before my career shifted. You'll love it. Mia is the owner and one of the best humans in the world. I vouched for you. You start on Monday."

"You're too much good."

He laughed and shrugged. "You're not lying. I just hate that I have to catch a flight back to Los Angeles tonight," he said as he paid the bill and dusted powdered sugar from his shirt. He was supposed to be with the band as we spoke, but when I'd called him, he'd promised to be there for me when I got back. I knew we wouldn't have much time to spend together, seeing how he was currently on tour for the next few months, so I treasured every moment he gave me.

"It's really okay," I promised. "You've gone above and beyond with everything. I cannot tha—"

"If you thank me one more time, I'll dump all of this sugar on you. Snow White, I'm always here for you, no matter what, because that's what family does. We show up."

We stood up and started walking down the streets of the French Quarter. I'd forgotten how much I loved it, the life and energy of New Orleans, from the voodoo shops to the voodoo donuts, from the random human 'statues' on Bourbon Street to the live music at all hours.

It felt good to be back, felt right.

"So, we have all day before I gotta get to the airport. Any requests on what you want to do?"

"Well..." My hand wrapped around the key necklace I hadn't taken off for the past six years. The key a shy boy had given me years back still rested against my skin. "There is one thing."

"Here we are," Ray said, pulling up to the house on the corner of Maplewood and Chase. My heart was in my throat as I stared at the red brick home with a freshly mowed lawn and a large oak tree out in front, the branches filled with vibrant green leaves. Ray reached out and touched my shoulder. "You sure you want to do this? Six years is a long time. A lot can change, Snow."

I nodded. "I know, but still if I don't find out what happened, it will eat at me every day."

I climbed out of the passenger seat of the car and headed up to the front porch. Birds danced along the street, singing their songs of freedom as my heart remained chained to the memories of the boy who'd once seen me.

My fist hovered over the door as my mind battled my soul. My mind told me to run away and leave the past in the past, while my soul reminded me of Elliott Adams.

My heart pounded as I imagined what he'd look like. Was he still the nerdy, skinny boy with thin-framed round glasses? Did he still have his stutter? Did he still smile so gently that his dimple only showed a little bit?

I finally built up the courage I needed and knocked on the door. Then I waited.

And waited.

And waited.

I glanced back at Ray, who was staring my way with a frown on his lips.

When no one answered, my heart dropped into my gut. I shrugged toward Ray, and started walking back to the car. Just then, I heard the door creak open. "Hello?"

I spun around, my body filling with hope, but it quickly vanished when an older Caucasian gentleman opened the door. "Can I help you?" he asked.

I gave him a tight smile and cleared my throat. "Hi, yeah. I was actually, um, I, well..." My voice was shaking, along with my hands, and the words wouldn't form at all. I only took a breath when I felt Ray's hands on my shoulders, giving me comfort.

"Hi, I'm Ray, and this is my daughter Jasmine. She used to have a friend who lived here. We were wondering if you might know him. Elliott..." Ray looked my way for the last name.

"Adams," I said, still shaking.

The older gentleman lowered his brows and shook his head. "I'm sorry, the last family that lived here moved over five years ago. I've been here ever since."

My heart...it broke.

"Do you, um, do you have any idea what might have happened to them? Or where they went?" I asked.

He frowned, rubbing his hand over his bald head. "I'm sorry, no."

"It's okay," Ray said, shaking the guy's hand. "Thanks for your time."

"I wish I could've been more helpful," he told us.

"You've done more than enough," Ray replied, giving him a smile.

He walked me back to the car and opened the passenger door for me to climb inside. He shut the door, then hurried over to his side of the car and hopped in. "I'm sorry, Snow."

"It's fine, no worries."

"Are you okay?"

I laughed. "Of course." I shook my head back and forth and gave him a big smile. "It was a long shot anyway. I just had to try."

We drove back to the apartment and hung out until it was time for Ray to head to the airport.

"Are you sure you don't want me to drive you?" I asked.

He smirked and cringed. "You've been driving on the wrong side of the road for the past six years—I think I'll take my chances with a taxi." He hugged me tight. "Anything you need, though, you call me, okay?"

"Okay."

He walked into the hallway then called back to me. "And, Snow?"

"Yeah?"

"You're in New Orleans, one of the best places in the world to re-define yourself, to rediscover yourself. Go find the music. Go find your soul."

## Chapter Twenty-One

# Jasmine

Later that night, I put on a pair of jeans, a black shirt, and a leather jacket. I was going to do exactly what Ray had advised me to do: I was going to go searching for my soul.

I went to see my favorite parts of the city—well, not my favorite *parts*, my favorite *part*.

I walked down Frenchmen Street and filled my lungs with New Orleans air. I traveled down the alleyway behind the bars and allowed myself to remember as the music from inside filled my ears.

There was such a peacefulness about those bars, that alleyway.

It used to be home to me, my safe haven.

I closed the dumpster and climbed on top, like we used to do. The sky was cloudy, and even though I couldn't see a single star, I began to count them, because I knew they were there, just like I knew somewhere out there, a boy named Elliott still existed.

I thought about him often...only every single day for the past six years.

I always felt silly letting Elliott still exist in my memories. It had been ages since I'd last seen him, since he'd last written me, but still, I kept the key he'd given me around my neck. *So you know you always have a home to come back to.*

I didn't have a clue why I kept it after all these years. For protection? For memories? For pain? For hope? I didn't know, but during some lonely, dark nights, it was that key that kept me going. It was the reminder of a time when things were good.

It was a reminder that maybe someday things could be good again.

So, whenever he did run across my mind, I'd wish for our paths to cross again. I'd selfishly ask the universe to do whatever it took to bring Elliott back into my life. I wanted to see him by any means, just for the knowledge that he was doing better than I was.

Where had he and his family ended up? I knew I was no one he needed in his life. I was so far from the girl he once knew, but still...I wondered about those eyes and who they stared at each night.

I prayed for my personal gain. I wished and hoped for his hazel eyes to somehow, someway, lock with mine. I just needed to see the man he'd become, even if only for a moment's time. I wondered about his music and whose ears heard his sounds. I wondered if he was happy.

I hoped and prayed he was.

After a little too much time living in my memories, I stood up from the dumpster and headed to Frenchmen Street. There were dozens of people out that night, the same way the streets had been packed when I was a teenager. People were shouting, dancing, and loving on the energy.

When I heard a saxophone, chills raced down my spine. I turned on my heels and started in the direction the sound was coming from. My mind was racing as I took off in a bit of a jog toward the sound that seemed so familiar to me. The sounds were leading me to the corner.

To our corner.

To the place where I'd sung my soul and Elliott had played his heartstrings.

The sound was splendid, surreal, and I was out of breath when I reached the corner. Still, he wasn't there.

An older man stood on the corner playing music, and he played as if his life depended on it. A crowd had formed around him, cheering him on.

I began to choke up. While I listened to his notes cry into the air, I tried to compose myself.

*Stop it, Jasmine,* I warned myself. *You're being ridiculous.*

But I couldn't help it. His music was beautiful. I just wished it were coming from another person. I hated myself in that moment for the way I remembered.

Why would I miss a boy who never wrote me back?

Why did I care after all this time?

I sat down on the curb as the older gentleman played the saxophone. He played it so well. He went to war on the instrument, making love to every note. He performed like the music was his source of oxygen. He played as if it were the last time he'd ever play again. He left his soul on the battleground of music, and he owned his story.

As I watched him surrender himself to his songs, I surrendered myself to my feelings. I cried that night, first a few tears, and then I fell into heavy sobs. I wasn't able to stop myself. Everything that had happened to me over the past six years, over the past week, was flooding out of my system. I couldn't stop the tears from falling as he played. I couldn't stop the pain from shaking me.

When he finished, everyone walked off to find their next adventure, yet I stayed put, still crying.

He placed his saxophone in his case, he walked over to me, and bent down slowly, joining me on the curb. I turned my head away from him, embarrassed by my emotions.

He didn't judge me, though. He just reached into his pocket, pulled out a handkerchief, and handed it my way. Taking it, I wiped my eyes dry. "I'm sorry," I told him, mortified.

He gave me the softest smile, and his gentle brown eyes displayed his soul. "Baby girl, you're too young to be feeling so much." I laughed and kept wiping my eyes, still trying to catch my breath. As I tried to speak, he shook his head. "Just give it a minute. Feel what you need to feel. You can't rush feelings. You just gotta let yourself ride the wave of them."

I didn't know why, but that comment made me break into more sobs, and he kept sitting by my side. He was a stranger who allowed me to be strange that night.

Once I pulled myself together, I blew my nose in the handkerchief and held it out toward him.

He snickered. "Keep it."

"Thank you."

"What kind of music do you perform?"

I raised an eyebrow. "What makes you think I'm a musician?"

He gave me a knowing smile. "It's New Orleans—everyone's a musician," he joked. "Plus, I noticed the charms on your bracelet."

*Ah, makes sense.* "I've spent the past several years singing pop music, but soul is what keeps me up at night."

He nodded. "That makes sense. I saw how you heard me. I saw how you witnessed the pain of the music as I played, and I felt your sorrow. You lost?"

I grimaced. "Trying to find my way back."

"You know what my wife, God rest her soul, used to always say to me when I was lost?" He began to stand from the sidewalk and held his hand out to help me up. "'Find the music when life makes no sense.' You did the right thing, ya know, feeling tonight."

"Thank you." I smiled, rubbing my hands up and down my arms. "For your music."

"Welcome. I got a question for you, though."

"Yes?"

"What's your truth?"

"My truth?"

"Yep."

"I'm sorry, I don't know what that means."

He shifted around and turned to face me more. "What drives you? What motivates you? What breaks you and heals you all at once? What keeps you going each day? What's your truth? What are the saddest parts of your soul? What causes your heart to shatter?"

I laughed lightly. "I don't know how to answer that question."

He nodded. "Most people don't. It's worth thinking about, though, don't you think?"

I just grinned.

He smiled right back.

"People around here call me Teddy James, but my friends and family call me TJ. You can call me anything you want." He winked at me.

"I play here every evening, if you want to stop by. I don't promise you perfection, but you'll get heart."

"That's all I need, really. Thanks, TJ. I'm Jasmine, and I know this is going to sound crazy, but your music...it just reminds me of..." My words faded away, and I scrunched up my nose. "Did you ever know of a boy named Elliott Adams?"

TJ's eyes widened, and a small smile found his face. "*Jasmine,*" he sang. He took my hand into his, and his smile stretched wide. "Did this Elliott boy ever call you Jazz?"

My stomach knotted up. "Yes."

He lowered his brows and leaned in closer. "I have a question for you."

"Ask anything."

"What does that key around your neck stand for?"

I looked down at it. I hadn't even noticed that at some point I'd wrapped my fingers around it while talking to TJ. I wondered how often I did that unconsciously.

"I don't know, exactly. Hope, maybe?" I grimaced, glancing down at the piece of metal.

"Where did you get it?"

My eyes glassed over. "You know him."

TJ reached into his pocket and pulled out a heavy set of keys. "It was a family tradition of mine. It started generations back, the key swapping. Whenever someone was going through a hard time, or a major life change, you gave them a spare key as a reminder that they'd never be alone." He started combing through his keys. "This one was from my mother the day my father passed away. This one was from my wedding day. My grandmother gave it to me as a blessing for a warm home and warm love. This one was from my father when I went to fight in the war. Each key holds special meaning. Each key also carries a form of hope, hope on the good days and on the bad, through the sun and through the storms."

"I love that so much."

"This one"—he unhooked a key from his set and placed it in my hand—"was given to me a long time ago by a thirteen-year-old boy named Elliott Adams when I lost my wife to cancer. We'd been neighbors all his life, and I looked at him and his sister as my own niece and nephew. I was that close to their family, and when he gave me this key, it saved me. He handed it to me as I sat in my living room crying, and he said, 'Don't worry, Uncle TJ, I know she's gone and you feel lonely, but you're not gonna be alone because you got us. You always got us.'"

Tears filled my eyes as he spoke of Elliott. My heart began beating faster and faster. "I went to his old house and he wasn't there."

"Yeah, no. After the incident, he and his mother moved across town."

"What incident?"

TJ looked down at his hands and his bottom lip twitched a little. "You went to school with him, right?"

"Yes."

"Do you remember a bully Elliott had named Todd Clause?"

My stomach knotted up. "Yes."

"I'll never forget that name. I'll never forget how he stole so much from that poor family." TJ teared up, and he tried to keep himself together. "After you left, the bullying got worse." He told me everything. He told me how they attacked Elliott and used him as bait, how they forced him into the dumpster, how he had to listen to them abuse his sister. He told me how once he was free, it was too late, how he blamed himself each day, how the corner we stood on housed the ghosts that haunted Elliott every day.

The more he explained what had happened to Katie, the closer I grew to wanting to vomit.

"Oh my God..." Tears formed in my eyes as TJ told me how Elliott's sister had literally died in his arms. I couldn't imagine what something like that could do to a person's psyche. I couldn't envision the daily battles going on inside of Elliott's heart and soul. I was sure he blamed himself for what had happened to his sister, but it wasn't his fault. None of it was ever his fault.

"It was my fault," I whispered, my voice shaky.

TJ raised his eyebrow. "What was your fault?"

"All of this, everything that happened. The only reason those guys were bullying Elliott so hard was because he stood up to them for me. If it wasn't for me—"

"No," TJ disagreed swiftly, cutting me off. "Those boys were bullying Elliott before you even came into the picture. Don't you ever blame yourself for what those monsters did."

The ache in my chest wouldn't go away. "I'm sure he blames himself, though."

"Yes," TJ agreed. "He does."

"I kept emailing him," I told him, my body shaking with nerves. "He never wrote me back."

"He became a recluse. He kept to himself, not opening up to anyone anymore. He still shows up for things sometimes, but when he's there, he's not *there*. It's almost as if his mind is emptied. He's a ghost, as if he died right there with his sister all those years ago."

"TJ?"

"Yes?"

"Where is he?"

A weighted sigh fell from his lips. "Jasmine, it's important for you to know, he's not the same person he was when you knew him. He's... different, colder, much more of a loner, and he doesn't have much space to let people in. It's hard to explain. If you do see him, don't be surprised if it doesn't go the way you think it should, because it won't."

I understood what he was saying. I understood the warning he was giving me, but still...

I needed to see those hazel eyes.

"TJ?"

"Yes."

I took a deep breath. "Where is he?"

## Chapter Twenty-Two

# Elliott

I liked my job well enough.

It paid my bills and kept me busy. Plus, during my breaks, I could work out, and any time I could work out, I took advantage of it, which was why today sucked.

"I'm so-sorry, what?" I leaned forward in the metal chair toward Marc. He sat at his desk, which was covered in protein bar samples, paperwork, healthy recipes, and two-gallon water jugs. It was a mess, just like most of the stuff in the broken-down gym, but Marc, the owner, didn't seem to care much about shaping it up.

The gym had been passed down to him from his father, and it was clear that he wasn't passionate about the project. After he graduated college with a theater arts degree, finding a job that paid enough for rent in New Orleans was almost impossible. When his father offered him the gym, he took it with arms wide-open.

Marc wasn't a business man, but with his theater degree, he could sometimes act the part.

"Yeah...I'm sorry. You're fired." Marc looked down at his paperwork and shuffled through it, avoiding eye contact. That was how he handled everything—he avoided dealing with issues directly, and then he'd later complain and place all the blame on the employees when really, it was his own lack of leadership causing the decline of the facility.

"Oh?" I replied.

He placed the paperwork down. As he looked up, he shrugged. "That's all you're going to say? Oh? Don't you want to know why you're fired?"

"Will it change your de-decision?"

"No."

"Then, no." I started to leave, but he kept talking.

"You made three clients cry yesterday," he told me.

"They were acting weak." They'd all had three more sets of chest presses in them, and they'd failed to complete the task. "I thought my job was to push our clients."

"Exactly—*push*," he agreed. "Not destroy. I mean, listen, you're the best personal trainer we have when it comes to the actual fitness aspect. You're well-versed in the equipment and how to demonstrate the correct way to use it. You have a solid education in fitness and wellness, and you know technique inside and out for how to transform a body. Hell, you did it to your own body. Physically, you're a Greek god. Your muscles have muscles and your body is fucking insane, but emotionally...? You don't give the right emotional support for people on their health journeys."

I stared blankly. "You're firing me because three people cried yesterday?"

"Yes—no. I mean..."—he groaned—"Elliott, don't you see that you can't be there for people in an emotional, compassionate way if you're so cold?"

"No?"

He cocked an eyebrow. "Is that a question?"

"No."

He sighed, baffled. "Most of our clients here are looking to lose weight. Many have struggled with weight loss and self-worth issues for most of their lives. Can you see how having a trainer shouting at them that they aren't strong enough isn't the best approach?"

"But it's true—they aren't strong enough."

"Words aren't always necessary," he stated.

"I hardly speak to them. I hardly speak to anyone," I replied. It was true, too. I kept my words to a minimum. Most people didn't have a clue that I even stuttered, which was exactly the point. I hardly stuttered anymore, anyway. Stuttering was a weakness of mine, and over the past few years, I'd made it my mission to not reveal any weaknesses to anyone. I took a lot of speech therapy, and currently my stutters only came out when I was thrown off or upset.

"That's another issue," he told me. "Everyone says you're weird."

"Weird?"

"Like, you're mute, unless you're calling people weak. You don't engage with the clients. When they're good, you don't tell them."

"How will that help them?"

"It's called positive reinforcement. It's beyond helpful."

"I'm not going to do that," I told him.

He nodded. "That's fine, because you're fired."

"Oh?"

"Dude, why do you say everything like it's a question?"

I remained silent.

He stared at me. "You can leave now." I pushed myself up from the chair and before I left his office, he called out one last time. "Make sure to clean out your locker, too. The new trainer is coming in in about thirty minutes."

I headed to the locker room and collected all my things. As I walked out toward the weightlifting section, I overheard a few people celebrating the fact that I wouldn't be back again. They all hated me, which was shocking.

How could they hate a person they didn't even know?

I kept to myself for the most part, hardly spoke a word, and still they made up stories in their heads about the creature I was. It bothered me a bit that I could be the monster in someone else's story.

I never wanted to be a villain.

All I wanted—all I ever wanted—was to be the hero of a story, yet somehow, over time, I lost my way, and I was certain I was too far gone to ever go back.

In the back corner of Daze Jazz Lounge on Bourbon Street, no one bothered me. I sat in the booth every night, drinking whiskey and writing in a notebook. I was never bothered, always alone, except for when Jason wandered over.

He wandered over each night to sit across from me with a bottle of Jim Beam in his hand. He'd always cap off my already full cup and strike up a conversation. "What do you mean they fired you?"

"That's all there is to it," I said, flipping a page in my notes.

"What an asshole," Jason said, growing more upset than I was. "You worked your ass off there. Marc is such a dick."

I shrugged.

"*Dammit!*" he hissed, hitting his hand against the table. "I know you're nonchalant and don't give a shit about much, but that's messed up," he complained. "Listen, if you need extra cash flow, you can work a few shifts here, whenever you need to."

I gave a half-smile and thanked him. Jason's father owned the bar, and I lived upstairs in the apartment overhead. Jason used to live up there, but when he moved in with his fiancée, Kelly, he offered me the spot. It was almost half the price of my rent at the time, so I'd snatched it up.

"Also, did you get my messages about the bachelor party?" Jason asked.

"You sent me ten messages."

He smirked. "It was eight, you dramatic asshole. So, does that mean you're in?"

"Out."

"Come on, how often is it that your best friend gets married? You're the best man!"

"I do-don't party. Your fraternity pals hate me."

"They don't!" he lied.

"They think I'm weird."

"You are!" he agreed. "But you're my ride-or-die weird best friend, and if they have a problem with that, fuck them. If you want, I'll uninvite them all and you and I can just have our solid bromance and go get drunk on our own."

"Isn't that what we do here?"

"Yeah, but we'll do it with, like, strippers!"

I chuckled. "I'm gonna pass, but I'll be at the wedding."

Just then, Jimmy Shaw stumbled into the bar, breaking us away from our conversation. He'd been stumbling into the bar for the past few months since finding out his wife was leaving him. We both turned toward him as he fell into a booth and placed his head down on the table.

"Hey, Jimmy!" we both called out.

He kept his head down and waved.

"You okay?" we asked.

He stuck his thumb up then proceeded to sob. Jason grimaced. "If you're okay, I'm gonna go take the Jim Beam over to that sad sack. It looks like he needs it more."

I agreed and watched Jason go console Jimmy. My best friend was a good man through and through. He'd been that way our whole lives, too. Every time I tried to keep to myself, he'd kick the door down and barge right in.

As Jason took care of Jimmy, I went back to my whiskey and my notes.

I might've been a recluse, but with whiskey, my notebook, and Jason, I was never really alone.

# Chapter Twenty-Three

## Jasmine

I saw him first, but he'd argue that was a lie.

He kept to himself, sitting in a corner booth at Daze. A pencil balanced behind his ear as he flipped through a tattered notebook and sipped on whiskey. He'd been sitting in that corner booth since I'd arrived two hours ago and hadn't once looked up. The only person he took note of was the bartender, who wandered over every now and then to top off his drink.

I sat in the booth across from him, glancing over every now and then, sipping on my drink of choice for the night: vodka.

I used to drink tequila, but it made me too emotional.

I once tried bourbon, but it made me too sick.

So, vodka was my safest bet.

He was different in almost every way. He was huge, built, fit, and shredded. His black T-shirt clung to his body in all the right places, and his lips didn't have a smile on them, but those eyes...

Those sweet, sad, hazel eyes were exactly as I remembered, except now they weren't hidden behind glasses.

Many drunken women wandered up to Elliott's booth, trying to grab his attention, but he never gave it to them. He just nodded them away and kept his head down, focused on his notebook. Every once in a while, he'd take his pencil from behind his ear and write something down.

"You sittin' alone?" a drunken man said, stumbling to my booth, sliding in across from me.

"Oh, well, actually—"

"Let me buy you a drink," he blurted out, reaching out to touch my hand, his covered in oil and grease. His white T-shirt was stained with the same filth, as if he'd lived under the hood of a car for the past ten years.

"No, it's okay, really. Thank you," I said, trying my best to keep calm while I pulled my arms closer to my body.

"Co-come on," he begged pitifully, reaching out even more. "Let's get a drink and have a good time together."

My lips parted to speak, but I stopped when another voice spoke up. "Jimmy, move on." I looked up at the corner booth, where Elliott was still marking up his notebook but speaking to Jimmy.

Jimmy sat back a little and groaned. "Come on, Elliott, don't be a—"

"Jimmy," he said, his voice even sterner, still looking down. "Move on."

Jimmy grumbled but stood and walked away.

"Thank you," I said to Elliott.

He nodded once, still looking down. "Jimmy means no harm. He's just landed on hard times."

"Haven't we all at some point?" I lightly chuckled.

For a split second, he glanced my way, then he returned his stare back to his notes.

Then, he paused.

He sat up straighter.

Narrowed his hazel eyes.

Then, he closed the notebook.

When his head rose and his body rotated toward me, my heart started aggressively pounding against my ribcage, uncertain of what would happen next.

He stood up first and then I followed his suit, smoothing my hands over my leather jacket.

"Jasmine," he said as he breathed out, his eyes filled with confusion.

"Elliott."

"What are you..." he started, but his words trailed off.

A small twitch found his bottom lip, and he stuffed his hands into the pockets of his black jeans. My eyes danced across his face, taking in every part of him, trying to note the things that had changed, trying to grasp the parts that remained the same.

Most things had changed.

His beard was trimmed short—I'd never seen him with facial hair, and I instantly loved it. His left arm bore several tattoos, and I tried to take in every single one.

He was so grown up now.

There weren't many parts of him that were the same, but those eyes...

Those beautiful hazel eyes...

He picked up his whiskey glass and drank the final drop before putting it back down. "What are you..." He paused, shutting his eyes. "What are y-you doing here?" His small stutter made my heart twist.

"Looking for you." I didn't know what else to say, what else to feel. My eyes watered over, and the fire in my gut began to burn me from inside as the whole situation became overwhelming. Seeing him sent a wave of emotions through me. "I'm sorry, I know this is weird and stalkerish and not what you might want, and I know this is a lot to take in, but I wanted to see you because"—my hands started shaking, and I couldn't find the words for what I needed to express—"because..." I twitched a little, growing nervous. "Well, because...because..." My eyes glassed over looking at the skinny boy who seemed so fragile. "Because..." My voice trembled, and Elliott narrowed his eyes my way.

"Jasmine?"

"Yes?"

"Breathe."

"I-I am."

"You're not. Trust me, I know what it's like not to breathe."

And there he was—the boy I once knew.

My heart...

It skipped.

It cracked.

It broke.

It healed.

"I didn't mean to just show up, but—"

"Jazz." His voice was low, the nickname sending chills down my spine.

"Yes?"

"Let me kiss you?" He said it in the form of a question.

I nodded. "Yes."

His mouth crashed against mine as he stepped closer, wrapping his arms around my body, pushing me up against the edge of the booth. He kissed me hard, kissed me deep, kissed me as if it were the last wish he held in his heart. His hands slid under my thighs and he lifted me up, placing me on top of the table, allowing me to wrap my legs around his waist—and just like that, I was back in his story. Yet, unlike our younger chapters where our fire flickered, these chapters burned.

His lips...

His touch...

His body...

His world...

Oh, how I longed to return to the world of Elliott, where everything made sense and I never questioned what love meant.

He tasted like whiskey and memories I'd almost forgotten.

I gently moaned into him as he made love to my lips. Our bodies pressed against one another, two people twisting into a fantasy of yesterdays.

He remembered his promise.

He remembered saying he'd kiss me once we met again.

He remembered his words.

But this kiss...

This kiss was even more. It was more than I'd thought I would receive and probably more than he'd known he would give. It was painful, ugly, sad, and somehow still beautiful.

Our kiss was the apology for all we'd missed.

He slowly pulled back, my hands resting against his chest, his hands still wrapped around me. His teeth slowly grazed against my bottom lip as he rested his forehead against mine. Our breaths were uneven, and I wondered if it was his heartbeats or mine that were so wild and free. He licked his lips slowly, and held me so tight.

TJ was wrong.

He was the same. He was the same gentle boy whose touches healed me. He was the same quiet boy who held me when I needed him the most. He was the same sweet light in a world filled with darkness.

I breathed him in and held him so close, feeling like if I let go, he'd vanish into thin air. "I'm so sorry, Elliott." I cried into his shirt, pulling him closer to me as our lips touched. "I'm so sorry about Katie."

He let me go.

He stepped backward, and when our eyes met, his stare was filled with confusion. Then each time he blinked, his eyes became duller... tougher...colder.

*Hard.*

"What?" he asked quietly.

"I... TJ told me what happened. I'm so sorry, I can't believe she's—"

"Shut up," he barked out of nowhere. Every gentle part of him was now gone. My head started swirling, thinking I'd made it all up, as if our embrace, our kiss was simply a mirage in my tired mind.

"What?" I remained baffled, climbing off the table. "El—"

"No," he ordered and didn't say another word. He gathered his notebook, and walked away, disappearing up a staircase. My heart was racing in my chest, and confusion filled my head.

Elliott had welcomed me back into his life.

Then, in a flash, he'd vanished into thin air.

## Chapter Twenty-Four

**Elliott**

J*azz.*
My favorite kind of music.

My mind was drunk the second I made it up the staircase to my apartment. I needed to clear my head and return it to the state of numbness I preferred it to stay in. Set up in my living room was a punching bag I used every day. I put on my boxing gloves and slam my hands against the punching bag, over and over again until I felt nothing.

Working out was my method of escapism, and even though I tried my best not to think, Jasmine Greene still slipped into the cracks of my mind between every kick, every punch, every set I completed.

She looked beautiful, but that wasn't a surprise. I couldn't get her eyes out of my head.

*No. Stop*, I told myself, punching the bag repeatedly.

There was no reason for me to think about her. She was a part of my past, and I didn't live there anymore.

But that kiss...

Her lips...

Her taste...

Her touch...

"No," I said aloud, hitting the bag repeatedly. When a knock sounded on my door, I swallowed hard. I took off the gloves and went to open it, half hoping I'd see Jasmine, half hoping I wouldn't.

"What in the goddamn hell was that?!" Jason barked, charging into my apartment.

A sigh of relief washed through me upon seeing my best friend. I tossed my gloves back on and returned to hitting the punching bag.

"Hey, asshole! Speak up! What was that?" he demanded.

"What are you talking about?"

"Oh, I don't know—maybe I'm talking about the girl you just tongue-fucked down at the bar."

"I didn't tongue-fuck her," I told him, building up a sweat.

"The hell you didn't. You tongue-fucked her better than I actually screw my fiancée. Kelly would kill to be tongue-fucked like that!" he exclaimed, tossing his hands up in the air. "What just happened?"

"Nothing. It was just a girl I once knew."

Jason jumped in front of the punching bag and cringed as my fist stopped inches away from his face. "I'm going to need you to stop your Avengers training and give me more details than that."

"Remember when you were in Nebraska with your mom? And I told you I met a girl?"

"Yes, I fondly remember your hallucinations of the girl who didn't exist."

"Yeah, well, that was her."

His jaw dropped. "Shut up."

"What?"

"You can't sit here and lie to me by telling me that was the type of girl you were pulling back in high school. No offense, buddy, but I remember you in high school, and you were just about the ugliest person I'd ever seen, besides myself," he joked. "There's no way in hell that girl was your girl."

I shrugged. "She was."

"Holy shit. She's hot."

I didn't reply. I placed my hands on Jason's shoulders, moved him to the side and went back to punching and kicking.

"Maybe she can be your plus-one to the wedding," he joked, nudging me in the side.

"Nope."

"Maybe she can be—"

"She's nothing," I cut him off. "I don't even know her anymore."

"That public tongue-fuck told a different story."

"Yeah, well, I had an off moment."

"Are you gonna see her again?"

I slammed my hand into the punching bag. "Nope."

"Why not? Look, man, I know you got this whole 'I hate the world and everything that exists' emo phase going on, but...there was something there. There was—"

"Last time I saw her was right before K-Katie..." My voice trailed off, and I took a breath. "I won't see her again."

"Oh." Jason frowned. "I see." He shrugged his shoulders and gave me a pat on the back. "Well, at least you guys had one final good bang before calling it quits. What's that like, anyway, huh? Having sex in public? I feel like I should bleach my bar tables."

"Jason?"

"Yeah?"

"Shut up."

"Okay."

But of course, he kept talking, because Jason never knew how to shut up. "But you do need a date to the wedding."

"I don't."

"Yes, you do. You're the best man. How would it look having the best man not have a date to my wedding?"

"Um, like he doesn't have a date?"

"Come on, Elliott. I can set you—"

"God, no," I told him. "No more setups."

He cocked an eyebrow. "Is this because of Susie and her extra toe? Because I'll be honest, I didn't know she had an extra toe when I set you up with her."

I smirked. "Just not interested."

"Well, fine. You can come to my wedding dateless as long as you come to my bachelor party."

"Dude, like I said downstairs, I'm not coming to your bachelor party." I'd already told him that a million times, but he kept asking each day hoping I'd give in. After high school, Jason had gone off to college to join a fraternity and had some of the best years of his life. He met his fiancée, Kelly, at one of their frat parties sophomore year, and they'd been together ever since. Jason was infatuated with her. It didn't take long for him to propose after they graduated, and ever since then, all he talked about was the wedding. He was an extreme groomzilla.

It wasn't shocking to me, though. That was how Jason was about everything. When he did something—he did it big. When he fell in love, he fell hard. When he planned a wedding, he planned it huge—which was exactly why I didn't want to go to his bachelor party. It was going to be extreme.

"You know your friends c-can't stand me anyway," I told him. "I'm not a party guy."

"Yes, but I am a party guy, and I'll party enough for us both. I just want you sitting right there beside me, being your lame-ass self day-dreaming about macros and protein shakes."

I wished I could agree to his request, but I couldn't. I knew his friends would want to go hang out on Frenchmen Street, and I hadn't been back there since the incident with Katie.

I was almost certain I'd never go back there.

"I'll be at your wedding," I promised him. "Standing right by your side."

Jason groaned. "Okay, but if you could not look so hot and tempt-ing, that would be great. It's my time to shine, beer belly and all, okay? I better get back to work."

As he walked away, he said one last time, "That Jasmine girl's beautiful, though, Elliott—like, out of this world."

I didn't reply, but I knew he was right.

# Chapter Twenty-Five

## Jasmine

The next afternoon, I headed back to TJ's corner. He was already there playing, and I sat down on the curb, taking it all in. When I closed my eyes, I could feel the hairs on my skin standing up. I felt his music in every inch of my being, and when he stopped playing, I just wanted him to continue.

"It was that bad, huh?" TJ asked, sitting beside me.

"Do I look that defeated?" I joked.

"Just a little. I'm sorry it didn't go the way you wanted it to go."

"It's okay," I told him. "Nothing lost but a try."

"Did he give you anything at all? Any kind of...greeting? 'How are you?' 'Where have you been?' Anything?"

"He kissed me," I told him. TJ's eyes widened, surprised by my confession. "He kissed me, and I kissed him back, and we were great, and it was real, and it reminded me of why this city changed me in the best ways. And then, he stopped."

"What? He just...stopped?" His brows lowered. "Out of nowhere?"

"Completely out of nowhere. We were good—great, really—and then I told him I was so sorry about what had happened to Katie, and—"

"Ah," TJ cut in. "You brought up Katie, the kiss of death—or well, ironically, the death of the kiss. Any time Katie is brought up in a conversation, he shuts down."

"How do I get him to open up again?"

166

He shook his head. "You don't. Once you dip your toe into the pool of Katie apologies, you're pretty much done for. Do you know the last time I saw him?"

"No."

He frowned. "Me neither. Same with his mom. He answers when she calls, but she cannot recall the last time they saw one another, and he's never the one to pick up the phone and ring her. It's strange, really, how when Katie died, part of Elliott did, too."

"He was there last night," I swore. "I saw him. I saw him behind those hazel eyes."

"It comes in sparks," he told me. "And seeing you probably ignited the flame he's spent so many years trying to extinguish, but the moment he felt anything, he had to put it out again."

"That's so strange."

"And sad. My favorite memories include him. I taught music for all my life and teaching Elliott was the highlight. He just understood things I never said. Plus, my wife and I always wanted children but couldn't have any of our own. Caring for those two kids was so fulfilling for us, and it broke my heart to lose them both."

"I'm so sorry."

"It's okay. It's just odd, getting older. The older you get, the lonelier and longer the days seem. That's why I like coming here to play. It gives me a bit of meaning."

"What do you do when you're not here playing?"

He smiled and stood back up. "I sit at home, waiting to play."

That broke my heart, the idea of him just sitting and waiting for nightfall to come.

"Don't frown, young lady. It's really okay," he said, trying to comfort me. "Life happens. Sometimes you just have to go with the waves."

I believed that, too, but sometimes the currents just seemed too high.

I listened to him play for the rest of the evening, and when he finished, I stood up and thanked him for his music.

"Thank you for taking it in," he told me, placing his saxophone into a case. "It's nice to have someone to talk to during my breaks."

"I'll be back tomorrow."

Tomorrow turned into every tomorrow. I watched autumn brush through the city, painting the trees with burnt leaves. Ever since meeting TJ, I'd been sitting on that corner with him, listening to him play. I'd started working at Eve's, and I made sure to take my break around his music time. TJ was the highlight of my return to New Orleans. If it weren't for meeting him, I wasn't sure I would've been okay.

Plus, when he played, I swore I heard Elliott's heartbeats in his notes.

"How am I so far?" TJ asked, taking a break from playing his saxophone and sitting on the curb beside me.

I smirked and replied, "Your music is better than yesterday, and yesterday was the best I've ever heard you play."

I'd made a lot of mistakes in my life, but listening to TJ play his music wasn't one of them. Every evening he'd sit on a metal chair at the corner of Frenchmen Street with his saxophone, and he'd play his music for the passersby on their way to and from the strip of bars.

When people stopped to listen, they tossed him a few dollar bills. Some danced in the streets to his sounds, tourists recorded him with their cell phones, and a select few acted as if he and his music were nonexistent.

I never understood that—how could people walk past music and pretend they hadn't just seen a glimpse of heaven?

TJ was in his eighties, and he'd been born with soul. People didn't learn to play music the way he did—they came into the world with many lifetimes of heart and soul already embedded inside of them. TJ dressed in the best suits and ties, and he seemed to be a legend on Frenchmen Street. He was a staple of the street's nightlife.

For several weeks, I wandered out to the corner each day and sat on the curb to listen to him play. He always had the biggest smile on his face and he had such a positive outlook on life. Plus, his jazz music had healing powers. It could make the saddest person find a moment of hope.

Around seven-thirty each night, TJ took a break, grabbed two water bottles and two hot dogs from Dat Dog on the corner, and then sat beside me on the curb. He'd hand me a hot dog, and we'd eat the meal together.

"Anything you think I could do better?" he asked me, biting into his food.

"Yeah, stop buying a girl dinner every night."

"Can't help it. I'm a gentleman."

I snickered. "You might be the last one of those left."

"I hope that's not the truth. You need to marry yourself a good gentleman."

"I think I'm gonna avoid the whole marriage thing."

"Oh no," he groaned. "Don't tell me you don't believe in love."

I shrugged. "Depends on the day you ask me."

"What *do* you believe in? Do you believe in God?" he asked.

"That one's still up for debate, but I like the idea of him."

"Fair enough. What about aliens?"

"Maybe," I said, taking a sip of water. "But not like E.T. or anything. I more so believe in aliens who like, take over people's bodies and control their every action, making them do things they wouldn't normally do."

"Oh?"

"Mhmm. I'm ninety-nine percent sure my mom was overtaken by an alien."

"I've known you for weeks now, and that's the first time you've ever mentioned your mom. You talk about your father a lot, but never your mother."

"Oops," I murmured. "A lapse in judgment. It won't happen again."

"Why do you think she was taken over by aliens?"

I smiled and shifted around on the curb, signaling that I didn't want to talk about it. TJ picked up on my signal and didn't dive any deeper. That was one reason I liked him so much—he never pressed for more information about my past. He always told me it was called the past for a reason and there was no need to bring it into the present if it only hurt the person to talk about it.

"Oh! Guess what!" I exclaimed, clapping my hands together. "I have a gig on Friday."

"No way!" TJ said, slapping his leg. "I was waiting for you to get back into the soul music scene."

"Yeah, I've been practicing on my own. It's been so long since I've sung what I wanted to." I smiled and nudged him. "You should come see me just in case I suck so at least I'll have one friend there."

"Wouldn't miss it for the world."

"Thanks, TJ."

"What about other friends, though?" he asked. "This old fart can't be your only friend, right?"

I shrugged. "I never had an easy time making friends. My mom didn't leave much time for building relationships outside of the studio."

"There's that mom word again." He nudged me.

I bit my bottom lip. "Another slip of the tongue. Anyway, the last time I really had a solid friendship was a long time ago, but that's ancient history."

"But history nonetheless." TJ lowered his eyebrows. "I miss him too, ya know."

"It's weird. It's been so long, but still... When I met him, I didn't even know I needed him. When Elliott was my friend, I felt like I was unstoppable, like I was good enough."

"He had that effect on everyone. I just wish we could repay him for all he's done. Anyway, your show—where's it at?"

"Eve's Lounge Friday at six." I wrinkled my nose. "You might be late to your corner to perform, though."

"No worries." TJ knocked on the concrete. "This corner ain't going anywhere."

# Chapter Twenty-Six

## Elliott

My mother had called me fifteen times in the past week and had left fifteen messages, which was three less than the week before. Each time she sent me a message, I sent her a text telling her I was okay.

On Wednesday night, I stood in my apartment lifting weights when I heard a knock at my door. When I opened it, Mom was standing there, holding grocery bags in her hands with a bright smile on her face. "Hey, Eli," she said sweetly.

I blinked and saw Katie in her eyes.

"Hi, Mom." I stepped to the side and she walked inside. "What are you doing here?"

"You didn't answer my calls. I was worried."

"I texted you back."

"I didn't text you, I called," she said nonchalantly, placing the bags on the dining room table. "So you should've called back."

"Sorry."

"It's fine. I'm used to it."

As she started unloading the groceries, I raised an eyebrow. "I went shopping the other day. I have food."

"Not homemade food," she said, pulling out Tupperware. "I bet your fridge is just packed with chicken and broccoli." She walked over to the refrigerator, opened the door, and then cocked an eyebrow. "And salmon."

"I'm trying to tone up some more," I explained.

"Yes, well, one day of cake won't hurt you," she said, going back to unpacking the bags. She'd brought enough food for an army.

"Actually, it will. I'm on a sugar cut," I told her, glancing at my watch. "And I'd love for you to st-stay, but I have to get to work."

"That's funny," she replied, grabbing two plates from my cabinets and setting them on the table. "Because I stopped by the gym and they said you were fired."

"I was going to tell you—"

Her eyes softened. "Do you need money?" she asked, pulling out her wallet.

"No, I'm good."

"I'll help with rent," she said, flipping through her cash.

"Mom, stop. Really, I'm okay."

She shook her head back and forth. "Let me help."

"I don't need it. I actually have to go to an interview I forgot about…"

"Elliott." She grimaced. "There's no interview."

"Mom…"

"Please," she begged, tossing her hands up in defeat. "Look, I know you don't want me here. I get that you don't want to be around anyone, but, sweetheart…" Her voice cracked. "It's your birthday. And you shouldn't be alone on your birthday, okay?"

She was seconds away from tears, and I cleared my throat. "Okay."

"Okay. Now sit down."

We sat at the table, and I said, "I'm still not eating sugar this week."

"That's fine. I only brought enough cake for me." She grabbed one of the Tupperware containers and slid it across the table to me. "I made you two turkey legs."

A quiet moment passed before she spoke again.

"I know it's hard for you each year when I show up to spend your birthday with you, but I'm your mother, Eli, and you're my son. So, as long as I'm here, you're never going to spend your birthday alone, okay?"

I didn't reply, but she heard me clearly as I ate the meal she'd prepared.

*Okay, Mom.*

# Chapter Twenty-Seven

## Jasmine

The night of the show, my stomach was filled with nerves, even though there were only nine people in the entire bar.

Three of those people were employees.

I sat at a booth drinking hot tea, my foot tapping the floor ceaselessly as I waited for it to be time for me to perform.

"If you shake any more, your leg's gonna fall off," TJ scolded, walking into the bar and plopping down in the booth across from me. He sat his saxophone case on the table then placed his hat on top of that.

I smiled. "I was getting nervous you weren't going to make it."

"I always show up, maybe not always on time, but I always show up." He nudged my shaky hand. "You're too uptight. Relax."

"I can't," I replied. "It's been too long since I've performed music for me. It's terrifying."

"It's just like remembering how to ride a bike," he told me, squeezing my hand for comfort. "You can't mess it up."

When it was my turn to go on stage, I drew in a cleansing breath and walked over to the microphone. As the bar's band began to accompany me, I closed my eyes and lost myself to the music. As I sang, I held out every note and gave it my all, losing myself in the moment and feeling my soul heat up as I returned to my favorite world—the world of soul.

I performed four songs, and TJ stayed the whole time, his eyes glued to my performance.

When I finished my cover of "Fall for You" by Leela James, I thanked all nine people who'd listened to me sing.

Hurrying over to TJ, I slid back into the booth, feeling on top of the world. "So," I said, sipping on my now chilled tea that still sat on the table. "How was it?"

He cocked an eyebrow. "You've never ridden a bike, have you?"

My jaw dropped. "What?"

"That wasn't good."

I narrowed my eyes, bewildered by his comment. "What are you talking about? Everyone in here loved it!"

"Everyone in here is a complete idiot," he said, standing up from the booth. "It's ironic, really, for a soul artist to have no soul."

"TJ—"

"You hit every note you were supposed to," he told me. "You sang it exactly how you were supposed to, and yes, everyone here loved it, but they love all music here. This is what New Orleans is made of—talent, but you're more than talent, Jasmine. You're more than love. You need to be more." He gave me a gentle grin and tapped his finger against my nose. "You need to be magic."

"How do I do that?" I asked. "How does one become magic?"

He stood up from the booth and placed his hat on his head. "You follow me, and we start your training sessions."

"I thought you retired from teaching."

"Yes, I did." He nodded and lifted his saxophone case. "But then I heard your voice. It's not there yet, but the way you sing...the way your eyes cried to tap into that magic that lives inside of you—that makes me excited. It makes me want to teach again," he told me, shaking his head back and forth. "I haven't felt that passion in so long, not since a boy with a stutter performed for me."

I inhaled deeply and exhaled slowly. "When do we start?"

"Tomorrow at noon." He grabbed a napkin and a pen, scribbled down his address, and handed it my way.

"Perfect."

"Don't be late."

"I won't. Do I need to bring anything?"

"Only a notebook and your deepest, darkest fears," he said as he walked away. "And, Jasmine?"

"Yes?"

"You were never supposed to be a pop artist. This music, this style... this is you. You are the definition of soul."

His words meant more to me than he'd ever know, and I couldn't wait for our first lesson.

When I pulled up to TJ's home, I instantly fell in love. It looked exactly like all the stories he'd told me about his house. There were two huge oak trees at the front of his yard, and the leaves were slowly transforming into vibrant reds and sunburnt oranges from autumn's soft kisses. A few leaves shook from the branches and danced down to the unkempt yard. There was a large wicker fence surrounding the home, and inside it looked like a forest had overtaken it. A stone bench sat in the middle with weeds growing up the sides, and there were three gnome statutes guarding the entrance—one dressed as an alien, one as an angel, and another as Chuck Norris.

Three perfect reasons why TJ was quickly becoming one of my favorite humans to ever exist.

"It used to be beautiful," TJ told me, walking onto his front porch and nodding toward the yard. "When my wife was around, she made sure it was kept. I let it go."

"It's still beautiful in its wild form." I smiled, walking up the steps.

He grinned and nodded some. "If only we could perceive everything from that viewpoint. Come on in. I'm making you tea."

His house was beautiful, filled with memories and history. There was one wall covered in postcards from places all around the world. I stopped and studied them all, smiling at the display.

"I promised my wife I'd show her the world, and we saw it," he told me, walking my way with a mug of hot tea in his hands. His eyes stared at the wall and a small smile found his lips. "But nothing was as special as coming home. Nothing felt as right."

"Your wife was beautiful," I told him, smiling at the pictures on the fireplace. There were dozens of photographs, memories captured in ink, exhibiting the life of Theodore James. It was a gorgeous life, and I felt lucky to even be allowed to peer inside of it. The picture on the edge of the fireplace made my heart jump to my throat. It was a little Elliott holding a saxophone that looked five times too big for his small frame.

"That was the day he received his first baby," TJ explained. "That was the moment he fell in love with jazz."

Elliott's face beamed with that love in the photograph. His smile was stretched far, and you could almost feel his excitement shooting through the frame.

"I miss that smile," I confessed.

"We all do," he agreed. "But we aren't here to talk about him right now. Today, we focus on you."

I took off my jacket and placed it on the arm of his sofa before I sat down with my notebook in my hand. "I did some vocal warm-ups on the way over, if you want to skip that."

He narrowed his eyes and leaned against the fireplace. "We're not going to sing today," he told me. "We aren't going to sing for a while."

"What?"

"You have a lot of work to do before you can dive into singing." He nodded toward the notebook. "Write down the hardest parts."

"The hardest parts?"

"The parts of you that scare you. Your deepest truths—write those down. Write down every demon that ever haunted you at night. Write down the shadows, the fears, the sharpest pains."

"What does this have to do with me singing?"

He sat down in a chair across the way and clasped his hands together. "How well do you know yourself?"

"What do you mean?"

"What's your truth?"

I snickered. "TJ, you know I don't—"

"What's your truth?" he asked again.

I tensed up. "My life isn't a sad story," I told him. "I'm happy."

"I know, but what's your truth?"

Every time he said that, I cringed a little. I didn't have a clue what he was getting at, or why he kept asking me that same question, though I did know he wasn't doing it to be cruel. He had the gentlest look in his eyes, and that was what bothered me the most—how he looked at me and saw parts I pretended weren't there.

"I know you're happy. You smile all the time, Jasmine, but sometimes I see it...that quiet storm that lives behind your eyes. I see the thunder that's ripping you up inside as you try your best to pretend you've never even felt raindrops. Burying your hurts and your fears isn't going to keep them from emerging. It's only going to silence your real voice that's begging to escape."

"I..." My voice trembled, and I shook my head back and forth, looking down at my notebook. "I don't think this is what I want to do, TJ. I don't want to dig that deep."

He studied me for a moment before giving me his soft smile. "One can't truly heal if they pretend the cracks don't exist."

I gave him a tight smile and nodded once but didn't say a word.

He let out a defeated sigh and nodded. "Okay, then let's do some vocal warm-ups."

The following weeks began and ended the same. I rehearsed with TJ, I went to work, and listened to TJ perform, and I'd always end the night sitting behind the bars, reminding myself to breathe. TJ did his best to work with me, but it was hard. I made it hard.

There was a wall around me that I'd built up, and I hadn't known it existed until he'd tried to push it down.

I was happy.

I knew I was—I'd fought to feel that way. I had earned my happiness.

But he was right. On my journey to making it home, I'd hit a few bumps and gained a few bruises. The bruises I thought I had healed, TJ could still see. That scared me. What scared me even more was the idea of diving deep inside of myself, asking myself what those bruises meant, remembering what had caused them. I liked to hover over my emotions, touching them a bit but keeping the majority locked away.

If I hadn't fallen apart in front of TJ the first day I met him, he probably wouldn't have known about the rainclouds that sometimes danced over me each day. If I hadn't shown him that side of me, maybe he would've believed I was okay.

My music did suffer from me not opening up more, though I'd never really noticed how much I held back until TJ made me aware.

I just pretended it was okay, even though it wasn't. TJ pretended with me, too, even though he didn't want to. He believed in me more than I believed in myself, but he wouldn't push me to open myself up unless I was ready.

The saddest truth was that I wasn't certain I'd ever get to that point. I wasn't certain my voice would ever discover its true magic. I wasn't certain I'd ever be ready to stare at my cracks and call them beautiful.

But still, I was happy. It just turned out that every so often, the cloud above me would release a few raindrops—not heavy showers, not a deluge, just a few drops.

I could handle a few drops. Who was I to complain about a few raindrops when I knew others, like Elliott, were dealing with hurricanes?

Every person had lyrics in their life that were too painful to sing.

But others' lyrics were far worse than my own.

I was a lucky one.

I was happy.

## Chapter Twenty-Eight

### Jasmine

"Got PB&J today, young lady," TJ said the next week, sitting down beside me after the first half of his performance.

"I'm pretty sure it was my day to get dinner, seeing how you did yesterday."

He shrugged. "My mistake. I'm sure you'll get it tomorrow. By the way, I think our lesson was good today," he told me.

"I feel like I'm letting you down," I confessed. "I know I'm not giving you my all, and I know that's my own fault. It's like I have a mental block."

"Give all you can, and I promise you that's enough. When you're ready, you'll be ready. We're not here to be perfect, so for right now, let's just be good."

"Thank you, TJ."

"Any time."

We finished eating our meal, and TJ stood up and went back to his music. I stood up to go back to work, but something made me hesitate.

His sounds were different this time—sad, almost. His music was quieter than before, still beautiful, but more like a whisper. As I got ready to head into work, my heart flew to my throat in panic. TJ's saxophone dropped to the brick road, the impact intense. The sound it produced when it hit made my skin crawl.

"TJ," I whispered, confused as my stare shot up to his. His brown eyes were bugged out and his hands flew to his chest. *No...* I rushed over to his side as his knees buckled from beneath him. "TJ, no, please..." Tears flooded my face as I wrapped my arms around his body, trying to help him up. He shook in my hold and my tears kept falling, hitting his sweet, scared face. His gaze burned into mine, and I swallowed hard, shaking him, begging for him to stay awake, to stay with me, to not fade away into the night.

His breaths were heavy. He wheezed and huffed as a crowd formed around us. A few people called 9-1-1, and others shouted, terrified, filled with worry and fear.

And my voice said nothing.

It cracked, it burned, and still, no sound came out until I could only say the four words that sat deep in my heart. "Please don't leave me."

The paramedics came and pulled me away. I fought and clawed and shoved them, wanting nothing more than to hold on to TJ. I needed to hold on to him for a little bit longer. I needed to be there when we found out he'd be okay.

He had to be okay. He was Theodore James, the most talented musician, the most wonderful man, and my friend.

But they refused to let me hold on to him.

I watched them relentlessly. I watched them check his pulse. I watched them try to make his heart beat again. I watched them try to save him as they loaded him into the ambulance.

"Let me come!" I shouted, trying to push my way through, but they wouldn't allow it. There was no way they'd let me inside, and every second I fought them was a second they could've spent helping TJ, so I stepped backward and let them go.

"Tulane Medical Center," the paramedic shouted before they closed the doors and drove away.

As they left, my heart collapsed.

I grabbed his saxophone, placed it into his case, and hurried down the streets of New Orleans. I couldn't breathe. My legs forced me to run as I tried to find air to fill and empty my lungs. I raced to the corner, flagged down a taxi, and waited...and waited...and waited.

Once at Tulane, I rushed through the doors of the emergency room and hurried to the front desk.

"Excuse me, I'm lo-looking for a man who was just brought in. He had a heart attack or stroke or something on Frenchmen Street, and, and I-I need to know he's okay." I fumbled my words, my whole body shaking as I hugged TJ's saxophone case to my chest.

"Slow down, slow down. What's the patient's name?"

"TJ—um, Theodore James. He's in his eighties."

"What's your relation to him?" she asked, typing away at her computer.

"I'm his friend."

She paused her typing and peered at me over her screen. "Any blood relation?"

"No, we're just friends."

"I'm sorry, I can't give out a patient's information without an actual connection. All I can tell you is that he was brought in and is in the ICU."

"But—"

"I'm sorry, ma'am. That's all I can say. Do you know any of his family members? Can you get in touch with someone?"

"I only knew about his wife, and she died. I just, I..." Tears swelled in my eyes, and she reached out and placed a comforting hand on my forearm.

"Maybe just hang out in the waiting room for a bit to see if a family member arrives?"

"Okay, thank you."

I walked over to a chair in the waiting room and did exactly that—I waited.

It was going to kill me, the waiting. Whenever I blinked, I saw TJ falling in my mind. His terrified eyes were imprinted on my memory.

I rocked back and forth, wiping away the few stubborn tears that fell from my eyes.

Over the past few months, I'd been graced with TJ's presence, and losing him wasn't an option. When the waiting became too much, I stood up and rushed out of the building, going to the only place I could think to go.

"Elliott!" I exclaimed, out of breath as I rushed into Daze. He was sitting in the same booth as the last time, and he looked up with a hard stare my way.

He stood slowly and shook his head. "I thought I said—"

"It's TJ," I told him.

"What about him?"

Tears fell down my cheeks as the words fell from my lips. "I think he had a stroke. He's at the hospital. I was there with them, but they wouldn't let me know how he's doing because I'm not family, and I don't know if you know anyone we can call or—"

"Let's go," he said swiftly, gathering his notebook and walking past me. "I'll drive."

He led me to his car, and I climbed into the passenger seat. As we drove, nerves swirled in my gut, and Elliott manifested his in his tight grip on the steering wheel. "Was it bad?"

I started choking on my breath, replaying the look in TJ's eyes. "Yes."

He rubbed one hand on the back of his neck. "We'll stop by my mom's house. She's his medical power of attorney."

"He doesn't have any extended family?"

"No. Just me and my mom."

We didn't speak any other words, and when he pulled up to the house, he hurried inside to inform his mother of all that was going on. When they came back to the car, Elliott hopped into the driver's seat and his mother rushed into the back.

"I can't believe this," she murmured, holding a folder, which I assumed contained TJ's medical records. Her breaths were wild and untamed. "But he'll be okay," she told herself. "He'll be okay."

"He'll be okay," I told her, echoing her words. "I promise he'll be okay."

"Don't make those kinds of promises," Elliott said harshly under his breath, only loud enough for me to hear.

His mom glanced up for a second and wiped her eyes. "Eli?"

"Yes?"

"Who is the woman sitting in the front seat of your car?" She cleared her throat. "Is it your girlfriend?"

My stomach flipped, and Elliott groaned. "What? No. It's TJ's friend."

"Well, it's nice to meet you, TJ's friend. I just wish it were under better circumstances. I'm Laura."

I twisted around and smiled at her. "Nice to meet you, too, Laura. I'm Jasmine."

"Jasmine," she said quietly, turning to stare at her son. "Like...Jasmine, Jasmine? Like...Jazz, Jasmine?"

Elliott's eye twitched. "Yes."

"Oh my God...I didn't know she was back," she bellowed. Then she turned to me. "I didn't know you were back in New Orleans. Eli, how come you didn't tell me she was back?"

"Per-perhaps we should f-focus on TJ right now," he scolded, my heart skipping beats right alongside his stutters.

"Of course," his mother agreed. "It's just surreal, is all."

Surreal wasn't a strong enough word for what any of this was.

# Chapter Twenty-Nine

## Jasmine

The second we arrived at the hospital, Laura rushed to the front desk to get more information after telling Elliott and me to wait for her in the waiting room. We sat beside one another, not speaking a word.

He made sure to leave a seat between us.

Every now and then, Laura glanced back at us, giving us a soft smile before turning back to the desk.

"Okay, thank you," she told the receptionist. Then she hurried back over, sat down between us, crossed her legs, and smiled. "Sorry, it was a lot to take in."

"No worries."

"He suffered a pretty big stroke and is having a hard time with his heart." She must've seen the worry in my eyes, because she placed her hand on my forearm. "It's okay. He's in the ICU right now, and will be for a few days."

"And he's awake?"

She shook her head. "Not right now, but he will be. He will be okay."

"How can you say that?" Elliott questioned. "How do you know?"

"I don't know for sure," she said softly. She shrugged her shoulders and shook her head. "But sometimes I have to lie to myself to keep from falling apart. Sometimes lies are the only thing that keep me getting out of bed each morning."

The honesty in her confession shook me.

She lied to herself so she could keep going through life. I knew that feeling all too well.

She cleared her throat, and her gentle eyes met mine. "He's going to be okay, right?"

I nodded. "Right."

Hours passed, and TJ was still unstable. After I grew sick of sitting in that chair, I stood up and walked around the hospital for a bit. I called Ray to update him on what had happened, just to have someone to talk to, and he insisted on coming home.

"No way," I told him, my hand wrapped around the key necklace. "You have a show in Portland tomorrow."

"I know, but over the weeks, I've listened to you tell me how important this guy is to you. If you need me…"

"I'm okay for now, I promise. The moment that changes, I'll let you know. I just needed to talk to you, I guess."

"I'm glad you called, Snow. Always call. I'll always answer."

I agreed, and as we hung up, I headed to the cafeteria and grabbed three coffees. Walking back to the waiting area, I noticed Laura was off to the side talking to a nurse, and Elliott was in the same spot, with his head lowered as he stared at his clasped hands.

"Coffee?" I asked, handing one his way. "Cream and sugar is already inside."

He glanced up then back at his hands. "I don't take sugar."

"Oh, well, here." I handed him my cup. "I drink it black."

"I'm good."

"Come on…" I nudged his arm. "We could all use the energy."

"I'm fine."

"Eli…"

"I said I'm f-f…" He closed his eyes, and his hands made fists. I saw the pressure building up in him the same way it had when we were kids, the panic that was overtaking him as he tried to push out words. "*I'm fine!*" he snapped, making me jump back a bit. When he looked up and our eyes locked, I saw his truth—not his harsh reaction, but his sadness. He stared at me as if he were walking through a dream, uncertain of what he saw.

*It's me, though.*

He was seeing me, and I saw him right back, even though he tried to hide.

"I'm sorry, I didn't mean to yell...it's just my words sometimes..."

I nodded. "I remember."

He turned away again and murmured, "Th-thank you, anyway."

"You're welcome." I sat back down, leaving a chair between us, because I knew that made him feel more comfortable. What probably didn't make him feel comfortable was the amount of time I spent staring at him, but I couldn't help it.

Even with his hardness, he still looked like home.

I wondered if he kept replaying our kiss in his head like I had the past few weeks. I wondered if I kept crossing his mind the way he crossed mine.

"Eli," I whispered, leaning his way. "When we first saw each other..."

He parted his lips to speak, but then he stopped himself. His hard stare forced every hair on my body to stand up. I didn't know what to do. My mind began to swirl. I wanted to hug him and hold him and hit him and cry.

"Listen," he started coldly. "What happened between us...that kiss..."

Just then, Laura came back with a bright smile on her face. "I have good news—they said he's awake. He's been moved to a room, and we're able to visit him now."

"Is he okay?" I asked, taking my thoughts from Elliott and giving them to TJ.

*He's awake.*

Those were officially my new favorite words.

"He is. He has an oxygen mask, so he can't speak, and his hands are shaky, but he's awake. He's doing okay. Let's go visit."

"Yeah." I let out a deep breath and nodded. "Let's go."

When we arrived in his room, he was already falling back asleep, and we all agreed it would be best to let him sleep through the night.

"I'll stay here with him tonight, if that's okay," I asked the nurse. She agreed that it was fine. Laura thanked me and gave me a tight hug.

Elliott grabbed a notepad and scribbled something down, then handed it my way. "My number, in case anything changes."

I took it and thanked him.

As they prepared to leave, Laura walked over to TJ and gave him a small kiss on the forehead. "I'll be back tomorrow, TJ," she said softly. "Before you even wake, I'm sure."

She released a breath as she walked away, and as she passed by Elliott, I watched him grab her hand and squeeze it for comfort.

Laura looked up at her son, and tears started rolling down her cheeks. She seemed thrown off by the small touch—stunned.

"I'll drive you home," he whispered.

"Thank you."

"Of course." He walked to TJ and gently touched his shoulder. As he stared down at the older man, his mentor, his family, Elliott's eyes softened for a split second. Then, he stepped away and turned to me. "Jasmine."

"Yes."

He didn't say a word, but there was a small nod of appreciation, and I read it loud and clear.

"You're welcome, Elliott."

They left, and I made myself comfortable. In the middle of the night, TJ awoke, and when he saw me, he tried to speak, but he couldn't. His hands moved to the oxygen mask, which he tried to remove, but I stopped him. I rushed to his side to soothe him, taking his hand in mine. "You're okay, TJ. You're okay. You're not alone."

He began to breathe a bit easier, and his eyes slid shut. When I was certain he was okay, I allowed mine to do the same.

# Chapter Thirty

## Jasmine

I arrived back at Daze around five in the morning. When I walked inside, I glanced at the back booth where I always sat, and I saw Jason sitting there with a bottle of Jim Beam and two glasses. His head was down and he was sleeping, so I walked over and tapped him.

He stirred for a moment before rubbing the palms of his hands against his eyes. "Hey," he said as he yawned.

"What are you doing?" I asked.

"Waiting for you. How's TJ?" he asked, taking the bottle of whiskey and pouring it into the two glasses.

"He'll be okay," I said, sitting down across from him.

"What about you? Are you okay?" He slid me the glass.

My hands wrapped around it, and I shrugged. "I'm always okay."

"Yeah, yeah, I know, but between you and me...are you really, though?"

I grimaced and swirled the whiskey around. "He could've died."

"He didn't."

"But he—"

Jason reached across and placed a hand on my forearm. "He didn't, buddy. He's still here."

I nodded slowly. *He's still here.*

"I c-can't even remember the last time I saw him before today," I confessed, my chest tight. "How shitty is that?"

"I think we're all just doing the best we can, brother. Don't be so hard on yourself."

But how could I not? I'd almost lost one of the closest people to me, and I couldn't even remember the last time I'd seen him, the last words we'd spoken. TJ had spent his life taking care of my family, and I walked away from him as if it were nothing.

He could've died, never seeing me again.

"Don't worry about yesterday, Elliott. You were given another chance. You can still show up tomorrow."

I frowned, shooting back the whiskey. "You can go home."

"Meh." He shrugged. "I kind of already made myself comfortable here. Plus, Kelly hates my snoring." He nudged my arm one last time. "Are you okay, Elliott?"

"No." I shook my head, and for the first time in years, I spoke the truth. "Not tonight."

# Chapter Thirty-One

## Jasmine

When morning came, both Elliott and Laura were back bright and early. TJ was in and out of being awake for a few hours, and he no longer needed the oxygen mask, which made me happy.

"A welcoming party for little ol' me?" TJ remarked, lying helpless in the hospital bed. His speech was a bit slurred—the doctors had warned us about that—and he looked so tired. Seeing him that way made my stomach knot up with fear. His eyes were slightly open, and I noticed a small shake in his left hand, but I tried my best to not reveal my concern.

"You scared me, TJ," I said, walking over to him and kissing his forehead.

"You scared all of us," Laura agreed.

"Even the dark shadow standing far away in the doorframe?" he asked.

We all turned to see Elliott, who was keeping his distance. His hands were stuffed into his dark jeans, and there was hardly any emotion to be read on his face. "Even me."

TJ opened his mouth to speak, but instead of words, he began to cough, making us all hurry to his side. He shook his head, saying he was okay.

"Just take it slow," Laura instructed. "Son, can you get that cup of water on the windowsill for him?"

Elliott walked by me, slightly brushing my arm, and my soul began to burn.

I shook my head, trying to force the nerves away. I turned back to TJ as he sipped the water. "I was getting nervous you weren't going to make it."

"I always show up, maybe not always on time"—he winked—"but I always show up."

A nurse stepped into the room, somewhat surprised to see us all standing there in the small space. "Hi, I'm Nurse Rose. I'm in charge of watching over TJ for the next few hours of my shift, and although I'm sure you're all excited to see him, I'm afraid we're going to keep it to family members only at this time."

"Don't you s-see it, Rose?" TJ murmured. "This is my sister and my niece and nephew. It's pretty clear. We all look alike."

Rose smiled. "Yeah, I see that, TJ, but still, I think perhaps only one of them at a time to visit will help. You need your rest."

"We'll wait outside," I told Laura. Then, I approached TJ and kissed his forehead once more. "It's so good to hear your voice."

"Are you okay, Jasmine?" he asked, making me laugh. He was worrying about me as he lay in a hospital bed.

"Quit worrying about me, friend. I'm always okay, TJ."

"We'll get back to your music lessons soon," he told me.

I laughed. "No rush. You just get some rest."

He agreed, and I watched as Elliott moved closer to him. He placed a hand on his shoulder and gave him a small smile. It was so small that if I hadn't been addicted to staring at the familiar stranger, I would've missed it.

"If I knew all it would take to get you to visit was a stroke, I would've done it ages ago," TJ joked.

"I'm ha-ha—" Elliott paused and shut his eyes. His face turned slightly red and veins popped out a bit in his neck as his hands formed fists. "I'm h-happ—" he tried again, but the words weren't forming for him at all. There he was—the shy boy I'd once known.

He reopened his eyes and frowned.

TJ placed his right hand on Elliott's tense fist. "I'm happy, too, son." And just like that, with TJ's touch, Elliott's body began to relax.

TJ provided that same kind of comfort for me. I was certain it was like that for everyone who knew him.

The two of us left the hospital room and headed into the waiting area then sat beside one another. This time, there was no seat between us. We were so close, but still felt miles apart.

The silence around us was eerie. My mind was swirling with things I wanted to say, but I wasn't certain how to say them. Even so, I'd try.

I crossed my legs and cleared my throat. My lips parted to speak, but he found words before me.

"How do you know him?" he asked, referring to TJ.

"I'd go to his corner every day before work and listen to him play. He also recently started giving me music lessons. He's, um..." My words trailed off, and he stared forward. A tear rolled down my cheek, and I quickly wiped it away. "He's one of my favorite people in the world," I told him.

Elliott clasped his hands together and studied the floor.

"Why that corner?" he asked.

"What?"

"Why did you go to that corner?"

I snickered lightly. "Don't ask questions you already know the answers to."

"You still sing, though?"

I nodded. "TJ said you don't play anymore."

"No."

"That's the saddest thing I've ever heard."

He looked so defeated, so tired. Elliott was too young to be so broken down by the world, too young to know the level of sadness I saw in his eyes.

But then again, so was I.

I had so many things I wanted to say, but seeing his hard exterior made me feel uncomfortable speaking up at all. I wanted to ask and tell him everything.

*Where have you been?*

*What makes you cry?*

*What makes you smile?*

*What do you do for a living?*

*Did you miss me?*

*I missed you.*

Most of all, I wanted to hold him, to hug him, to remember him, but I knew I couldn't.

I couldn't because I knew that was the last thing he wanted. His body language told me that. We sat quietly for some time, saying everything in our minds, but nothing out loud until I couldn't deal with the silence any longer.

"I thought I'd never see you again," I confessed, fully raw to my own emotions. "And then when I did see you the way you kissed me—"

"That was a m-mistake," he cut in.

"It didn't feel like one."

"And yet, it was." He shrugged before he stood up and walked away, without thought of turning around. He left me completely baffled.

I stayed in the waiting room as long as I could, waiting for Elliott to return, but he didn't come back. I went back into TJ's room for my visit, and when we finished our talk, Elliott was still missing. That sat heavily in my heart for more than one reason. I left the hospital and headed into work, dazed and confused.

Elliott Adams had changed so much, and yet he was still so much the same.

He'd been broken into so many pieces, and yet he was still fully himself.

# Chapter Thirty-Two

## Jasmine

It was a rainy Saturday when TJ was released from the hospital. Laura and I took him to his house while Elliott went to a job interview. TJ argued that he'd be okay, staying alone, but that wasn't true. His balance was off-kilter, and we all worried about him being by himself.

Laura and I spent the morning with TJ, arguing about the living arrangements. He was going back and forth with us over what would happen over the coming weeks.

"It's really okay, TJ. I can take some time off work and help look after you more," Laura told him, trying to ease the guilt he felt for crashing into her life.

"No, no, no. The last thing you need to do is uproot your life for me. You're already dealing with so much, working two jobs day and night. Taking care of me is too much, and I know my insurance doesn't really cover nursing assistance, but that's okay. I'll be okay on my own."

"TJ, you fell this morning at the hospital," she admonished. "You can't be alone."

"I can help him during the day," I chimed in.

"No, it's not your responsibility. I'm not your child. Besides, that doesn't fix anything. I'd still be alone at night. I might as well be alone during the day, too."

"TJ, that's crazy," I told him. "There's no way we're leaving you alone."

"You have to." He shrugged. "I'm old. It's okay."

"That's exactly why it's not okay. You fell this morning, and I was there to help you. What if it happens again?" Laura asked.

"It has happened before, and I was able to help myself up."

His words felt like a sucker punch. "You've fallen before, TJ?"

"Oh my gosh, why didn't you tell me?" Laura hammered him.

"Because I knew you'd worry," he replied. "You have so much on your plate, Laura. You don't need to worry about me."

"Now we're definitely not leaving you alone," she said firmly.

"There's no way not to," he argued.

"I can take nights," a deep voice said, making us all turn to the front door. Elliott was standing in the foyer with his hands stuffed into his pockets.

TJ's brows knitted. "What are you doing here?"

I felt Elliott's eyes dance across me before his stare met TJ's. "I just got a job at a gym not too far away. The hours are eight to four, so I can be with you during the evenings."

Laura's eyes watered over, and she placed her hands against her heart. "You'll help?" she asked, unsure how to fully grasp what her son was saying.

"You'd do that for me?" TJ asked, seeming confused by Elliott's offer.

"Yes."

"Why?"

The discomfort Elliott felt was apparent. Opening himself up was something he struggled with, and everyone standing in the room knew it. There was this battle we witnessed between Elliott and his soul each time he came near. It was as if he wanted to express his true self, but he feared opening up would be damaging.

"You'd do the same for me," he finally said. "You did do the same for me. When my d-dad walked out, you stepped in."

*Oh, Elliott...*

TJ knew he couldn't turn that offer down. It'd been years since Elliott had showed any kind of desire for connection, and he'd be a fool to shut him down.

"I'm going to see if I can hang a p-punching bag on the tree in the backyard?" he said as a question.

"Okay, son." TJ nodded, clearly stunned.

As Elliott walked away, the three of us followed him with our stares. Laura's hand was still resting over her heart, and tears were rolling down her cheeks. "My son's home."

"Not yet," TJ disagreed, shaking his head a little. "But he's working on it."

We got TJ settled into his place, and Laura brought over a new walker to help him get around. It took a few days for us to get into the groove of caring for TJ, but over time, it became easier. The hardest part was watching him struggle to return to his normal self. TJ believed things would come back to him a lot easier than they were. Sometimes his mind was fogged, and he grew dizzy from time to time. Walking was tough for him, but the biggest pain to his heart was that he couldn't play his music.

One afternoon, I found him standing over his saxophone, running his fingers along it.

"You okay, TJ?" I asked, but he didn't reply. I walked over to him and placed a comforting hand on his shoulder. "TJ."

He shook his head back and forth, and when he looked at me, his eyes were heavy with sadness. "Yes?"

"Let's get you to bed for a nap. You need rest. I'll probably be gone by the time you wake up to get to work, but Elliott should be here to help you for the night. I'll check on you after my night shift, okay?"

He nodded as we walked toward his room. He hated that I had to help him into his bed. He hated that he needed help at all. TJ was always the one to give help, not receive it, and I could tell this was a hard transition for him, but still, he said thank you, and still, he praised God. His belief in something greater than him when the days were dark was shocking. I wished we all could've been more like him in that way—hopeful, even when darkness roamed.

Once he was settled in, I went to work on cleaning the house. As I straightened up the living room before heading to work, I glanced out the window and saw Elliott standing across the street. His back was to me and his hands were stuffed in his pockets as he stared at the house in front of him, the house where he'd spent most of his childhood.

I walked over to the front door and looked his way. People walked past him, but he didn't move an inch, almost as if he didn't see them at all.

"Elliott!" I hollered, stepping onto the porch. He didn't turn around. I walked down the steps and hurried over toward him. It was as if he were frozen solid, unable to move at all. The closer I got, the more my stomach filled with nerves. "Eli," I said softly, placing my hand on his shoulder.

He jumped out of his skin, and when he turned my way, his eyes were glassed over with emotion. His feelings—his true feelings—were on display as he stood there studying the place he had once called his home. With one swift breath, he stepped backward. His glassy eyes changed back to his hard stare.

"What is it?" he barked.

"I just..." My words faded away as my mind tried to hold on to the broken pieces I saw in his gaze. I recognized that. I understood the sadness he harbored somewhere deep inside his soul, because it matched my own. What I didn't understand was the harsh side he was committed to presenting to the world, to me. "I just wanted to check that you were okay."

"I'm always okay." He brushed past me toward TJ's house, and I sighed, following.

"It's okay if you're not okay," I told him. "I know I wouldn't be okay coming back to the place I grew up, being around the memory of Kat—"

"*Shut up!*" he barked, turning around to face me in the middle of the street.

"What?"

He moved closer, his strong build reminding me how small I was in comparison. He hovered over me, inches away from my face. His warm breaths brushed against my skin as he spoke. "Just don't."

"Elliott—"

"You don't know me anymore, and I have no desire to r-r-rebuild a friendship. I didn't come back for you," he told me, his tone so cold.

"I never said you did," I whispered, feeling embarrassed.

"You look at me like you believe I did, though, like this—like *we* mean something, but we don't. You mean nothing to me and I mean nothing to you, all right? I came back to help care for TJ and t-that's it. Nothing more, nothing less. Do you understand?"

I nodded and my shoulders rounded. Each second, I felt smaller. "Yes."

"Good." He turned around and walked toward the house, then he stopped once more. "And Jasmine?"

"Yes?"

"Never mention my sister to me again—ever."

He left me standing in the road as my mind tried to catch up. I was completely stunned, frozen still, the same way he had been moments before. Then, as I discovered my thoughts, as I realized what I should've said to him, I stormed back into the house.

"No," I whisper-shouted toward Elliott, knowing TJ was sleeping.

"Excuse me?"

"I said no. You don't get to talk to me like that. You don't get to belittle me and tell me to shut up because you're sad—and don't lie to me and say you're not sad, Elliott, because you are. You are sad, and I saw it. In that split second when you first turned around, I saw the real you, the hurt you, and I'm sorry I brought her up. That was me crossing the line, but you don't get to tell me to shut up for checking on you. You don't get to tell me who I can and cannot be. If you want to ignore me, if you want me to ignore you, fine, but don't ever tell me to shut up again. I'm not the girl you get to tell to shut up."

"You're right." He shifted around in his shoes as his eyebrows lowered. "I'm sorry."

I stepped backward, a bit taken aback by his apology.

I hadn't expected it at all.

"Oh?" I muttered.

"I don't—" He paused, and the corner of his mouth twitched. "I didn't mean to..." He stuffed his hands into his pockets, lowered his stare, and cleared his throat. When his head rose, he locked eyes with me, and that softness I'd once known was back in his stare. "I don't know how to exist around you," he told me, so raw, so truthful. I saw him, saw how much it pained him to tell me that before he walked away, leaving me stunned.

He confused me so much. It amazed me how he could be so hot and cold in a span of seconds. I wasn't certain how to take it, what it meant, but I did know I felt exactly the same way he did.

I didn't have a clue how to exist around him.

Yet still, even with his shadows, I craved for him to stay.

# Chapter Thirty-Three

## Elliott

I suffered from nightmares during sporadic moments of each day. Each time I looked in the mirror, it bothered me my face sometimes reminded me of my sister's. Every room I stood inside of at TJ's had some sort of memory of her attached to it. The hallway toward the bedrooms even had markings of our heights since we were two years old. His house was my second home, where we celebrated all holidays, birthdays, and random Tuesdays.

Katie lost her first tooth in TJ's kitchen, and she got scolded for failing her first test in the dining room.

Everything I touched was a reminder of her. The worst thing, though, was crossing paths with my mother. I had Katie's eyes, but Mom had her eyes and smile. She had her wild, curly hair. She had her heart, her personality, her love.

Everything beautiful about my mother matched my sister's soul, and it broke my fucked-up heart every time she looked my way.

Not only did I suffer from nightmares during the day, whenever I closed my eyes, I'd fall into dreams that were always covered in shadows. I'd be back in that alleyway, listening to them mock Katie, listening to them abuse her. Sometimes I'd become aware that I was dreaming, but still I couldn't wake up. I needed to wake up. I couldn't watch her die again. I couldn't...

*I stumbled to my feet and rushed over to Katie. Her breaths were shallow and her eyes widened, panicked. "Eli," she murmured, and I wrapped my arms around her.*

*"It's okay," I told her, panicking as I noticed the blood on my fingers from where I'd touched the back of her head. "You're okay, you're okay."*

*She started to shut her eyes, and I shook her.*

*No...*

*"St-stay here, Katie. Stay h-here."*

*"Eli," Katie cried, pulling at my shirt. "Eli...Eli...E—"*

I shot up from TJ's sofa, shaken awake from the dream that was too real. My body was drenched in sweat, my heart rate was through the roof, and I couldn't pull back the image of Katie dying. She died again in my dream.

She always died in my arms.

"Eli," a voice whispered, making me turn my head to the left. Jasmine was standing there with wide eyes filled with panic and worry. "You were shouting in your sleep."

I squeezed my eyes shut and shook my head back and forth.

She shifted around and gave me a tight smile. "I came back from work early tonight and realized I left my house keys here. You can head home if you want. I can stay the night."

I stood up from the sofa and glanced at the time. *Midnight.* "Okay."

"Are you..." she started, but she paused, knowing the answer.

*No.*

I wasn't all right.

I'd never be all right again.

I headed to Daze. Jason was working behind the bar, and I sat down on a bar stool across from him. The moment he looked my way, he frowned and poured me a glass of whiskey on the rocks.

"Nightmares?" he asked.

I nodded.

"Awake or sleeping?"

I shot back the whiskey. "Both."

He poured me another glass. "Do you want to talk about it?" He always asked me that.

"Nope." I always replied that.

He leaned forward against the bar and cocked an eyebrow. "Do you want to listen to me talk about my wedding and how we picked out the flower displays today?"

I snickered and pinched the bridge of my nose. "Yes."

Jason got a goofy grin and pulled out his cell phone to show me photos, because of course he'd taken photos. "She wanted peonies and buttercups, but I was definitely much more old-fashioned and wanted roses, but not like, red roses, burnt orange roses, with some stephanotis tossed into the mix. I felt like those would read more November, autumn wedding than red roses. We ended up doing the best of both worlds and mixing them all together." The way his face glowed with excitement was the best thing I'd seen in a long time.

No one was more excited than Jason to become someone's husband. Kelly was the luckiest girl in the world to have someone like him. Their wedding wasn't until autumn of next year, but he and Kelly were already planning as if it were next month.

As he continued talking about his wedding day, I was thankful for the break from reality he gave me. Sometimes all your soul needed to rest was whiskey, peonies, and a best friend who loved you, scars and all.

As weeks went by, TJ had a harder and harder time adjusting to his new situation. He hadn't meant to become so hard, but life was making it impossible for him to feel strong. He was always the one who cared for others.

He didn't have it in him to be cared for at all.

"No, no, no!" I heard one evening at TJ's, making him a snack. I hurried into his music room and found him on the floor, struggling to stand up.

"TJ," I muttered, rushing to his side to help.

He waved me away, his face stern and grumpy. "No! Don't touch me," he said, trying to get himself up. He couldn't do it, and I ignored his protests as I helped him to a chair.

"What are you doing?" I asked him, confused as to why he was even in the music room.

He shook his head. "I wanted to read music," he told me. "I just wanted to read my music." His walls were covered in music books from floor to ceiling, lesson plans he'd used on many students throughout his life, including me. It had been years since he'd taught music, but even when he had retired, he had still been able to play his own tunes—up until now.

"You could've asked me to get them," I told him.

"*I'm tired of asking people for help!*" he barked, which was shocking. TJ was never one to yell. Scold, yes; yell, never. His eyes fell to his left hand, and I watched the shakiness that possessed it. His brows knit together and he sighed, sitting back in his chair. "I'm sorry, it's just...I can't play my music anymore," he murmured.

"Maybe with some physical therapy, you'll get it back."

"I'm eighty-one years old and suffered a stroke, Elliott. I can't even hold up the instrument." He sounded completed defeated. "I'm never going to be able to play again."

"Well, that's okay."

"What?"

"Music isn't everything."

TJ's face turned slightly red. "What did you just say?"

"I said music isn't everything."

"Are you joking?" he asked me. "Music is the only thing."

There had once been a time I'd believed that, too.

"You know what I see when I close my eyes?" he questioned, shutting his stare. "I see notes, bars, melodies, lyrics. I see music. When I breathe in, I think of jazz. When I breathe out, I crave it, and without being able to play my saxophone...without my music..." A tear rolled down his cheek, and I tried to ignore the way his emotions brought me discomfort. "Without my music, I might as well be dead."

I choked out a cough. "You don't mean that. Look, I know it seems hard, but music isn't everything. I used to play the sax then I gave it up, and I'm okay."

He opened his eyes and gave me a hard stare. "You had a choice to not play the saxophone. You chose to walk away from it. My music was ripped away from me, stolen away. You and I are not one and the same."

I lowered my head, feeling guilty at his pain, but I wasn't certain what to say. He asked me to leave, and I did as he requested. As I walked out of the room, I listened to TJ start to sob uncontrollably. I wouldn't be able to fix him, because I knew nothing about being fixed. All I knew was how to stay completely broken, so I reached out to a person who was better fit for helping him.

The moment I called Jasmine, she was on her way. It was her day off and she was just sleeping at her house, so it didn't take her long to arrive. She jumped into the first taxi she could get and was at the house in a flash. "Where is he?" she barked, her eyes wide with worry as she came into the living room to join me.

My eyes danced down her body, noting the fact that her trench coat wasn't tied. She glanced down at herself, noticing the fact that she was still in tiny shorts and a tight tank top with no bra, exposing her nipples through the fabric. She gasped, quickly tying the coat shut. Her cheeks turned red, and I looked away.

"Sorry," I muttered.

"Sorry," she replied. "I just rushed out of the house, not thinking."

"You can borrow some of my clothes if you'd like. I brought workout clothes but haven't used them yet."

"That would be great," she agreed.

I headed off and grabbed the white tank top and black sweatpants. She took them and headed into the bathroom to toss them on. When she came out, a small smile formed on her face, and her smile forced my heart to beat. She looked beautiful. The clothes were way too big, totally ridiculous, and they looked absolutely perfect on her. The band of the sweatpants was rolled down multiple times to sit correctly on her waist, and my eyes moved to her hipbones, which poked out a small bit.

*Jesus...*

My gut twisted as I tore my stare away. "He's in the mu-mu-music room," I stuttered. "He's been in there the whole time."

"Thanks," she said, hurrying in to see him. She closed the door behind her, and I sat down on the sofa, waiting to make sure TJ would be okay.

It took some time, but Jasmine ended up walking TJ to his bedroom and putting him to sleep. When she reemerged, I stood up from the sofa and stared her way.

"He's okay," she told me. "He just had a small panic."

"I didn't know what to do. He..." I swallowed hard. "I didn't know what to do."

"Thanks for calling me."

"Thanks for coming."

"Always. I can stay for the rest of the night if you want, since I'm here."

"Okay, sounds good."

We stood still for a moment, staring at one another, unable to look away. The right side of her mouth curved up, and the left side of mine did too until I realized what I was doing. Then it curved back down.

She was in my head again.

"Okay, well. goodbye, Jasmine." I gathered my stuff to leave.

She kept smiling. "Goodbye, Elliott."

I walked out the front door, and she followed behind me to lock up. Before I stepped off the porch, I turned to her and narrowed my eyes. "What's wrong with him?" I asked.

"He just feels worthless. His music gave him worth, a purpose, whatnot, and for that to be gone...he's just lost."

"How did you c-comfort him? What did you say to him?"

"Nothing."

"What?" I asked, confused.

"I didn't say a word. I just sat there with him."

"You didn't say anything?"

She shook her head. "No. Sometimes people don't need words, Elliott. Sometimes they just need the space to feel what they need to feel, with someone present as a reminder that they're not alone."

## Chapter Thirty-Four

### Jasmine

One night in late November, I sat behind the bars, listening to the music of Frenchmen Street after my shift at work. It still amazed me a bit how much it felt like home back there in those dirty areas. As I listened to the music of the bluegrass bar, I closed my eyes and took deep breaths. When I sat behind those bars, I did the most overthinking I allowed myself to do. Ninety-eight percent of the time, I was perfect. I was happy and healthy, and my mind never went to dark places.

But during those two percent, my mind did wander.

Mama hadn't called me once.

Whenever I spoke to Ray, I'd ask him if she'd reached out to him, but the answer was always no. I shouldn't have been surprised. The way she and I had left things had been rough, so it wasn't shocking when I had no emails or messages from her at all.

But still...

If I had a daughter, I'd at least want to know she was safe.

If I had a daughter, I'd do better than Mama.

"Jasmine."

My eyes shot open at the sound of my name, and when I saw Elliott standing in front of me, my gut tightened. "What are you doing here? Oh my gosh, is it TJ? Is he all right?" I asked, hopping off the dumpster.

"He's fine. I had my mom stop by to stay with him for the night. He told me you come here after you're done at work. I just..." His eyes shifted around in the alleyway, and his hands were in fists.

*Oh my God...*

"Eli, is this where it happened...?" I whispered.

He shut his eyes for a second and nodded. "Yes."

"Have you been here since?"

"No."

"What are you doing here? Are you okay? What's going on?" I asked, rambling off questions, seeing the intensity of the moment for him. Sweat lined his forehead, and he grimaced.

"I need your help."

"Anything," I told him. "Anything you need."

"TJ's lost, and I want to help him. He had a b-bad night tonight, and I need to do something. I can't keep watching him be so broken."

"You came here...into this alleyway...because you're worried about him?" I asked. He nodded. "Eli...why would you do that? I can only imagine how hard it is for you to be here."

"When we had no one, he stepped up. When we had nothing, he saved us." His voice shook. "My father walked out, and TJ stepped in without q-question. When Katie..." He paused and swallowed hard. "When Katie died, TJ stayed and helped my mom when I ran away. He always saved us, and now he's broken, and I want to help him."

"How can we do that? How can we help?"

"H-he thinks his music died. We just need to prove to him that it didn't."

"How?"

He began to tell me his plan of action, and every word he spoke made my heart do cartwheels. Every idea he tossed out was perfect. In that moment, he was the sweet boy who stood up for me, for his sister, for his mother. Elliott was exactly what he'd always been—caring.

"Do you think it will help?" he asked.

"I think it will."

"Good," he muttered. "Good, good. Okay, well, goodbye." He started off, and my heart was in my throat.

"Elliott, wait!"

He turned around to face me. "What is it?"

My mind blanked. There was a slight tremble in my body, and I rubbed my hand up and down my arm. "Never mind. Go ahead. Good night."

"What is it?" he asked again. I stepped forward and then back. My body was battling my mind, and he saw the struggle I was dealing with. He walked closer to me. "Jasmine?"

In a flash, I leaped toward him and wrapped my arms around his body. I pulled him into a hug, and I was certain he'd push me away. I was invading his space, and everything I'd learned about him lately told me he wouldn't appreciate it, but I couldn't help it. Knowing where he was standing, knowing how hard it must've been for him to come back to that alleyway...I couldn't not hold him. I couldn't just let him walk away and feel alone. My hug was a reminder that he wasn't alone out there. My hug was a safety net just in case he needed to fall.

He didn't push me away, but he didn't hug me back. I could feel his sadness, his pain, his heart. I could only imagine how long he'd been drowning in his sadness.

Then, out of nowhere, a miracle happened. His hands wrapped around my back, and he pulled me in closer to him. He allowed me to hold him, and he held me right back. He didn't let me go, and that simple fact made me want to cry. Elliott Adams, the boy who hardly opened up to anyone anymore, was allowing me to get close to him. I held on so tightly to him, because I could tell how much he needed to be held that night.

I was so thankful he held me back.

## Chapter Thirty-Five

*Jasmine*

Winter moved into New Orleans quickly, and the cold weather swept through along with it. Elliott and I had spent the past few weeks working on his surprise for TJ, and it was all coming together so nicely. I'd have been lying if I'd said it wasn't nice to be spending so much time with him, too. Even though we didn't talk a lot, just being near him seemed like a treasure, seeing how he kept so many people far, far away.

A week before Christmas, I sat bundled up in my pajamas, watching holiday movies alone, drinking hot cocoa. Mama had never made a big deal of holidays, and we used to work through most of them, so even though I was alone, it felt special to just sit and watch festive movies in reindeer pajamas.

When the front door handle started wiggling around nine that night, I jumped out of my skin, turning around to see who was there. Instead of a person, I saw a tree.

"What in the world..." I muttered before the tree was pushed farther into the apartment and a smiling Ray popped up from behind.

"Merry Christmas, Snow White!" he hollered.

"Oh my gosh! What are you doing here?" I rushed over to pull him into a hug.

"It's almost Christmas. Did you think I'd miss our first Christmas together?"

I laughed. "You're Jewish."

"Yeah, but decorating trees always sounded fun." He lifted the tree and dragged it farther into the living room. "Also, side note, there's about seven hundred dollars of decorations in the car and two more smaller trees for the dining room and kitchen."

"Seriously?" I smirked, my hands pressed to my chest in excitement. "A tree for the kitchen?"

He shrugged. "For our first Christmas. We can tame things down next year."

"We'll celebrate Hanukkah next year," I told him.

"How about next year we light the menorah and decorate the Christmas tree?"

I smiled wide, nodding. "Deal."

We stayed up late, adorning the apartment and laughing with one another, singing every Christmas song under the sun. By the time we finished, it looked as if we were standing in the middle of the North Pole. We had pretty much nailed Christmas.

"So, what do you think? You think I should try to cook a ham and a turkey for Christmas day?" Ray offered.

"Good God, no." I laughed, plopping down on the sofa. "I was actually thinking maybe we could have people over for dinner? Just a few friends, like TJ. He's been through so much these past few weeks, and I know he's feeling a bit down in the dumps, so I think a holiday dinner with loved ones could cheer him up, maybe."

"That sounds like a solid plan. I can still definitely help cook," he started.

"No, seriously—I don't want anyone dying on my watch," I joked.

He threw a couch pillow at me, and I tossed it right back.

"I'm glad you're back."

He smiled. "Me too."

The next morning when I arrived at TJ's house, Elliott was standing on the front porch with a mug in his hand. "Black coffee," he told me, handing it my way.

I smiled at his thoughtfulness. "Thank you. How's he doing this morning? How was last night?"

"He's good. I put on a Miles Davis documentary for him to watch, and it seemed to ease his mind for a bit."

"Good."

"Well, I'll see you," he said as he started to leave.

"Wait, random question—do you have plans for Christmas?"

He shook his head. "We don't really celebrate since Katie..." He stuffed his hands into his pockets. "Why?"

"Oh, well, I was thinking it might be nice to host a dinner and invite you all over. Ray is back in town, and I figure you, your mom, and TJ could come over."

"I normally have drinks with Jason on Christmas," he explained. "It's not really plans, but...he kind of makes me do it."

"Oh, well, okay." I shrugged. "I just thought I'd ask."

"Okay. Thanks?" he said it in the form of a question, and my heart flipped upside down.

"Yup. Thanks again for the coffee. I hope you have a great day." I opened the front door.

"Maybe he and his fiancée, Kelly, can come too?"

When I turned around, Elliott's eyes were still on me, and in those eyes, I saw something I hadn't seen from him since I'd been back in town—hope. "Of course. The more the merrier."

"My mom will want to help cook," he told me.

I smirked. "Good, because I'll need all the help I can get."

"What time?"

"Um, how about noon?" I asked.

Was he actually agreeing to come?

"Sounds good. I'll spread the word, and we'll be there."

"Thanks, Eli." I gave him a smile, and I wasn't certain if he realized his slip-up, but he one hundred percent gave me a smile back.

"Snow, breathe." Ray laughed as I moved through the apartment like a mad woman on Christmas Day. I kept setting and re-setting the dining room table—the napkins needed to be folded perfectly, and the silverware needed to shine.

"I just want everything to be perfect," I told him, double-checking that all the food was in the right place for Laura to help me prepare the meal.

"It will be perfect," he told me, standing on a small step ladder to re-hang the mistletoe that kept falling every other day. "It's already perfect. Just breathe."

I complied, and when I released the breath, it caught in my throat as the doorbell rang. "*Ohmygosh*, they're early! They weren't supposed to be here until twelve!" I exclaimed, racing my hands through my hair.

Ray snickered and put the ladder away. "It's eleven-fifty-three." He walked over to me as I hurriedly removed my apron, revealing my black Christmas dress. His hands slammed against my shoulders, and he shook me gently. "Breathe."

I let out a breath then rushed to the front door. As I opened it, I saw a smiling Laura pushing TJ in a wheelchair. "Merry Christmas!" She smiled brightly, wheeling TJ inside. Jason and Kelly followed right behind them, holding Tupperware containers in their hands. "Sorry we're early."

"What? Are you? I didn't even notice," I replied, shrugging nonchalantly as Ray chuckled in the background.

"I brought spiked eggnog!" Jason exclaimed, his voice dripping with pride.

"Don't drink that, unless you want to die a slow death," Kelly joked.

"Duly noted." I smiled, glancing out the door. "Where's Elliott?"

"He's just parking the car. The main road was pretty packed, so he drove around," Laura explained.

When I turned to Jason and Kelly, they were frozen solid, staring at Ray with their jaws on the floor. I snickered seeing their reaction. "Everyone, this is my dad, Ray Gable. Ray, this is everyone." I went around introducing them all, and Ray shook each of their hands.

"It's so nice to meet you all." Ray smiled warmly. "I can take all your coats and put them in the guest room."

"Holy shit!" Jason shouted, still stunned.

"Holy shit!" Kelly echoed, her mouth still open. "Your dad is Ray Gable?"

I smiled, seeing the small wave of pride that hit Ray. Being recognized by fans was the best Christmas gift he could ever receive. "Yeah, he is."

"No need to make such a big deal about it." Ray smirked, standing a bit taller than before. "I'm just a normal everyday person, like you. I use the bathroom and pump my own gas. Here, let me take your coats."

Kelly giggled and started twirling her hair. "Oh, Ray." She blushed, nudging him in the arm playfully.

Jason chuckled and twirled his short hair too, still starstruck. "Oh, Ray." He blushed, also nudging him in the arm.

I hadn't known Kelly for more than two seconds, but it was completely obvious that she and Jason were two peas in a pod. It was cute to see how alike the two were. "Does Elliott know your dad is Ray Gable? He's your biggest fan," Jason said, handing his jacket to Ray. "After me, of course."

Kelly nodded rapidly. "Yeah, he's totally your biggest fan," she said, slipping out of her coat and handing it to Ray. "After me, of course."

I could see it happening all too clearly: Ray's ego expanding.

He turned to Laura for her jacket, and she smiled wide. "I'm sorry, I have no clue who you are," she said sweetly, and that ego balloon of his? It popped even quicker than it had inflated.

"It's okay," Ray said, silently licking his wound. "I'm more of a mid-lister. I'm not Adam Levine."

Laura's eyes lit up. "Oh! I love Maroon 5! Do you know them?"

That made me giggle.

Laura and Kelly headed to the kitchen to set up and start preparing the meal while Ray tossed the coats into a room, and Jason pushed TJ into the living room.

"Merry Christmas."

I turned to the door to see Elliott standing there with a bottle of champagne in his hand, wrapped in a bow.

My emotions began to swirl. "Merry Christmas."

He took off his gray newsboy hat, followed by his black pea coat and scarf. He looked so handsome—handsome beyond words—and my heartbeat noticed. Elliott wore black slacks and a burgundy button-down dress shirt with black suspenders attached. The way the shirt hugged his muscular arms was enough to get any woman pregnant on sight.

"You look..." I started, but my words faded away. I blinked once and tried my best to move my stare away from his body, but it was harder than it seemed.

"You look..." he started, but his words trailed away, too, then he smiled. I smiled back. I was so happy we were to the place where we equally smiled at one another.

"Who do we have here?" Ray said, walking back over to the front door as I closed it behind Elliott.

"Ray Gable." Elliott nodded, holding his hand out toward him. "There's no way I'd forget you. Nice to see you again."

"See me again?" Ray asked, confused.

"Yeah, um, we met him when we were kids. Remember the boy I used to play music with on the corner?" I asked.

Ray nodded, cocking an eyebrow. "Yeah, uh, did this guy...eat him or something?" he joked, referencing Elliott's improved build.

We all laughed and laughed then Elliott and I just stood there staring at one another. I wondered if his heartbeats were as wild as mine.

"Okay, um, let me..." Ray squeezed into the space between Elliott and me. "I'll take your coat, Elliott."

We both broke our stare and cleared our throats.

"I'm gonna go help the girls in the kitchen," I said, pulling myself away from the butterflies Elliott Adams always provoked in me.

"Yeah, uh, I'll be in the living room," Elliott said quickly, handing me the bottle of champagne.

The afternoon slowly came together. After an amazing meal, the guys all hung out around the television, but instead of football, the musicians were wrapped up in watching their favorite music concerts of all time on YouTube. The same way the average man discussed the Green Bay Packers and the Dallas Cowboys, those guys discussed Prince and Michael Jackson.

"They're such nerds." Laura laughed, tossing plates into the dishwasher. Just then TJ's laughter filled the space, and it sent chills down our spines. "It's good to see him smiling."

"Yes," I agreed. "I'm glad he's enjoying himself."

"Both of them," she said, nodding toward Elliott, who wasn't smiling as big as TJ, but still, the small smirk was visible.

"He looks a little happy, doesn't he?" I asked.

She teared up and nodded. "Happier than I've seen him in a long time...because of you."

"I doubt it's me," I told her. "He's just finding himself again."

She shook her head back and forth and placed a hand on my shoulder. "I wish you could see the way he looks at you when you're not paying attention."

"What?" I asked, baffled.

Kelly nodded. "I've known the guy for four years now, and this is the first time I've ever seen him look...I don't know..." She shrugged. "Hopeful?"

"Even the fact that he's in there talking about music... Years went by where he wouldn't even mention it. He locked it away because it made him feel good, and Elliott didn't think he deserved anything that made him feel good."

I smiled as the three of us continued to clean up.

"Jasmine," Elliott called me, nodding me over.

"Hey, is it time?" I whispered.

He nodded, glancing at his watch. "I think we should head over there so we aren't late."

"Sounds good."

He cleared his throat, getting everyone's attention. "Excuse me, everyone, but I, um, Jasmine and I prepared a Christmas gift for TJ, and we'd like to present it now."

TJ raised an eyebrow. "A gift? For me?"

"Yes. It's just, it's not here. We have to go to it. If everyone could meet us at Frenchmen Street in fifteen minutes, that would be perfect."

Jason's eyes bugged out and he walked over to me, lightly tugging on my arm. "Did he just say Frenchmen Street?"

"Yes. Why?"

He shook his head back and forth. "He hasn't been to Frenchmen Street since Katie..." He dragged his hands over his face, shocked. "What kind of magical unicorn are you, woman?"

I laughed. "You know the corner TJ plays on?"

"Yes."

"Can you make sure he's sitting right there for us?"

"Absolutely."

"Thank you, Jason." I smiled.

"No," he murmured in disbelief. "Thank you."

# Chapter Thirty-Six

## Jasmine

I glanced around a building on Frenchmen Street, toward the corner where TJ normally performed, and I saw everyone was in place. As I turned back around, Elliott was right next to me.

"All set?" he asked.

"All set."

He nodded then turned around to everyone else standing behind him. There were hundreds of people there, all holding instruments, ready to perform. In true New Orleans fashion, the second Elliott waved his hand, everyone began to play and march.

The street filled with celebration as we proceeded together, dancing in the streets, waving ribbons, and singing loud and proud in the name of one person: Theodore James. As we marched in his direction, chills raced up and down my spine. The energy of the night, of such a wonderful city was surreal.

The moment we reached TJ, he had tears in his eyes as he scanned the crowd. The hundreds of individuals were his students. He'd touched each and every one of their lives with music, had taught them how to play, how to express, how to soar. He'd helped every single one of them tap into their magic. He'd helped each person find their truth.

As the music went on, each person danced up to TJ and placed a key in his lap. Tears spilled down his cheeks as all his students gifted him with a key out of love, respect, and honor. He grew more and more overwhelmed as the keys began to pile up. They were a reminder to him that even through the hard times, he was never alone. Even through the darkness, he always had a home.

Whenever I thought of home, I didn't think of a place; I thought of people, the ones who shaped us into the people we were meant to become, the ones who loved us with our scars and told us those scars were beautiful, the ones who allowed us to make mistakes and still loved us fully.

TJ's home was large and filled with light, and that night, he felt it fully.

When the music slowed down, everyone cheered his name. Just as TJ was about to speak, Frenchmen Street was filled with a sound that sent chills down everyone's spines.

Elliott and his saxophone.

My stare moved to him, stunned as he began to play.

His sounds were so painfully raw, so real. The way his fingers danced across the instrument and summoned the notes made me want to break down into tears. I kneeled next to TJ, giving him comfort as he grew overwhelmed listening to Elliott play. Ray embraced Laura as she, too, fell apart to her son's music.

I was overtaken by memories of Elliott as he played. He was a million times better than I remembered, and I remembered his music with each note...his music that healed me when I was young and taught me what it meant to be beautifully sad...his music that had shown me my way six years before when I was lost.

His music made the world soar.

"It's our song..." TJ whispered, squeezing my hand. "Etta James, 'At Last'...it was our wedding song," he cried. "Did you know he was going to play it?"

"No," I told him. "I didn't even know he planned to perform tonight."

*Oh, Elliott...*

I stood up slowly and cleared my throat, walking over to stand beside him. I closed my eyes and began to sing along. My words fell into harmony with the notes and bars that danced from his saxophone. I became wrapped up in his sounds as my voice sang the breathtaking lyrics.

I let go fully, giving myself to the music, giving myself to Elliott Adams and his soul.

Once we finished, the streets filled with silence, and Elliott's hazel eyes locked with mine. My heart was beating at unknown speeds, and I wondered if his was doing the same. He walked over to me, took my hand in his, and lightly squeezed it.

"Thank you," he whispered.

"Always," I replied.

He then walked over to TJ, reached into his pocket, and pulled out a key. As he handed it to the closest man he had to a father, he smiled. "I know you think you lost your music after the stroke, TJ. I know you're lost, but look around. Look at all these people here, all the lives you've changed, all the lives you've saved." He took a deep breath, and when he opened his eyes, they were filled with emotion. "You saved us all. You didn't lose your music, Uncle TJ. Don't you see?" Elliott explained, gesturing toward the crowd. "You *are* the music."

## Chapter Thirty-Seven

**Elliott**

"That was the sweetest thing I've ever seen," Kelly exclaimed as she, Jason, Jasmine, and I sat in the back booth of Daze. After celebrating TJ in the streets with everyone, the four of us were still wide awake and had headed over to the lounge to have drinks.

"I've never swooned so hard in my life," Jason agreed, wrapping his arm around Kelly. "And, Jesus! Elliott, your music. It's been too long since I've heard it."

"And your voice, Jasmine!" Kelly squealed, sighing in pleasure as she poured more of Jason's spiked eggnog into four shot glasses.

"Yeah, yeah! That voice," Jason agreed. He lifted his shot in the air. "To Jasmine and Elliott!" he cheered.

We all lifted our glasses in the air.

Jasmine smiled my way and gently nudged me in the shoulder. "To your music."

I tilted my head toward her. "To your voice."

We took the shot down and before we knew it, we were having drink after drink, shot after shot, celebrating Christmas.

I couldn't remember the last time I'd celebrated anything.

Every now and then, Jasmine would check her cell phone. I'd noticed her checking it religiously all evening. Whenever she looked away, a flash of sadness would hit her, but she'd shake it off fast. Only I noticed, really, because I'd been spending the past weeks noticing her all the time.

I wondered what she was searching for on that phone.

Jason and Kelly did most of the talking. I'd never taken the time to really get to know Kelly, but the more I learned, the more I saw how the two were a perfect match. They thought the same way, laughed the same way, and loved each other out loud. They were the definition of a public display of affection, and they displayed it nonstop.

"If you guys were wondering," Kelly said, pouring herself and Jasmine red wine, taking a break from the eggnog. "Planning a wedding is the most stressful thing in the world."

"Do you know how many different types of vanilla frosting there are at Cake & Pie Bakery?" Jason asked.

"*Oh, oh!*" Kelly laughed, tossing her hands up in the air. "You have no clue how many different types of vanilla frosting there are at Cake & Pie Bakery! Should we tell them how many?"

"Let's tell them how many."

"Thirty-four different types of vanilla frosting," they said in unison.

"And we tried every single one," Jason said.

"Even though we knew we were getting chocolate, but free frosting samples aren't something anyone should pass up," Kelly explained.

Jasmine laughed, and I loved the sound. "I've always wanted to pretend I was getting married so I could go eat cake."

"Ohhh, do it! You have not lived until you've tried thirty-four different types of vanilla frosting," Kelly replied. "But you know the worst part about planning a wedding?"

"The seating chart!" they said, again speaking in unison.

"Betty can't sit next to Nancy because they both dated Eddie, and Eddie can't be at a table that has seafood. Jackie can't be near her sister, Sarah, because she got the house after their mom died, even though Sarah took care of the mom. Mark fucking hates Eva, and Eva's awkwardly in love with Mark. Jane wants nothing to do with Rob because he voted for Trump, and Rob wants nothing to do with Harley because she's still 'feeling the Bern' and has Vermont bumper stickers on her car. Don't even think about putting the twins at the same table, because they are their own people and don't want to be paired together for the rest of their lives." Kelly talked and talked, and it was possible that she spoke even more than Jason did, which was shocking.

"It's pretty exhausting, and not cheap at all," Jason said, pulling her closer to him. "Let's just elope."

She laughed. "Yeah, my parents would *love* that. They are already *super* pumped that I'm marrying a democrat."

"True, true. Okay, no eloping."

Kelly pressed her hands to her cheeks and shook her head. "Oh gosh, we're talking too much about boring basic people stuff. Sorry, you guys."

Jasmine just giggled, because Jasmine was drunk. It seemed that every time she didn't see what she was hoping to see on her phone, she'd take another shot.

*Blame it on the eggnog.*

"Okay, okay, no more wedding talk. Let's do something fun! Let's play Never Have I Ever," Kelly said, clapping her hands together.

"What's that?" I asked.

Jasmine's eyes widened. "You've never played Never Have I Ever?" she asked, stunned.

"No?"

She smirked and giggled. "Is that a question?" She was a giggly, smiley drunk, and it was the most adorable thing I'd ever seen. Her cheeks were rosy, her eyes doe-wide, and she also became extremely touchy-feely.

I wasn't complaining.

She kept smiling and giggling. "Don't worry, I've never played either."

"Never Have I Ever is a drinking game where someone says, 'Never have I ever' then they say a simple statement. Anyone who has done that thing at some point in their life takes a drink. Then we go around and around in a circle until we pass out from drinking," Kelly explained. "You go first, Jas."

Jason nodded. "Okay. Never have I ever skipped school."

We all drank.

"Never have I ever cried during a Disney movie," Jasmine said.

She, Kelly, and I drank.

Jason cocked an eyebrow toward me. "Dude."

"Have you never seen Brother Bear?" I choked out.

"Oh, shit. Yeah." Jason took a drink. "You're right."

"These questions are too boring. Let's get real. Never have I ever had a threesome," Kelly said, raising the bar.

When I turned to Jasmine, her eyes were on me, and when I didn't drink, her lips curved up.

Jason jumped in. "My turn—never have I ever lost my virginity on a dude ranch in the back of a shed that had five purple umbrellas hanging from the ceiling."

"That's awkwardly de-de-" I paused and shut my eyes. *Descriptive—say it. Say the word.* "De-de—" My blood pressure built, embarrassment from feeling like a damn fool for being a grown man and still being unable to say such words. It felt as if everyone's eyes were on me, waiting for me to push out the syllables, waiting for me to figure out what I was trying to say. Right as I was about to have a breakdown, I felt a hand find my thigh under the table. I looked up to see Jasmine giving me a gentle smile, and I took a breath. "That's awkwardly descriptive," I pushed out.

I placed my hand on top of Jasmine's and lightly squeezed. *Thank you.*

She smiled as if she'd heard me, and replied, *You're welcome.*

Kelly cleared her throat and nonchalantly took a sip of her drink. "It was during Bible camp, and it wasn't a shed, it was a stable, and there were two horses watching the whole time, thank you very much."

Everyone started laughing, and then the game went on. I noticed Jasmine's hand still resting against my thigh. Her fingers kept kneading my muscles, moving closer and closer to my inner thigh, and my breaths grew deeper.

"I have one," she said, holding her glass up with her free hand. "Never have I ever fallen in love while covered in horse shit."

I laughed out loud.

Actually laughed out loud.

Jason's and Kelly's eyebrows were cocked high and their stares were bewildered, but I ignored them as I lifted my glass, clinked it with Jasmine's, and we both took a sip.

"Um...what the actual heck?" Kelly asked incredulously.

"You two had a really fucked-up friendship, didn't you?" Jason remarked.

The night went on with more shots of tequila and more laughter. Jasmine became more and more touchy-feely, and even though I knew I wanted her, I was also fully aware of how intoxicated she had gotten.

"I think it's time to call it a night." I smiled at my friends.

Jason agreed. "Sounds like a plan. I'll get us an Uber," he told Kelly, who was giggling with Jasmine over something only they understood.

When Jason and Kelly headed out, Jasmine turned to me, tripping over her feet a bit, and smiled. I caught her before she tumbled. She blushed and pressed her hands against my chest. "Can I stay the night?"

"Of course, if you'd like. I'll sleep on the couch."

"*Orrr*," she sang, tracing her finger along my chest. "You can sleep with me."

I chuckled, shaking my head. "You're drunk."

"Yes, but rumor has it that I'm much more flexible when I'm drunk."

*Oh, God.*

She was beyond drunk.

"If you heard what you just said and were sober, you'd probably be ten shades of red. C-come on, let's get you to bed."

Her eyes were heavy, and she pulled on my shirt. "No, let's do it here," she begged, pleading for me to take her right then and there. Her hands wandered down to my crotch, and I eased them back up higher.

"Jasmine." I grimaced. "You're drunk."

"Please, Eli. Please...I want you," she whispered, slowly starting to unbutton my shirt. "Don't you want to feel me, taste me, have me?"

*God, yes.*

My body reacted to every touch she gave me, craving her in every imaginable way. There were so many nights I'd imagined what it would be like to be on top of her, beneath her, behind her, inside... Jasmine was everything I'd ever dreamed of, physically, mentally, and emotionally. She was the one I wanted at the beginning of each day and at the end of each night, but she wasn't ready.

"Come on, Elliott," she said softly against my ear. "Please?"

I took a breath.

*No.*

She wasn't in her right frame of mind. She couldn't truthfully express what she needed. She was only there offering me the physical when I needed the total package. I needed Jasmine—mind, body, and spirit.

I needed her to be fully aware of what she was doing.

Otherwise, the sex would be just like all the other men she'd been with in the past—*hollow.*

"We can't," I told her as her lips grazed my neck. My eyes rolled to the back of my head, and my skin crawled as she touched me. "Jazz, don't."

"Just...please, Eli..."

"No." I finally forced myself away from her. I shot myself across the room and shook off the effects of the drug she'd forced into my being. "We can't."

"Why?" she asked, clearly embarrassed, though she tried to hide it with a fake confidence. "I know you want me."

"I do."

"Then why won't you sleep with me?" she questioned. "Why won't you fuck me?"

"Because I care about you."

Her eyes glassed over and she shook her head. She then said the most heartbreaking thing I'd ever heard in my life. "People don't care about me, Elliott. People just take pieces of me and then throw the rest away."

In that moment, I witnessed the storm behind her eyes.

How long had it been there?

How long had it been building in her heart?

She lied about being happy because it was easier than acknowledging how sad she'd become. Some days it was better to lie than to face the darkest truths.

Her heart was broken, and I hated that I hadn't noticed until she was drunkenly stumbling around in front of me.

She pressed her body against mine and begged me to touch her, to love her, to pretend I didn't see the storm dancing behind that chocolate gaze, but I saw it. I saw her, and it broke my fucking heart.

"Kiss me," she whispered.

"No."

"Fuck me," she begged.

"I can't."

Tears filled her eyes, and she started pounding her hands against my chest. "I hate you!" she shouted. She hit me harder and harder. I held my hands up and let her hit me, because I knew it wasn't me she was shouting at. It wasn't me she was hitting; it was the demons she pretended weren't even there. Alcohol had a way of doing that—pulling out the parts of you that you didn't want to see.

After a few more seconds of pounding, her anger shifted to pain. She started crying softly at first, and then she slipped into heavy sobs. Her hits slowed down, and she fell against my chest. She started pulling on my shirt, and my hands were still in the air. As she cried, I wanted nothing more than to be her comfort. I wanted nothing more than to wrap up all her hurts and put them into my own soul.

"Tell me what you want, Jasmine. I'm here. Tell me what you need me to do."

"Hold me?" she whispered.

"Yes."

"Love me," she begged.

*Always.*

My arms quickly dropped around her frame, and I pulled her darkness against me. I held on to her for what felt like forever, and still, it wasn't long enough.

I carried her up to my bedroom, laid her in bed, and tucked her in. She wiped at her eyes, which looked like raccoon eyes with her smeared makeup. "Are you sure no sleepover?" she murmured, making me smirk.

"Maybe tomorrow."

She turned in the bed and hugged a pillow as I went to turn off the light. "She didn't call me, or email."

I leaned against the door and raised an eyebrow. "Who?"

"Mama," she whispered, her sobbing coming back. "It's Christmas, and she didn't write me. She never writes me back. I've written her every day since I came here, and she never writes back."

"She's a fool," I told her.

She laughed, hugging the pillow tighter. "You didn't write back either."

"I'm an idiot."

"It's okay, Elliott Adams. I don't get why Mama won't write me, because I've always tried to make her happy, but I get why you didn't write back. It was because I'm the reason Katie died."

My chest tightened and ached. "What did you just say?"

"They bullied you because of me." She yawned. "If I weren't alive, none of that would've happened. Maybe Mama was right—maybe she should've never had me. Then everyone would be okay."

Before I could reply, she was out cold, lightly snoring.

Why would she think that? Why would she think Katie's death was on her?

My heart broke for Jasmine. I couldn't imagine what she'd been through, dealing with her mother's scorn, having a mother who wished her own daughter dead.

My mother would have given her own life to have her daughter back.

Over the past six years, I'd been dealing with my own storms, never once thinking of the pain anyone else around me was going through.

Jasmine was broken, too, just like me.

Only normally she hid it behind her smiles. Now she'd shown me her darkness.

She was sleeping, but I didn't leave right away.

I smiled her way and tried to be the bravest man I could be. I told her none of this was her fault. I told her she was the definition of love. I begged her not to blame herself for something the devil had laid on her doorstep.

Then, I fell asleep right outside the bedroom door, because I selfishly didn't want to be alone.

# Chapter Thirty-Eight

## Jasmine

I woke up alone in Elliott's bed, feeling like a fool. I had a splitting headache and felt beyond nauseous. *Too much eggnog, too much wine.*

"Ugh." I pushed myself up to a sitting position and smoothed out my wrinkled dress. I tried my best to tame my hair, but not even a hair tie and a high bun could make the monster on my head less wild.

My eyes met the nightstand beside me, and when I saw a glass of water, crackers, and two Advil, I silently thanked Elliott for putting up with me the night before. I wished it was one of those drunken nights where I forgot everything I said and did, but unfortunately, it wasn't. I remembered everything, every embarrassing thing I'd done and every embarrassing thing I'd said—throwing myself at Elliott...begging for sex...humiliating myself.

I remembered the way I told him to fuck me.

*Oh my God, I told Elliott Adams to fuck me.*

I remembered the way I fell apart too...

After popping the Advil into my mouth, I stood up. I collected all my stuff, and when I opened the bedroom door, I began tiptoeing to the front door, thankful I didn't see Elliott.

I wasn't ready to face him.

"Avoiding me?" Elliott said, walking out of the bathroom right as my hand landed on the doorknob.

I turned around to see him shirtless, drying his hair with a towel. I gave him a tight, uncomfortable smile. "No, no. I was just going to go check on TJ."

"I called my mom—he's okay."

"Oh, okay. Well, I better get back to my place to help Ray clean up after yesterday. It was a mess."

"Jazz..." he started, his eyes growing so soft. "Last night—"

"I drank too much," I cut in. "I never really did good mixing alcohol, so I'm really sorry for anything I said or did."

"You did nothing wrong."

"I did. I made a fool of myself, and, I'm sorry."

He stepped closer, and the hairs on my arms stood on end. "What happened?"

"What...what do you mean?"

*Closer.*

"What happened to you?"

I closed my eyes. "Nothing. I'm sorry, really, but I'm okay. It was just too many shots."

"You're not okay."

*Closer.*

"Elliott..."

"You worked with TJ, right? He trained you?"

"Only for a little while." I rubbed my hands up and down my arms. "Why?"

"What's your truth?" he asked me.

I tensed up. "What are you talking about?"

"Every person TJ has ever trained had to dig deep. They had to put a mi-mirror up every day to get to that place, to find their truth. It's hard, and it's scary to go to those places, but you have to find your truth."

I swallowed hard. "I can't. I can't do that."

He nodded once and slid his hands into the pockets of his gray sweatpants. "I get that. So, let's box."

I snickered. "What?"

He walked over to his living room and picked up a pair of boxing gloves. "If you don't want to talk about it, at least get it out of your system."

"By boxing?"

"Yup." His stare stayed somber. "By boxing." He handed me the gloves, then walked behind the punching bag, holding it still. "Ready?"

I slid the gloves onto my hands. "This is ridiculous." I laughed lightly. "I'm really okay, Elliott."

His eyes locked with mine, and his voice was low. "Ready?" he asked again.

I stood up straight. "Ready."

As I began to hit the punching bag, Elliott coached me. "Whatever eats you up at night, hit it. Whatever drives you up the wall, pound it out. Whatever hurts, make it hurt back."

I started out feeling dumb, but the more he coached me, the harder I swung. Then it got to the point where I couldn't stop. I hammered into the punching bag nonstop, my breaths uneven, my heart rate sky-rocketing. I started kicking the bag as Elliott continued.

"What pisses you off? What drives you nuts? What hurts?" he asked.

*Everything.*

Tears rolled down my cheeks as I kept swinging, emotions swallowing me whole, and it wasn't until my legs started to give out that I stopped. I stepped backward, about to fall to the ground, dripping with sweat, when Elliott was there to catch me.

"I got you," he whispered, helping me over to the couch to sit. "I got you."

As I caught my breath, he grabbed a glass of water for me. "Thank you," I told him. "I actually feel...lighter."

He smiled. "Good. And just so you know, Jasmine, I'm always here if you need to talk."

"It's really not that serious," I told him. "I just spent so much time keeping things to myself to try to make my mother happy...I never really realized how sad it made me. I gave her my all and it still wasn't enough."

"What made you leave?"

I sighed, thinking back to it.

"You don't have to tell me if you don't want to," he sincerely swore, but I shook my head.

"No, it's fine, really. It's not a big deal. You're going to think I'm stupid."

"No, I'm not."

I combed my hair behind my ears. "We spent years going for a big record deal. I was ready to give up, but Mama said I just had to work harder. So, I did. I spent more time in the studio with Trevor, and I'd pass out in dance studios. I hadn't been eating a lot, was hardly sleeping at all, but I wanted to make her proud. I wanted her dream to come true, and then it did.

"This past July, we were offered a record deal, and it was huge. It was everything we'd ever wanted and more. Of course, we threw a huge party. Trevor rented out this club and invited everyone they knew—which was a crazy amount of people. During the party, while we were all having a good time, I headed to the bathroom. It was a one-person restroom, and, um, as I was washing my hands, the door opened, and it was Trevor. I told him to leave, and as I tried to walk past him, he grabbed me and placed his hands under my ass and squeezed it. I kept shoving him and saying no, but he was hammered—of course—and he wouldn't listen. Then he groped my chest and I kneed him extremely hard then got away. When I found my mom, I was crying and shaking, feeling violated, and instead of her love, I got her anger."

"What?" he asked, baffled.

"Yeah. She, um, backed him up and told me it was my fault."

"How could she do that?"

"Ya know, if I didn't dress like a slut, people wouldn't treat me like one, that kind of thing. I wore the outfit they chose for me. I did everything they told me to, but still, it was my fault her boyfriend crossed that line. I was the one at fault."

A vein popped out of Elliott's neck as he pounded his right fist into the palm of his left. "What a sick bastard," he hissed. "If I ever see him..."

"It doesn't matter," I told him. "I got away."

"No, you didn't."

"Yes, I did. I broke free. He didn't really touch me...and then I left. I got here before anything happened."

"Jazz...something did happen. What he did to you—"

231

"It could've been a lot worse," I said emphatically, shaking my head back and forth. "He didn't rape me, he didn't..." As those words left my mouth, my body began to shake. "It didn't go too far. I was lucky."

Elliott leaned in and took my hands in his. "What he did to you was wrong. What he took from you without your permission, how he put his hands on you was disgusting."

"I got away. I ran away before he could take more. Others have had it way worse."

"Listen to me, just because others have been hurt in different ways, that doesn't make your pain mute. You're allowed to feel hurt. You're allowed to feel violated. You're allowed to want to scream, to shout."

"My mom was right—my dress was short, too low-cut..." I said, feeling sick as I spoke the words.

"You could've walked into that club naked and he still wouldn't have had the right to lay a hand on you. Do you understand me?"

I nodded, though I still felt unsure. I'd spent my life being told everything was my fault, that the weight of Mama's suffering came from my faults, and now Elliott sat in front of me, telling me I was wrong, that I wasn't to blame, that Mama's faults were hers and only hers. He was telling me everything would be okay.

It was as if he'd taken the weight of the world from me.

"You said something last night that b-bothered me," he confessed. "You said Katie's death was because of you."

"Yeah."

"You believe that?" he asked.

"It crosses my mind, or at least I believe it's sometimes hard for you to be around me, because I'm a reminder of the worst time of your life. I get that, though. I understand."

He narrowed his eyes and stared down at the carpeted floor. "The day after I t-took you out on our first date, Katie came to me, smiled, and said, 'I was wrong about that girl, Eli. She's a good thing.'" He brushed his hands against the back of his neck and looked up, locking his eyes with mine. "She loved you for me."

"Eli..."

"I'm hard," he told me. "Over the years, I've been cold and short and mean sometimes, and yet, you still showed up. You still smiled at me, because you're good. You're a good thing, and that's hard for me be-because you remind me of my past, but you're not a reminder of the worst times." He shook his head. "You're a reminder of the best time of my life, and I didn't think I deserved you," he confessed. "For the longest time, I didn't think I deserved to feel good."

I reached out and took his hands into mine. "You do, Eli. You deserve to be happy, more than anything."

"It's hard to be around you sometimes," he whispered.

"Why's that?"

His eyebrows knit together and he lowered his voice. "Because you make my heart beat."

"And what's wrong with a beating heart?"

He slightly shrugged his shoulders. "The more they beat, the easier they break, but that's the thing about you, Jasmine—I've been dead for six years now, and then you show up and remind me how good it feels to be alive, what it feels like to breathe again. Don't you see why it's so important that you exist? Don't you see why the world needs you? Why the best decision your mother ever made was having you? You're the music in a mute world, and my heart beats because you're here."

# Chapter Thirty-Nine

## Jasmine

The connection between Elliott and me grew each day, and I couldn't have been happier about it. He was slowly opening up to me, to the world, and it was amazing to witness. TJ was also doing much better with his physical therapy, which was a blessing. Plus, he began training Elliott again, which brought TJ more peace of mind than anything else in the world.

I still couldn't get over how much Elliott had helped me shed light on my scars. I'd spent so much time pretending they didn't exist, so to have him help open me in a way I hadn't thought I could was amazing. He paused his life to help me navigate through mine, and when the time came for me to do the same for him, I was ready.

On the third Tuesday in January, I overslept by an hour and I hurried over to TJ's house to switch places with Elliott so he could get to work. When I showed up, he was standing in front of his old house, staring blankly ahead.

"Hey, Eli," I said, gently touching his shoulder.

He turned around to see me and gave me a half-smile. "Hey."

I rubbed my hands up and down my arms, trying to shake off the cold. I was shocked that he was standing there in a short-sleeved T-shirt and not freezing to death. "You okay?"

"Yes."

His body language told me differently. "Are you sure...?"

He nodded and cleared his throat, changing the subject. "TJ's having a rough morning."

"Oh." My gut tightened. "Because of the music? I really thought he was doing better, and his physical therapy is going well…"

Elliott stayed somber, and his forehead wrinkled. "It's not the music."

"Oh? Then why is he having a rough morning?"

"Because today's the anniversary of the day Katie died."

"Oh my God, Elliott…" My heart leaped into my throat, and without thought, my hand landed on his forearm to give some type of comfort. "Are you okay?" *What a stupid question to ask—of course, he's not okay.*

His head tilted down a little to stare at my touch against his skin, but for some reason I couldn't let him go. He probably didn't know it was happening. His mind swam in a sea of darkness as he stood there, and with my small touch I was able to witness the tiny tremble of his body as his sadness filled him up. He turned back to the house and stared. "I'm always okay."

"Elliott—"

"My mom is in there with him. She's s-s-sad too, because of me." He cleared his throat once more and pushed my arm away from him. "It's my fa-fault they're sad. It's my fault she's gone."

He was slipping back into his guilt, back into the cage he'd locked himself in for years.

"No. That's not true," I told him, my voice stern.

He inhaled sharply. "Can you look after them?" he asked. "Can you make sure they're okay?"

"Of course."

"Thank you." He stuffed his hands into his pockets and walked over to his car.

"Elliott, where are you going?"

"To my apartment."

"You shouldn't be alone today."

"Don't worry about me." He climbed into his car, not giving me one more word. As he started his engine and disappeared down the road, my heart began to break for him. He was so lost, so far from living life. He was merely sleepwalking through it.

I understood that feeling more than he knew.

I entered the house and found Laura and TJ sitting in the living room watching home videos. Katie's young face flashed on the screen, and she was smiling and dancing with a younger Elliott.

They looked so free, so happy.

"Jasmine," Laura said gently, standing up from the sofa. She walked over to me, and my eyes glassed over.

"I'm so sorry, Laura. Elliott told me what today was, and I—"

"He spoke to you?" she asked, stunned.

"Yes."

"He didn't say a word to either of us all morning," TJ told me. "He walked around like a zombie."

"He's hurting." Laura teared up and shook her head back and forth. "He's blaming himself. He always does this."

"What happened wasn't his fault," I told her.

"We all know that, but he doesn't. He won't allow himself to know that." Tears started falling down her cheeks, and she shook her head again. "He shouldn't be alone, not today, but he won't let anyone in."

I glanced back at the front door and crossed my arms. "Are you two okay together?" I asked.

She nodded. "Yes. We'll be fine."

"I'm going to go check on him, then, if you're both sure you're okay. I know he'll probably shut me down, but I just want to try. I know he won't let me in, but he shouldn't be alone."

"Oh, Jasmine. He spoke to you. Over the past six years on this day, he hasn't spoken a word to anyone. Don't you see?" TJ gave me a small smile paired with his heavy eyes. "He's already let you in."

My heartbeat sped up as I hugged each of them goodbye. I hopped into a taxi and headed over to Daze. As I walked in, Jason called toward the door.

"Sorry, we're not open today."

"I'm sorry, I just..." I started, and he turned around. A small, broken smile found his face.

"Jasmine. You're here for Eli?"

"Yes."

"He won't let anyone in today. It's been that way for years now. It's pretty much like talking to a brick wall."

I took off my coat and scarf. "He spoke to me earlier. He told me what today is."

His eyes widened, and then he showed me his forearms. "I know that doesn't sound like a lot, but it literally gave me goose bumps. I don't know what it is about you two, but there's something there. You should see the way he stares at you when you aren't looking," he told me.

I chuckled. "I've heard rumors about that."

He reached for a bottle of whiskey and walked over to me. "And you should see the way you look at him."

That statement gave me goose bumps.

"Come on, I'll take you upstairs." He led me to the staircase at the back of the lounge, then handed me the bottle of whiskey. "The offering of booze never goes unwelcomed, but if he doesn't let you in again, don't take it personally. He's just working through a lot of demons in his head."

"Thanks, Jason."

He nodded. "He's my favorite person in this world. I know he's closed off, and many people don't get him, but Elliott still shows love in his own way, you know? It's not as apparent as it is with others. It's much quieter, but I swear it's there. So, the fact that you showed up today to be with him...the fact that you care...he just needs more people like that, you know? More people who care about him even though he's broken. Thank you for that."

As he walked away, I swallowed hard, walking up those stairs. Each step felt as if I were invading Elliott's personal space. Each step sent a spark of fire racing down my spine. I knocked on the door a few times, and I wasn't certain he'd open it.

Just as I was about to turn around, the door creaked open, and Elliott stood there with his hard stare.

"What are you doing here?" he asked dryly.

He was talking to me.

*Good sign.*

"I, um, I just, I thought, I—"

"What is it, Jasmine?" he asked, his voice sounding defeated.

"Whiskey?" I asked, holding up the bottle.

"It's eight in the morning."

"If you have coffee, we can put it in that," I joked.

He didn't move an inch. His eyes peered into mine, and I gave him a slight smile. "I just thought you shouldn't be alone."

"I told you, I'm okay."

"Yes, but still..." I shrugged my shoulders and held the bottle up a little higher. "Whiskey?"

His mouth twitched, and then he stepped to the side, allowing me to walk inside.

I tried to hide my shock, but I took the opportunity when he gave it to me.

Elliott headed straight to the kitchen, pulled out two mugs, and started a pot of coffee.

I hung my coat and purse on the back of a chair then took a seat.

The only sound in the whole apartment was the brewing coffee, and once it finished, he filled the mugs then splashed each one with whiskey.

"Thank you," I said.

He nodded once.

"So," I started.

He leaned his back against the refrigerator and shook his head. "I don't want to t-talk." He swallowed hard and blinked his eyes closed. "Please."

"Okay." I shifted around in my chair, my fingers tapping against the side of the glass. "I don't want to cross a line by stopping by, Elliott, especially on a day like today. So, if you need me to leave, I can go."

His eyes stayed shut, and I watched him take a deep inhale.

He didn't say a word, but when he opened his eyes, they told me exactly what I wished his lips would say.

*Stay.*

I stayed with him throughout the morning, afternoon, and night. We moved from the kitchen to the living room, and sometimes back and forth, not once exchanging words. That day we used silence as our voices. We used darkness as our healing, and Elliott used me as his anchor. I understood Elliott that day, how he needed the silence yet still needed someone nearby.

He didn't need words. He just needed the space to feel what he needed to feel, with me present as a reminder that he wasn't alone.

When midnight hit, he stood up and walked to the front door. I tossed on my coat and my purse and followed his steps. Our goodbye was calm, just as it had been the day before. We didn't embrace, didn't even say goodbye. I just walked down the steps, ready to let go, but then he called me back.

"Jasmine."

I turned to see him looking down toward me. "Yes?"

"Ask me about her?" he said in the form of a question.

"What?"

He shifted around a bit before leaning against the doorframe, crossing his arms. "C-c-can you ask me about her?" he whispered.

I lowered my brows and gave him a small smile. "Can you tell me about your sister?"

"Yes."

I sat down on the steps, and he sat down at the top. My back rested against the stair banister. He didn't look my way, his stare fixed on his fists, but I couldn't look away from him. All my attention was placed on him and his heart.

"She loved the color purple," he told me. "Anything and everything purple was her favorite thing in the world. She believed in fairy-tales. She had braces for three years and would get taffy stuck in them at least once a week. She prayed each morning and d-did the same every night. She couldn't whistle, but she could jump rope like a pr-professional." He closed his eyes, took a deep inhale, and released the breath slowly. I watched as tears rolled down his cheeks and hit his hands. "She wanted to adopt kids someday. She h-hated the idea of some kids never feeling loved. She loved me more than I deserved and loved my mom the same."

I leaned in closer to him. "Tell me what you need from me. If you want me to go, I'll go. If you want me to stay, I'll stay. Anything you need, Eli, I'll do it."

He lightly squeezed my hands and stood up, pulling me to a standing position with him. He stepped down one step, so we were beside one another.

His lips parted, and he spoke the only word I needed to hear. "*Stay.*"

A sigh of relief fell from my mouth.

All I ever wanted to do was stay.

# Chapter Forty

## Jasmine

The following weeks felt like a fairy-tale. Elliott was showing up in ways I hadn't known possible, ways Laura had prayed for each day since the accident. Whenever we crossed each other's paths, we'd both act so nervous. Whenever I saw him, my heart skipped.

Whenever he stuttered, I swore I fell a little more head over heels.

I wasn't certain what we were, but I was just so happy he was back in my life. Some mornings when I'd arrive at TJ's, I'd find them in the living room for a saxophone lesson. I'd lean against the doorframe, and they never noticed me, because when those two rehearsed together, they gave it their all. It was a magical experience to watch. I swore TJ had to have been Elliott's father in a past life, and Elliott his son. They smiled the same way, scolded the same way, and loved the same way, too.

I saw it in TJ's eyes, too, the way he was slowly but surely redefining his purpose in life. That was the craziest thing about life—sometimes it shifted in directions we never thought it would go, but the greatest thing about humans was our ability to adapt.

TJ might not have been able to play his music anymore, but he sure did hear his sounds through a boy named Elliott Adams.

"You're going to be late for work." I smiled toward Elliott after he performed a Stan Getz piece.

He glanced at his watch. "Oh crap, okay. TJ, we'll pick up where we left off after work. I'll just leave my saxophone here."

TJ nodded. "Just work over those bars in your head at work, okay? You're almost there. You'll get them."

I loved watching those two interact.

Elliott walked by me and gave me a gentle grin. "He's smiling more."

"Because of you," I told him. We were all smiling more because of Elliott's smile.

"I'll be back around four. Have a good day, you two."

He headed out of the house, then suddenly came rushing back in. "Jazz, can I, um, talk to you outside real quick?"

"Of course." I stood and moved to the front porch with Elliott then closed the door behind me. "What's up?"

He squinted one of his eyes shut and rubbed his hands over his head.

"What's wrong?"

"Nothing's wrong, it's just..." He clasped his hands behind his neck and stood up straight. "Let's go on a date?"

Butterflies swirled in my stomach, and my cheeks heated up. "Is that a question?"

"No—well, yes...well..." He took a breath. "Will you go on a date with me this Saturday?"

"What?"

"You can say no. I just, I'm..." He bit his bottom lip, and his hazel eyes met mine. "I'm crazy about you, and I want to take you out on a date, but you can say no."

"Saturday is Valentine's Day," I told him.

He stuffed his hands into his pockets and swayed back and forth. "Yes."

"Are you asking me to be your Valentine, Elliott Adams?"

"I am asking you to be my Valentine, Jasmine Greene."

"Can I dress up?" I smiled.

"Please do."

"Okay."

"Okay."

We stood there and stared at one another, smiling like we were sixteen years old again. The butterflies and goose bumps from all those years ago remained, and just like he used to do, Elliott blinked once and said, "Okay, well, goodbye." Then he hurried away.

I walked back inside and sat back down on the couch next to TJ.

"Is everything okay?" he asked.

"Yes."

"What happened?"

My smile stretched. "He asked me out on a date."

"A date?" TJ exclaimed, clapping his hands together. "Thank you."

"For what?"

"For bringing him back home."

"It was a mutual thing." I smiled wide. "He brought me back, too."

On Saturday, Elliott picked me up from my apartment, and like the overprotective father he was, Ray was standing right next to me, staring him down. "Are you sure I can't drive you two to your date like I did back then, Snow?"

I smirked. "I think we'll pass on that this time around."

"Okay, but if he gets handsy..." he warned.

*My gosh, I hope he does.*

"Don't worry," Elliott said, staring up at the sky. "I won't even look at her."

"Good," Ray said approvingly. "That's a solid plan."

"Oh, also, your new song 'Walker's East' is one of the best songs I've ever heard in my life," Elliott told him.

Ray got his goofy big smile on his face and puffed out his chest. "Jasmine, if you don't marry this hunk, I will."

I blushed. "Good night, Dad. I'll see you later."

"Have her home by midnight," he ordered.

I laughed. "We might not be home by midnight. Don't wait up." I kissed his cheek and hurried over to Elliott's car. He opened the door for me and kept looking up at the sky. I giggled. "You two are the two most ridiculous men I know."

"Well, Ray looks like the type to kill me, and I don't want to lose my life before I take you out."

He hadn't given me any clues about the date, had just told me all I had to do was show up, and that's just what I did. We drove for a while, and when he parked the car, I looked around, confused. "Where are we going exactly?"

"You'll see," he replied, hopping out of the car then racing over to the passenger side to open my door. "Oh, and please don't take this as something more than it is right now, because it's just a part of the act for tonight."

"The act?" I asked as he took my hand and helped me out.

"Yeah." He reached into his pocket and pulled out a ring. "You gotta wear this on your ring finger."

I knew he'd said not to read too much into it, but I was a female, and we read into everything—and once we finish reading too far into something, we reread it five more times.

"Why am I wearing a wedding ring?"

"It's fake," he assured me as we started around the corner. "And this is why." He gestured toward the building, and I couldn't stop laughing.

"Seriously?"

"Yes. Today we are fake-engaged and we are going to try thirty-four different vanilla frostings at Cake & Pie Bakery."

"Oh my God, dreams do come true!" I exclaimed, jumping up and down. "Wait, I thought you didn't eat sugar?"

He shrugged. "I'll do it for you. I'll try anything with you."

"Careful what you say," I warned. "Because I like food, and you might get a little fat hanging around me."

We walked up to the door and before we entered, he turned to me. "Okay, so we're planning a wedding for the first weekend in June. The theme is rustic. We're super excited and can't wait to tie the knot. I think that's all you need to know. And, Jasmine?"

"Yes?"

"Act like you love me."

*Easy enough.*

We walked into the bakery, and we tried every single vanilla frosting they had in the place, along with six different chocolate frostings. The time with Elliott seemed effortless. When we laughed, we laughed loud, and when we were quiet, it was peaceful. We ebbed and flowed just like we had as kids.

It was so easy to be around him and fully be myself.

"My favorite was twenty-eight," I told him.

He grimaced and shook his head. "They all taste like a heart attack waiting to happen."

I leaned over, took his leftovers of thirteen and fifteen, and licked them up out of the cups. "Or they taste like heaven on earth."

"I don't know if I should be turned on or disturbed by you licking frosting from those little cups."

I picked up his chocolate number four and licked it dramatically slowly, twirling my tongue around the edges. "Mhmm," I moaned. "This is my favorite kind of chocolate."

Elliott huffed and cocked an eyebrow. "Really? *That's* your favorite kind of chocolate?"

I snickered at his comment. "I'm just saying, one night I tried to taste a different form of chocolate, and the supplier said the store was closed that night."

"It must've been around Christmas, because a lot of businesses close on Christmas day, but don't worry"—he leaned back in his chair—"I hear you can get candy half-priced after the holiday," he said with a smolder to his voice.

I cracked up laughing. "Wait, time out, sorry, just to be clear, we're talking about your penis, right?"

He nodded. "Yeah, sorry, did I take this the wrong way? Because I was ninety-nine percent sure we were on the same page."

"Oh yeah, I was definitely talking about your penis." I continued to giggle, wiping tears from my eyes. "It's just...you literally just said your penis was half-priced after the holiday season. Like, what's a full-priced penis of yours like? Do you charge for the meal before dessert? Is the tip included in the fees? How many customers a year sample the chocolate? What's the return policy? Did you know selling this form of chocolate is illegal in all states but Nevada? In the movie *Pretty Woman*, Julia Roberts sold white chocolate and had such a hard time with it. Does your penis have Yelp reviews, and if so, what is its star rating?" I couldn't stop the tears from flowing down my face.

Elliott bit his bottom lip and shook his head back and forth. "Jasmine?"

"Yes?"

"Can you stop saying penis?" he asked, a small, wicked smile on his lips.

"Yes, sorry. I swear I'm a grown-up." I cleared my throat, looked around the space, and then whispered, "Penis."

"Thanks," he joked. "I was trying to have swag, and you just killed all my c-cool points."

I was out of breath, laughing so hard at the situation. I was sure it had taken an awkward turn for Elliott, but watching him get nervous and seeing that playfulness in his eyes was so worth it.

"I'm sorry, I'm sorry." I exhaled, still wiping tears.

"Keep doing that," he told me with his smirk.

"Doing what?"

"Laughing. It's my favorite sound."

His comment made my laughter die down, and butterflies shoot to my stomach. "Stop it." I blushed, twisting around in my seat.

"Stop what?"

"Staring at me like that."

"Like what?"

"Like you're crazy about me."

He grinned, but he didn't say a word.

The owner of the store, Carol, came over to our table with the cheeriest voice. "So how was everything?" she asked as she collected the cups from the table.

"Out of this world amazing," I told her.

"That's good to hear. You two are adorable to watch together. How long have you been together?"

"Since we were sixteen," we said in unison.

His smile met mine, and it felt so good.

"That's so sweet. Well, listen, if you're interested in setting up a cake order, I'd be happy to help you out with that."

"No, we—" I started.

"Yeah, that would be great," Elliott cut in.

"What?" I asked.

"Just bring over the form and we'll fill it out together," he said with a completely straight face.

"Absolutely. And when you called in you said it was a June 2nd wedding date, right?" Carol asked enthusiastically.

"Yup," he told her.

She hurried away.

"June 2nd is my birthday," I stated, confused.

He nodded. "I know, I remember. I just figured, what's better than your favorite kind of frosting on your birthday cake? It's something to look forward to come June."

I was in awe of him.

"Stop staring at me like that," he said softly.

"Like what?"

He held his hands out to me and took mine in his hold. "Like you're crazy about me."

We placed our order for our fake wedding cake, and the butterflies that showed up in my gut refused to leave.

"Well, thanks for coming in." Carol grinned. "And if I can just say, I've been doing this for thirty-seven years, and I've never seen people who looked more in love than you two. I can see that you're wild about one another."

Elliott smiled and took my hand into his. "Yeah, she's a good thing."

We thanked Carol for letting us con her out of frosting, and then Elliott guided us to our next location. When we stopped in front of the Steamboat Natchez, my chest tightened.

"Really?" I asked, knowing I'd only been on that steamboat once, and it had been with him.

"I thought it would be nice. They're having a Valentine's cruise with live jazz music and dinner." The cruise was exactly like the time before, but this time there were many more people onboard to celebrate love.

We danced all night to the music, letting ourselves go and fully embracing one another's company. The live music was electrifying, and the crowd was lively. It seemed as if the wall Elliott had built up over the years was finally crumbling, and seeing the grown man he'd become was one of the best things that had ever happened.

Toward the end of the cruise, Elliott walked me to the edge of the boat. As I held on to the railing, he stepped behind me and wrapped his arms around my waist. The city of New Orleans was lit up as the boat moved down the Mississippi River.

When it reached the graffiti building we'd viewed as teenagers, Elliott's mouth gently brushed against my ear and he whispered, "You are be... You are..." His breath against my skin made my heart rate increase. I listened to the deep breaths he took before holding me closer. "You. Are. Beautiful," he said softly, making me turn around to face him.

"Eli...you said it. You said beautiful," I exclaimed. "You couldn't ever say that before."

"Well, yeah. I did practice every day for the past six years."

And there it was.

So small, so tiny, so real.

*Love.*

I knew I was young, and I knew it was stupid, but in that moment, I began to fall in love with a quiet boy who quietly cared for me. The boy who was scared and still strong. The boy who not only sheltered me but cared for me when he didn't have to at all. I hadn't known much about love, I hadn't known how it looked, felt, or tasted. I hadn't known how it moved, how it flowed, but I knew my heart was tight and currently skipping a few beats. I understood the goose bumps covering my arms. I knew this stuttering boy who was sometimes so scared, was someone worth loving for the second time ever.

I knew Elliott Adams was love, and I was falling into him so fast.

Truth was, I had never fallen out of love with him.

Only this time, unlike before, I refused to let him go.

"Jasmine?"

"Yes, Elliott?"

"I'm going to kiss you?"

I laughed lightly. "Is that a question?"

When his lips met mine, he gave me the answer I'd been wanting to receive. He kissed me slowly at first, tasting every part of me. He kissed me harder, and this time I tasted his hope. The more we kissed, the more my love grew. His arms wrapped around me, and he pulled me closer to him, deepening the kiss.

I kissed his lips as my hands fell to his chest, and I discovered his heartbeats.

After we headed home, we walked up to his apartment. We didn't say a word, but we stood in front of one another knowingly. As Elliott unbuttoned the cuffs of his shirt, I stepped out of my high heels. As he removed his shirt and revealed his toned abs, I let my hair down. I turned my back to him and moved my hair to the left side of my shoulder.

"Unzip?" I asked.

He did as I requested, his hands resting against my sides as he leaned in and nuzzled the curve of my neck. It was so faint, the feel of his lips against my skin. His kisses were whispers of a forever we'd always dreamed of.

The dress dropped to the floor, and I slowly drifted around to face him. His stare didn't dance across my body. His eyes were locked with mine. "You are beautiful," he said as he breathed out. His hand landed on my hip, and he drew me closer to him. "You are beautiful. You are beautiful."

His eyes were dilated, and my heart was beating wild as he brushed his lips against mine. He gently sucked on my bottom lip and chills raced down my spine. I was nervous, but it wasn't a bad nervous. It was the best kind of nervous, the kind of nervous one felt when dreams were coming true.

I inhaled sharply as he whispered to me, "I want you tonight, and then I want you in the morning. Say yes?"

My hands wrapped around his neck, pulling him down slightly. "Yes."

He placed his palms beneath my ass, lifted me up, and carried me to his bed. As he laid me down, he stepped back for a moment, taking me in. His eyes surveyed my body, and he took in every single inch of me as he unzipped his slacks and slid them to the floor.

He slowly lowered himself, his hands wrapping around my left thigh, my heart racing with anticipation as he touched me. His mouth fell against my inner thigh, where he rolled his tongue against my skin.

He worked his way up, taking his time, making me twist, making me turn, forcing me to fall victim to my moans. When his mouth met the edge of my panties, he slowly pulled them down my thighs, tossing them to the side of the room.

"Please," I begged as his tongue slowly swept against my core, making me thrust my hips toward him.

"Eli..." I muttered as he slid his tongue deep inside of me. As he tasted every part of me, I cried out, feeling two fingers slide into me, making me twist even more.

"Eli, please..."

He slid in another, moving his tongue to my clitoris as he licked and sucked and fucked me with his mouth. My body reacted each time he deepened his touch, thrusting his fingers into me fast and pulling them out slowly. My heart was insane, my mind blurred. I wanted him more than anything as he built me up closer and closer...

*Fast, slow, fast, slow, fast...*

"More," I begged, unable to keep quiet, unable to want him any more than I did in that moment. "Yes..."

He reached up and grabbed my breast with his free hand while his other took even more control. His breaths were growing wilder, his want matching mine.

"I'm going to...I'm going..." I breathed out, feeling a tremble down my back, my desires building to an uncontrollable level.

"No," he told me, pausing his fingers inside me. He moved up to my lips and kissed me hard, tugging my bottom lip between his teeth before he spoke. "Not yet." His pupils were huge, and I saw the way he craved me, how he wanted me, how he needed me the same way I needed him.

"Elliott..."

"When you let go," he whispered, positioning himself over me, sliding his tongue against the curves of my breasts. "I want to feel it. When you let go"—he breathed heavily as he slid his hardness deep inside of me—"I want you to tremble against me." His growl made me cry out in pleasure. "When you let go, Jazz," he hissed, grazing his teeth against my earlobe, "You better fucking scream."

As he slid into me, I felt every moment of happiness, of ecstasy, of bliss, of love.

He proceeded to have his way with me until my voice went hoarse.

It was still there, fully intact: our love song.

Our love existed in every second, and every touch we shared.

My mind was dazed as he pulled my hair. My heart was his as he thrust deeper and deeper into my body, into my mind, into my spirit.

A part of my soul had thought he'd move on after I left, but a bigger part of me knew the kind of love we had wasn't something that could ever be abandoned due to distance and time.

That night we did exactly what we'd always wanted to do—we became our own song. We made love in every room, in every corner, in every way. I loved him more and more as his breaths fell against me, as he whispered my name.

Every second, every touch...

"You are...are...you are my world," he promised with tired breaths, lying beside me in his bed. "You are my fucking world."

And he was mine.

My lover, my friend, my beginnings, my ends. He was everything I wanted to have and everything I had thought I'd never witness again.

I loved how we physically connected that night, but my favorite part was after the sex, when we lay there, tangled up in one another's arms.

Our eyes were heavy, but we couldn't let go of the feeling of bliss we discovered. I couldn't stop running my fingers across his chest, and he couldn't stop gently kissing my skin as we shared stories with one another. My favorite stories were the ones he shared about Katie. Before, he couldn't even speak her name, but now, when he shared with me, he smiled. It was as if the memories weren't destructive flames anymore. They were sparks of love, and he honored her name by speaking those memories out loud.

"She loved fried salami sandwiches. She sucked at cooking them, though, so they were really *burnt* salami sandwiches, but I swear she'd slather them with mayo and eat them all the time. There was a time she ate them for breakfast, lunch, and dinner for three weeks straight." He laughed heartily.

I smiled. "That's actually pretty disgusting."

"Yeah. Our house would smell like burnt salami for days. Mom would come home from work and holler, 'Katlyn Rae Adams, if you ever get married, please never cook for your husband. You'd be the death of him.'"

"It must run in your family—TJ tried to get me to eat peanut butter and roast beef once." I groaned. "Disgusting."

"Hey, don't knock it till you try it. Same with the ham and jelly sandwiches."

"Oh my gosh." I shook my head back and forth. "You hang out with him way too much."

"My mom hated his sandwiches but would still eat them all the time because it made TJ smile."

"Your mom is one of the kindest people I've ever met."

"She's too good for this world," he told me. "She's a saint."

"Does she date?" I wondered.

"Nah. She has a hard time getting close to people after my dad. He really did a number on her. I think she gets lonely, though. I asked her about it once and she told me she'd rather be alone and lonely sometimes than in the wrong relationship and sad. She was convinced that being in a bad relationship was ten times lonelier than actually being alone."

"Any person would be lucky to have her."

"I agree. If it happens someday, he better love her like it's his last breath—or else I'll kill him."

I smiled at how much he loved his mother. She loved him the same exact way. They were lucky to have one another.

"I've been a shitty son," he confessed, rubbing the back of his neck. "My mom would give up her world for me, and I spent the last six years trying to stay away for selfish reasons because I wasn't strong enough."

"What do you mean?"

"She looks just like her," he explained quietly. "Every time I see my mother, I see my sister too, from her curly dark hair to her smile... from her small figure to the way she laughs, the way she cries. So, I've avoided her."

"But that sounds like such a blessing," I told him, moving in closer. "Being able to see your sister in your mother's smile. It's almost as if she cheated death somehow. It's almost as if a part of her spirit lives on in such a beautiful way."

"I've never thought about it like that."

"Sometimes it's hard to see things in a different light when you've become so accustomed to the dark."

He pressed his lips against my forehead. "Jasmine?"

"Yes?"

"I love you. More than words can say, I l-love you."

The way he stuttered over the word love matched the skipping of my heartbeats.

"I love you too, Eli." I'd always had. I'd loved him when I was sixteen, and even though time passed, I had never let that love go.

That was what the key around my neck stood for to me.

The key was Elliott, and for all those years, he stayed right beside my heart.

He was home to me.

We didn't sleep together again that morning, but I felt his soul against mine. My favorite thing about Elliott was how he could make love to me with only his stare.

I loved how he loved me so quietly as our eyes drifted closed, giving way to sleep, and I loved how I knew he'd love me the same when we awoke.

# Chapter Forty-One

## Elliott

She woke up before me. When I stirred in bed, I glanced up to see her standing near the windowsill wearing one of my oversized T-shirts. The light from the sun spilled in, and I couldn't fully grasp what had happened.

I couldn't remember the last time I'd felt so happy.

She was really there. She'd come back to me.

She didn't have a clue what she'd done for me. I'd spent six years locked in a cage, and she was the key to my freedom.

"Good morning," I called, startling her, and she turned around to face me. In her hands was a notebook, one of the many that sat inside of my dresser. "What are you doing?"

Her eyes filled with worry, and she shook her head. "I'm sorry. I went into your dresser for a T-shirt, and I found this. It was open on top of everything, and I saw my name and—"

"It's okay," I told her, patting the spot beside me on the bed.

She joined me and sat up straight. "What are these, Eli?"

"Letters I wrote to you," I told her. "I, um...TJ used to have me write down my hopes and fears in notebooks, to help with my music. After what happened, I gave up pretty much everything. Everything that meant anything good to me, but I couldn't stop writing to you, even if you never read them. I think that's why it worked for me. I knew you wouldn't see them and try to make me feel better. I just bled onto the paper each night, writing down everything in my heart, everything I felt. Writing to you m-made me feel less alone, I guess. I was hard on myself, but at least in some shape or form I wasn't alone. You were always there with me. You were always around."

Tears fell down her cheeks, and I wiped them away. "Don't cry. I never want to make you cry."

"I'm sorry, it's just..." She sighed. "These entries...your pain... I'm so sorry, Elliott."

"Hey," I said, shaking my head. "I can breathe now. I can breathe."

My lips grazed over hers, and she nodded. "You wrote these letters, and I wore your key. This is us...this has always been us."

"This will always be us."

"My favorite part was how you ended each letter, your P.S."

I gently kissed her forehead, and we lay back down. I pulled her closer to me. "Also, I still love you," I whispered, repeating the words I'd written so many times.

"Also, I still love you," she echoed softly. "Can we just stay here? Can we ignore the world for a while?"

I smirked. "I wish, but I gotta get to TJ'. We have a music lesson, and he'll kill me if I'm late."

"That's not a lie."

I kissed her lips. "Let's see each other afterward?"

"Yes. Dinner tonight, with Jason and Kelly, maybe?"

"I'd love to, but maybe tomorrow? I'm a bit busy tonight. Actually, I was going to ask you—do you think you can hang over at TJ's tonight for a bit?"

She smiled. "Why? Is someone else sampling your chocolate this afternoon?"

"Depends. Would that make you jealous?" I joked.

"Jealous? Please, I hardly like you." She rolled her eyes. "You're hardly even cute, anyway. You're actually kind of ugly."

"Oh, is that so?" I stood up and lifted her into my arms. She wrapped her legs around me.

"Where are you taking me?" she asked.

"To take a shower with me so I can show you just how ugly I can be."

After we finished our shower, we got dressed, and just as we were about to leave the apartment, I got a call from Mom. "Hey, sorry we're running behind a bit. I'm on my way now."

"That's not it, Elliott," she said, her voice sounding somber.

"What's wrong?"

"I just need to talk to you. We need to talk."

"On my way." I grabbed my coat and my keys as Jasmine looked at me, concerned.

"What is it?" she asked.

"I don't know, but we gotta go."

We arrived at TJ's house, where he and Mom sat on the sofa. She brought us up to date with everything that was going on. "I should've told you right away, but I knew you two were out last night and—"

"You should've told us right away," I huffed, leaning against the doorframe with my arms crossed.

"I know, I know." She nodded. "I'm sorry, I was just stunned. I didn't even tell TJ until this morning, and he had me call you right away."

"This isn't your mother's doing, Elliott. Just remember that," TJ said.

"They left a note?" Jasmine asked, reaching out toward Mom, taking the piece of paper. Her eyes danced across the words, and a weighted sigh fell from between her lips.

"Yes. It was in my mailbox yesterday afternoon. I wasn't sure how to handle it...how to feel."

"Can I see?" I asked Jasmine. She stood up and walked it over to me.

*Ms. Adams,*

*I know this is crossing the line, and I hope someday you will forgive me for crossing it. After everything your family has suffered, it is ill of me to even reach out to you, but I knew if I didn't, I'd always sit with a pit of regret and guilt in my stomach for not trying.*

*As you know, Todd is facing life in prison with no chance of parole. My son's life is gone. He will spend the rest of his days behind bars for the act he committed six years ago. The day you lost your daughter, I, too, lost a child—definitely not to the same extreme as your loss, but still, there is a hollowness inside my entire being.*

*I wasn't a good mother.*

*I never showed up when I should have, and I focused too much on work to really give any type of love to my children. I grew up in a home where love wasn't common, and I seemed to carry that down in the way I raised my children.*

*I left them to their own destruction because I never gave them any order.*

*I figured if I had survived growing up in a house that was never a home then my sons would be fine too.*

*My older son was trouble, but not like Todd.*

*Todd was reckless. He was screaming for years for his father and me to notice him, and we ignored his shouts. We figured he'd grow out of it. We'd figured he'd make his way to college, still rebel, but come out with a career, a wife, and children.*

*Truth was, there was a darkness that hovered over Todd. It was a heavy cloud, and I realize now that I was the one who placed it there. I ignored his cries, so his days grew dark.*

*My son did the act, yes. He took your daughter's life, but if there's anyone else to blame, I know it's me.*

*I should've loved him better. I should've done more.*

*Five years ago, my eldest son moved away, and I haven't heard from him since. Three months ago, my husband took his own life. It was too much for him.*

*It's been too much for us all.*

*Todd wrote me a few weeks back, asking me to reach out to you and your son. He wanted me to express how heavy his heart is with what happened, how weighted his pain is.*

*He wanted to know if he could somehow express that to you.*

*He wanted me to ask if you'd be willing to visit him at the Louisiana State Penitentiary.*

*I know this is a lot, and if I do not hear from you, I will fully un-derstand and will not reach out again.*

*I again express my deepest sorrows for the loss of Katie. I know my apologies will never be enough and will always appear empty, but do know that they exist. Do know that there isn't a moment that goes by that I don't think of your suffering and wish I could ease it away.*

*I hope to hear from you soon.*

*If not, I understand and send blessings your way.*

-Marie Clause

"This is bu-bullshit," I hissed. "How dare she even write to you! How dare she reach out!" I hollered, my blood boiling. I was livid at her words, at her apologies. The nerve she had to actually walk up to my mother's mailbox and leave that kind of message for her—it enraged me.

"Calm down, son," TJ urged.

"No." I paced back and forth, my hands forming fists. "We should report this. We should let the cops know that these people, these *monsters* are crossing lines. They are going to pay for this. They aren't al-lowed to—"

"Her husband committed suicide, and her other son moved away, Elliott. It's not *they*, it's only her," Mom interjected.

"But still, she had no right to—"

"I'm meeting with him."

My heart snapped in half as I turned to face her. "What?"

She had tears rolling down her cheeks, and her body shook as TJ comforted her. "I'm meeting with him. I've already decided, Eli. I just called you over to see if you wanted to come with me."

"You're...you..." My mind was jumbled, and words wouldn't leave my mouth. She was talking insane. She was playing with the devil, the same devil who had taken away my sister—her daughter. "You can't."

"I am."

"Eli..." Jasmine started, standing up to walk toward me, but I tossed my hand up to warn her back.

My eyes peered into Mom's and I shook my head. "How could you do this?" I asked, baffled by her choices. We owed these people nothing. They had taken from us, not the other way around. "You're making the bi-biggest mistake of your life."

I marched out the front door, and it didn't take long for Jasmine to race after me and grab my arm. "Eli, wait!" she said, grabbing my arm.

I tensed up at her touch and couldn't look her way. No. She'd try to make me understand. She'd try to break through to me. "Jasmine?" I whispered.

"Yes."

"Let me go."

"No, Elliott. I won't. I can't. Let's go talk to her. Let's—"

"*Jasmine!*" I shouted this time, my blood boiling inside of me. I turned her way, and her eyes were wide with worry. "Let. Me. Go."

She slowly released her hold on my arm, and I stormed off, not looking back her way.

If I saw her, I would beg her to follow me, to help me escape my mind. I would ask her to make me understand.

But in that moment, I didn't want to understand. In that moment all I wanted to do was escape reality.

# Chapter Forty-Two

## Jasmine

"Jason!" I shouted, racing into the bar. He was setting up getting ready to open in a few hours.

When he heard his name, he turned to face me. "Jasmine? What's going on?"

"Is Elliott here?"

"Yeah, he stormed upstairs about ten minutes ago. Why? Is everything okay?"

"No." I shook my head. "It's not." I filled Jason in on everything that had happened, and the worry in his eyes matched my own.

"He's going to snap," he told me.

"Yeah, I know. That's why he needs us right now. He needs us close, otherwise he'll start building that wall again, but I'm sure he locked the door upstairs."

Jason grabbed his set of keys. "Don't worry, I got a spare. Come on."

We hurried up the stairs, and when we walked inside, there Elliott was, hammering away at his punching bag. He wasn't wearing boxing gloves. His fists were just pounding into the bag repeatedly, leaving cuts and bruises across his knuckles.

"Brother, what are you doing?" Jason asked, slowly approaching Elliott.

"You can't just ba-bar-barge in here," he barked as he continued to hit the bag.

"Eli." I grimaced. "We were worried about you. That was a lot back at TJ's. What's going on in your mind?"

He kept hammering, not replying.

"Eli, talk to us, please," I urged.

"I don't want to," he whispered.

"Come on, man, we're here," Jason offered.

"I don't want you here!" he shouted, hitting the bag one more time before turning to face us. His chest heaved, rising and falling faster and faster. "Leave."

Jason stood tall. "No."

Elliott's wild stare moved to me. "Leave," he repeated.

I mirrored Jason's stance. "No."

He grew angrier and angrier, his breathing erratic, his beautiful eyes filled with madness. "Fine." He pushed past both of us. "Then I'll go."

We called after him, but he wouldn't turn around. The moment he got outside, he took off running, not looking back once.

"We looked everywhere, Laura," Jason told Elliott's mom on the phone as we sat in his car. We'd just left the last gym we figured Elliott might go to, and we'd had no luck finding him. "We'll keep looking through." He paused. "No, really, you stay with TJ. He'll pop back up. We'll call if we hear anything. Okay, bye." He hung up and released a heavy sigh. "Well, this fucking sucks."

"I can just imagine his mind spinning. It's breaking my heart..." Elliott had been MIA for hours now, with no word. The sun had set a while ago, and still, he was gone.

"I know, me too. I just can't imagine where he might be." He exhaled audibly. "We checked every gym, every jazz bar, hell, even the music corner on Frenchmen Street, and nothing. I literally have no clue...maybe we should wait for him to cool off? I'm sure he'll return to Daze."

My mind was racing, and my gut was tight with nerves. "Jason, can we check one more place?" I asked.

He put his car into drive and nodded. "Just tell me where."

We parked the car and hurried to the alleyway on Frenchmen Street. Jason let out a sigh of relief as we stared at Elliott sitting on top of the dumpster.

"Thank God," he whispered. "Should we both go or...?"

"I'll go," I told him. "If you could let Laura know we found him, that would be great. Thank you for everything." I pulled him into a hug.

"Of course. Anytime."

He headed out, and I took a few moments to observe Elliott. His shoulders were rounded, and his hands gripped the edge of the dumpster. He seemed so defeated.

"Hey." I smiled, walking his way.

He looked up and gave me a broken grin. "Hey."

"Can I sit with you?"

He took a moment before he scooted over, making room for me to join him. "I'm s-sorry." His voice cracked. "I'm sorry for yelling at you. My mind was..."

"Hurting. Your mind was hurting, and I understand. You just worried us, that's all." I lay my head on his shoulder and scooted closer to him. "Talk to me?"

His body shifted a bit before he reached out to take my hand into his. "I just don't get it. I've been going over it in my head all day. I don't get why she'd w-want to visit him. I don't get it."

"Your mother's a beautiful woman, and she's smart. She wouldn't just make this decision without having a solid reason of her own. You know this. You know your mom."

"She's too good."

I shook my head. "We need more people like her. We need more people who are too good."

He grimaced and rubbed the back of his neck. "I still don't understand, though."

"I know, but maybe that's the thing, ya know? Maybe it's not for us to understand."

"What do you mean?"

"She has her reasons. She didn't ask you to come over for you to talk her in or out of going. She had already decided, Eli."

"Then why did she call me?"

"For you to hold her hand."

He swallowed hard and closed his eyes. "This isn't about Todd's or Marie's healing, is it?"

"No, it's about your mom's healing."

"Thank you," he whispered. "Thank you for not letting me wander too far."

"Always." I glanced around the alleyway and listened to the music coming from the bars. "Why did you come back here?" I asked.

"Because I wanted to stay angry. I didn't want to ease up on my fury about what happened, if that makes sense."

"It does. Is it hard for you? Being back here?"

"Yes," he confessed, pulling me closer. "But it's easier with you. Everything is always easier with you."

## Chapter Forty-Three

### Elliott

"What are you doing here?" Mom asked the morning she was going to visit Todd. She shook her head back and forth. "Now, Eli, I love you, but if you're here to talk me out of this…"

"I'm not."

"Then why are you here?"

I stuffed my hands into my pockets and swayed back and forth. "It's a two-and-a-half drive to the Louisiana State Penitentiary. I thought you might enjoy some company."

Her eyes widened. "What?"

"You didn't really think I'd let you do this alone, did you?" Tears fell down her cheeks and she covered her mouth with the palm of her hand, overtaken by emotion. I smiled. "Come on, Ma. Don't cry."

"I'm sorry, I'm sorry…it's just…" She took a deep breath. "I really need you today, Eli. I didn't want to ask, but I need you so much. For so long, I'd thought I lost you. For so long I thought you were gone."

"I'm back," I promised her. "I'm back, and I'm sorry it t-took me so long, because I've missed you. You're the most amazing human I've ever known," I told her.

"Eli…" Her eyes watered over, but I continued speaking.

"I spent years trying to get strong. I thought strength came from the physical aspects of life. I thought strength came from weightlifting, boxing, being able to fight back with my fists, but all this time, I was wrong." I cleared my throat, trying to hold in my own emotions as Mom's poured out. "I've learned that being strong is getting out of bed each day when your world's falling apart. I've learned that being strong is showing up on your son's birthday, even when he's distant.

"Being strong is loving the broken pieces of your loved ones. Being strong is crying yourself to sleep at night and waking each morning still believing in beauty. Being strong is forgiveness. What you're doing today—that is strength. You are all of t-this, Ma. You are my rock, my hero. Without you, I'd be nothing. When we lost Katie, you lost me, too, and I'm so so-sorry about that. I'm so sorry for all I've put you through."

"It's okay, Elliott. I'd do it again in a heartbeat if it meant you'd come back to us all. I'd walk through it all again for you...always for you."

I smiled. "I know you would, because you are the definition of strength." I walked over to her and pulled her into a hug, and she held on tight, as if she'd been terrified she'd never be able to hold me close again. "You have her smile," I whispered. "You have her smile, Mom."

"And you have her eyes."

I held her as long as she needed me to, and then I continued to hold her some more.

We drove to the prison, and when we arrived, a team was waiting to search us, making sure we didn't have any kind of weapons or illegal items. That was a wake-up call. I'd never been to a prison, and the moment we arrived, it felt terrifying.

Todd's mom was waiting for us inside. She was skinny, sickly looking, and I'd never seen a pair of blue eyes that looked so sad.

"Um, hi, I...um." She stuttered over her words and her body shook. Every part of her was broken; she was nothing like the woman I remembered. "I...thank you. Thank you for coming," she finally pushed out.

Mom didn't say anything, but she offered Marie a small smile.

My heart was racing as they signed us in for our visit. We walked through a set of metal detectors, and we were led down a hallway then placed in front of a glass partition. There were two seats in front of the window, and Marie waved for us to sit down as she stood behind us.

A staff member walked through the door, and Todd was with him. His hands were handcuffed together, and his feet were shackled, too.

I wanted to vomit, seeing him. I wanted to run away and never face the past again, but Mom needed this closure. She needed to let go, and maybe I didn't understand her way of healing, but I loved her enough to stay by her side.

Todd looked worse than his mom. His face was covered in facial hair, his skin was pale, and he was almost a skeletal. As he sat down, he cleared his throat. He lifted the telephone on his side, and Mom did the same. As he spoke to her, tears began to fall down her cheeks, and I could only hear her replies.

"Yes. Thank you. I know." At one point, she closed her eyes and took a deep breath. I took her hand and linked it with mine, giving it a squeeze. Once they finished talking, they both glanced over to me. Mom pulled the phone from her ear. "He wants to speak with you."

With hesitation, I took the phone in my hand, and placed it against my ear.

"Hello?"

"Hey, man..." Todd said nervously. He kept shifting around in his seat, unable to stay still. "Wow, you really be-beefed up, huh?" he stuttered, his nerves swallowing him whole. He laughed. "I mean, I doubt anyone's bullying you anymore."

I didn't say a word.

"Look, I know...there's nothing I c-can say to..." He tripped over his words, couldn't connect his thoughts, and it was a feeling I knew all too well. When he was finally able to grasp a few words, he looked up at me with glassy eyes and said, "I'm so sorry, Elliott."

Then he looked back down at his hands.

"I forgive you," I said, making him shoot his stare back up. Tears swam in his eyes. "What?"

"I forgive you. Not for me"—I nodded toward my mom—"but for her. I forgive you for her."

He broke down into uncontrollable sobbing, and I watched as he struggled to breathe. "Thank you, Elliott. Thank you."

I remained still as I spoke the last words. "I never want to hear from you again," I told him. "This is it. This is the end."

He nodded and continued to fall apart. As we stood up, Marie shook behind us, as she stared down at Mom's hand still in mine. Then she looked to her own son, who was trapped behind that glass. She was unable to hold him, unable to reach out and comfort him as he fell apart. So, she did all she could do: she fell apart too.

She covered her mouth as she sobbed heavily into the palm of her hand. Her tiny figure shook nonstop, and she was seconds away from falling to the ground with the heaviness of her heart. I watched it in her; I watched her soul burn.

She kept apologizing over and over again. She kept saying words I was more than familiar with. She kept blaming herself for what had happened six years before. She probably blamed herself for her husband taking his own life, too.

Her son sat behind bars, but the truth was, Mrs. Clause was living in true imprisonment. She was completely alone. She had nothing and nobody, not even one hand to hold for comfort during the hardest days of her life. As her legs were about to give out, as her breaths were dissolving, I rushed in and held her close. I held her close and she cried into me, falling apart while my arms did their best to keep her together.

I didn't know why I said it.

I didn't know why the words left my mouth.

I wasn't even certain I believed it, but I told her what she needed to hear.

I held her close, and whispered that it wasn't her fault.

The way she howled in sorrow afterward was enough to break my own heart.

We stayed with Marie until she was able to gather herself, and then we left as she sat down to speak with her son. I watched her place her hand against the glass partition, watched him place his opposite hers, and I released a breath.

I wrapped my arm around my mom's shoulder and kissed the top of her head as we walked away. "Thank you, Mom."

"For what?"

"For never letting me go."

That night she prepared dinner for the two of us, cooking all of Katie's favorite side dishes. We talked all night long, real conversation with laughter. I couldn't remember the last time I'd heard my mother laugh.

"I've missed this," she told me, making two cups of coffee as we sat at the table. "Some of my favorite memories were spent around this table.

"Same with me," I agreed.

"Is it hard for you? Without your sister here?"

"I actually think it was harder for me to be alone, than it was for me to be here."

She nodded. "You thought you deserved to be alone. You don't think that anymore, right?"

"Yeah, not at all. You all really helped me." Her eyes watered over, and I laughed. "Come on, Ma. Don't cry."

"I'm sorry, I'm sorry. It's just... I've missed you so much."

"I've missed you, too. You have the greatest heart in this world. You see things in the way that most wouldn't. What you did for Marie today...most people would've let her suffer."

"I know what it feels like to suffer. Plus, I couldn't help but think, what if it were you who committed the act of hate? What if my child made that level of mistake? How would I deal with it? I'd know I'd blame myself. It's the mother instinct. You overthink everything from day one. You live in guilt for everything from missing a school concert to forgetting to put the juice box in their lunch bag. If it were you behind bars... If I were never able to hold you again, I'd feel more imprisoned than anyone else. Marie is trapped in a world of loneliness and guilt for the remainder of her life. So, she needed today. I needed today."

"We all needed today, I think," I agreed.

"How you helped her, how you held her... That was good. That was so, so good. Eli, you're the best man I've ever known."

"Well, ya know. Every good part of me exists because of you."

After that night, we started up our dinners together each week, growing closer each time. The more I learned about my mother, the more reasons she gave me to love her. One Sunday night as we sat at the dining room table, she looked up at me with that smile that matched my sister's.

"I think we should expand our dinner nights," she told me. "Invite others. Our family is big—we might as well all eat together."

I grinned. "We're going to need a bigger table," I joked.

"Let's just host it at TJ's house. He'll love it."

## Chapter Forty-Four

# Jasmine

One morning after I stayed at Elliott's apartment, I rolled over in his bed to find him still sleeping. My hand had been wrapped around my key necklace as I stared at my emails.

Elliott stirred and then turned to face me. "Good morning," he whispered. He wrapped his arms around me, and pulled me into the curve of his body.

"Good morning."

He raised an eyebrow. "What's wrong?"

"What makes you think something's wrong?"

His mouth gently kissed the nape of my neck. "I know you, Jazz. What's wrong?"

"I heard back from my mom."

He sat up, alert. "What?"

"Well, not from her directly. I wrote to Trevor and he said I should come out to talk to them."

"Really?" Elliott asked, cocking an eyebrow. "He was that easy about meeting with you?"

"Well, not really. I might have lied to him and said I was thinking about trying for the record deal again."

"Jazz..." Elliott sighed. "I just—"

"It's been months and I haven't heard a word from her, Eli. She won't see me. So, yeah, I lied, and it was wrong, but my mother won't see me, and I need to try one last time." I took a deep inhale. "I know it doesn't make sense. I know that I'm probably an idiot for thinking that there's something there that isn't but—"

"I'll go with you."

"What?"

"You don't ever have to explain to me why you're doing what you're doing. Do you think you need to do this?"

"Yes."

"Then okay. We're doing this."

My hands raced through my hair. "You don't have to do this. I can go alone."

He gave me a stern look. "We don't do things alone. Not anymore. Does Ray know?"

I shook my head. "No. If I told him, he'd try to protect me. I know this is something I have to do without him."

"Well, let's do it then."

We waited two weeks before getting on a plane to London. The whole flight my stomach was in knots. When we made it to the hotel the night before meeting Mama, I cried into Elliott's shirt. My nerves were higher than they'd ever been. I wasn't ready to face Mama, but Elliott held me through all the tears.

I was so thankful he was there for me.

It was a Saturday afternoon when we walked up the steps to Mama's flat. When I knocked, Trevor answered the door, and Elliott placed a hand on my shoulder for comfort.

"Hi, Jasmine," he said coldly. His eyes moved to Elliott. "You got a bodyguard now?"

"This is Elliott. My..." My words faded off as I turned to Elliott.

"Boyfriend," he said reaching out to shake Trevor's hand.

"Shit, that's some grip," Trevor said, pulling his hand away and shaking it.

"Sorry," Elliott murmured. I smiled knowingly. That intense handshake was for me. I was glad he didn't break it—that could've caused a little too much trouble.

"Come on in, Heather's in the living room. We'll talk there. I'm gonna be honest. I'm shocked it took you this long to come back to your senses," Trevor said, shaking his head. He was wearing sunglasses inside. *Who wears sunglasses inside?* Trevor of course.

He led us to the living room, and my heart leaped into my throat. Mama sat on a sofa with her legs crossed. Her posture was tall and stern. She hadn't changed much from what I remembered. She didn't stand to greet me. She didn't even say hello.

All I wanted to do was hold her, hug her, and tell her that even with her coldness, I still missed her.

"Sit," Trevor order, gesturing toward the sofa across from Mama's.

I sat beside Elliott, and Trevor sat down next to Mama. He finally slid off his sunglasses. His eyes were bloodshot red. He was probably high, drunk, or both, but I didn't mention it. I wasn't there for him.

Trevor rubbed his hands together and cleared his throat. "I'm not gonna lie, Jasmine. You left us in a fucking mess. We were days away from celebrating the biggest deal, and you walked the fuck away. You screwed so many people over with that damn choice and getting back the same kind of deal is out of the question."

"How are you?" I asked, my stare on Mama. She stared back at me, her brown eyes that matched mine. I leaned forward, clasping my hands together. "Did you get my emails?"

She didn't say a word.

"Listen, this isn't a family reunion," Trevor cut in. "Just to be clear, this is all business."

"Is it, Mama?" I asked. "Has this always been just business?"

"Heather, leave," Trevor told her. She stood up like a robot, and turned to leave the room.

I shot up. "Mama, did I ever matter to you?" She paused her footsteps. Tears formed in my eyes. "Did you ever care?"

She turned slowly to look my way, and tilted her head. "All you've ever done was let me down."

"No," I said. "I didn't. All I ever did was try to make you proud."

"You failed."

My chest tightened at her words, but her blows didn't sting as much as they used to—I was getting stronger. "Is that what your parents said to you?"

"I beg your pardon?"

"You never talk about grandma or grandpa. I've never even met them. Did you let them down? Did you fail them when you got pregnant?"

"Shut up," she warned, but I wouldn't—I couldn't.

"You were only what, seventeen or eighteen when you were pregnant? Did they turn their backs on you? Did they call you a failure? Did they push you away?" Her bottom lip trembled. I knew I was hitting a nerve. "Were you supposed to be their star?"

"My parents were trash, and my career was my way out." Her voice cracked, but she didn't dare let a tear fall—that would show weakness. "My mother was a drug addict and got knocked up by my father—the drunk—at seventeen. I grew up in a trailer, and worked my ass off to get far away from that life."

"Then you got pregnant with me."

"Yes." She nodded. "I became my mother, and you became my biggest mistake."

"Hey—" Elliott started, but I shook my head.

"It's okay," I told him. It was my battle to fight, not his. I turned back to Mama. "I'm sorry about your parents and the way your childhood played out, but you're wrong about me failing you. You had issues before me. I am not your failure."

"Like hell you aren't!" she barked, marching over to me. "Everything you've ever done has broken my heart. You have let me down since the day you were born, taking away the only shot I had at a real career of my own. So, what do *I* do? I work my ass off to make you something. To give you what I've always dreamed of, and what do *you* do?! You toss it away because your feelings were hurt?! You're a child, and I wish to God you weren't a child of mine," she sneered with hatred in her voice.

I felt it—her hatred, but still, love existed inside of me.

My skin crawled at her words, but I didn't crumble. I didn't falter as she spat her words my way. "Tell me about my father," I softly spoke.

She stumbled a little. "What?"

"Tell me about my father."

273

"Your father was a monster, just like mine. He was a drug addict who took more from me than anyone, and then left me the moment he found out about you. He was weak. Just like you."

I shook my head. "No. That's not my father."

"Excuse me?"

"My father's name is Ray Gable. He's the lead singer of Peter's Peaks, and a great man. He has a heart of gold, and he'd do anything to make sure I was okay. Now, tell me about my mother."

"I'm your mother."

I shook my head. "No. You're not my mother." She didn't reply, and I cleared my throat. "My mother wouldn't treat me the way you have. My mother wouldn't push me to be something I never wanted to become. My mother would've loved me through all the bad times. She would've listened to me."

"You're so selfish," she hissed. "I gave you everything. You could've been a pop star."

"I never wanted to be a pop star. I sing soul."

"You don't. You were never a soul singer!"

"That's all I am!"

"I want you to leave," she told me. "I want you to leave and not come back. Ever."

I took a deep breath, and for the first time in forever I finally started to let her go. It was slow, and painful, but I knew with pain came healing. Over time things would get better and my breaths would become calmer, but at least I could walk away knowing I gave it my all. I tried, and that had to be good enough.

I turned to Elliott and gave him a small smile. "You ready?"

He stood up and placed a hand on my lower back. "Are you all right?"

"Yes. I will be. Let's go home."

We started walking away, and I heard her shout at me.

"You're making the biggest mistake of your life! Leaving your shot at a career for what? For love?! What a foolish child you are. You were always a fool."

I took a deep breath, and I felt it as it hit me--my truth.

I closed my eyes and turned toward her. As my lips parted, the words flowed freely from my lips. The song was "Palace", by Sam Smith, and it summed up everything I'd ever felt for Mama. It showcased my love, my need, my want to be her daughter. To make her proud. To be who she always wanted me to be. We built a palace of a career I never wanted to live in. And for years I lived in that palace because I wanted to be her princess, and because I loved her.

She was everything to me, she was my queen, but I knew it was time for the palace to crumble. I needed to let go of her, I needed to allow my heart to break, in order for it to heal. And to do that, I had to feel it all.

As I sang, I put my everything into the performance—my soul, my heart, my darkness. I gave way to every part of the harsh relationship between my mother and me. I remembered every second of pain and every glimpse of happiness. I relived it as the words fell from my lips.

I loved her and didn't regret it. I never would, but I was ready to move on. Therefore, I said goodbye. She'd be a ghost in my memories that sometimes brought me comfort, and other times she'd bring me pain. But no matter what, she was my past.

It was now time to let go and move on to my future.

When I finished singing, Elliott smiled at me, giving me comfort.

"You found it," he said.

I nodded. "Yes."

"Found what?" Trevor barked.

I looked over to Mama and released a weighted sigh I'd been holding all my life. "I found my truth."

Closure was an odd concept. In my mind, I always believed closure came when both parties spoke from their hearts, and let go together. I thought there couldn't be full closure if one party wasn't willing to open up and express their truths, but that wasn't what closure was—not really. Closure wasn't a fairy-tale ending with equal goodbyes. Closure was simply one person finding their voice, their own strength, and learning to let go by themselves.

Closure was one person writing the ending to a very toxic song, and never replaying it in their souls. The best kind of closure was being brave enough to start a new song with new lyrics and a beautiful melody.

Closure was moving on, and it was now time for me to do exactly that.

Elliott and I stepped outside onto the porch, and he held me in his arms. As I fell against his chest, I didn't cry. I just held on tight. "That was hard," I said softly.

"I know. You did good, though. I'm proud of you. Are you okay?"

"Yes," I told him truthfully. "I am."

"Good." He let me go and nodded toward the street. "Because I think he would've started a war if you weren't okay."

I looked up and saw Ray leaning against a car. My eyes shot to Elliott. "You told him?"

"I had to. Figured you could use your Dad today."

Ray smiled my way and walked over with his hands stuffed in his pockets. "You have a good day, Snow White?"

I smiled, and raced over to him, pulling him into a hug. "Yes," I whispered. "I had a good day."

Maybe it wasn't the norm, but I had a family. A family that my heart created, a family that cared for me through the darkness and the light, a family that would go to war for me.

My heart was filled with love, and the best feeling in the world was knowing that their hearts loved me, too.

# Chapter Forty-Five

## Elliott

Our first official family dinner took place on Katie's birthday. It only seemed right to remember her while we expanded our family, and everyone came to celebrate and process together. Kelly, Jason, TJ, Mom, Ray, Jasmine, and I all sat around the new table in TJ's dining room.

Everyone shared their favorite stories of Katie, but we didn't just live in the past with our conversations; we also looked to the future. We planned for tomorrow, because we were no longer trapped behind the bars of yesterday.

True freedom came once you learned the final stage of grief: acceptance.

I'd never thought I'd make it there, and I never thought I'd understand what true acceptance meant. It didn't mean just coming to terms with the tragedy that rocked your world sideways. It didn't mean tossing all that pain to the side.

It meant accepting a new form of happiness. It meant allowing yourself to cry, yet also being so joyful that you sometimes thought your heart would explode.

True acceptance meant learning to live again.

I was so ready to live.

"I better start cleaning up—it's getting pretty late," Mom announced, standing up from the table.

"Wait, can I just say something really quick?" I asked. "While we're all here?"

"Yes, of course, Elliott," she said, sitting back down.

I stood up. "I just wanted you all to know that having you stand by me through the past several years is more than I deserved. You all mean the world to me, and I'm so thankful to have you in my life. You've stood by me through the darkest of times, so I was hoping to now finally have you stand by me during a moment of light." I turned to Jasmine and reached out for her hand. As she placed hers in mine, I lowered myself down to one knee. "Jazz..."

Her eyes watered over. "Oh my God," she muttered, her body shaking.

"When we were kids, you asked me what jazz meant to me, and my answer is still the same: jazz is the re-reminder that whenever I'm alone, I'm not really alone. It's my best friend when the world is hard. Jazz is beauty. It's unique. It's powerful without even trying." I reached into my pocket and pulled out a small box.

"Eli," she said breathlessly.

"You were, are, and will always be my Jazz. You are every beat, every note, every bar. You are the lyrics, the harmony, and the melody. You were, are, and always will be my favorite song." I opened the box, revealing a key with an engagement ring tied to it. "So, I give you this. This is the key to my heart, and it's yours for the keeping, but I just need you to know that my heart is rough sometimes. Sometimes it beats unevenly. Some days it's battered and bruised, but I promise you, as long as my lungs rise and fall, as long as I am here, this heart of mine will beat for you. I will give my all to you, each and every day of my life. So please, Jazz..." I moved closer, placing my forehead against hers. "Marry me?"

Tears rolled down her cheeks. "Is that a question?" she whispered.

"Yes"—I nodded my head—"and all you have to do is say yes. So please...say yes?"

She placed her hands behind my neck, pulling me closer as her lips pressed against mine. "Yes."

With one word spoken, the whole house celebrated. That celebration was the beginning of a new life, not only for Jasmine and me, but for all of us. We were crafting a new song, with new lyrics, leaving the albums of the past behind us.

But we were fully aware that if we ever needed a reminder of our past, those songs were always stored in our hearts and our minds, ready and available for a replay.

After dinner, I walked outside and sat on TJ's porch, staring across the street at my childhood home. TJ's front door creaked open behind me and Jasmine appeared. She walked my way and sat beside me. Her head fell on my shoulder, and she stared across the street with me.

"Happy?" she asked.

"Happiest," I replied.

"You're my favorite sound," she whispered. Her doe eyes looked up at me, and a small smile found her lips. "You've always been my favorite sound."

For the first time in forever, I was finally able to step out from behind the bars of my past. I was learning how to stand on both feet, I was learning how to walk again. I could feel the light coming back to me, filling me up with hope, with love, with happy endings.

I'd spent six years locked in a cage, and Jasmine Greene was the key to my freedom.

She was my music, my life, my everything. When our love blended together, it produced the most beautiful sounds. When our love blended together, two songs became one.

I placed my lips against hers and gently whispered my greatest truth, "You are beautiful."

# Epilogue

## Jasmine - Two Years Later

"And there we go," Laura smiled as she finished tightening the corset on my wedding gown. She stepped backward and stared at me. "Wow."

"Does it look okay?" I asked, feeling overwhelmed and excited all at once.

"It looks more than okay. You're so stunning, Jasmine." She fanned her eyes, trying to stop from crying.

"Don't cry! You'll make me cry and we'll both ruin our makeup," I joked.

"I know, I know it's just...I always dreamed of this day, and I'm so happy you're the one who has my son's heart. I know you'll keep it safe."

"I promise I will."

She pulled me into a hug and held on tight. When her voice whispered against my ear, I couldn't stop the tears from rolling down my cheek. "I always wanted two daughters."

I held her even tighter than before. "I always wanted a mom."

"We ruined our makeup," she softly laughed against my ear.

"It's okay. There's always time for touch-ups."

"Are you having a good day, Snow White?"

Laura and I both smiled at the sound of Ray's voice. We turned around to see him peering into the dressing room. He was wearing his best suit and tie, looking dapper as ever.

"Wow," he breathed out. "You both look amazing."

"She's the showstopper," Laura remarked.

"Says the beauty queen." I smiled.

"Let me give you two time alone," Laura said. As she walked past Ray, their hands slightly brushed against one another.

"You are beautiful, Laura," Ray told her.

Her cheeks blushed over. "You don't look half bad yourself, Ray."

She left the room, and Ray's stare followed her until she was out of his viewpoint.

"What was that?" I bellowed, shocked.

"What was what?"

"That! What was that moment you and Laura just had?"

Ray smirked and shrugged. "I don't know what you're talking about."

"You definitely know what I'm talking about, Dad! Oh my gosh. You and Laura?!"

"Shh..." he hissed. "It's... I just asked her out to dinner, that's all. It's not a big deal."

"You do know Elliott is going to give you hell for this, right?"

He nodded, and walked over to me. "I definitely know. Especially seeing how I'd gave him hell since he was sixteen. But you know what? Some things—some people—are worth going through hell for, and I think Laura is one of those people."

That made my heart skip. "You both deserve happiness."

"Speaking of happiness..." He stood in front of me and crossed his arms. "Wow, wow, wow..."

My stomach knotted up with butterflies. "Stop..."

"Snow, you look like the princess I always knew you were. This is the happiest day of my life." His eyes watered over and he bit his bottom lip. "Elliott is the luckiest man alive."

"And I'm the luckiest girl."

"Oh! I have something for you." He reached into his back pocket and pulled out a small box. "Your gift from the father."

"Dad...you didn't have to get me anything."

"Yes, I did. It's nothing big, and it just goes with your charm bracelet."

I took the box and opened it. *Thank God for waterproof mascara.* "Dad…"

"It's a key charm—a key to me. And now, I give you my vows." He pulled out a piece of paper, and cleared his throat. "Whenever you need to come home, no matter what happens, I'm here. I know Elliott is going to be more than enough for you. He is going to provide for you in every way a grown man should. He'll stand by your side. He'll protect you and care for you, but, I give you me too, Snow. I'm always here. As your father, I promise you my love, always and forever. I'm always going to be the first man in your life, and as I walk you down the aisle today and hand you off to your happily ever after, I want you to know I'm here in the shadows cheering you on. You're the best blessing I've ever received in my life. You're my world. Through sickness and health, till death do us part, for the rest of our lives, I'll be here for you. For always." He lowered his paper and wiped the tears falling from my eyes. "I love you."

"I love you, too, Dad."

He kissed my cheek. "Good. Now. Let's go get you married."

The moment we walked down the aisle, I felt my heart heal. Elliott was standing at the end of the walkway waiting for me to meet him. Ray's arm was linked with mine as we traveled down the aisle. My body was overtaken by pure joy as we grew closer and closer.

*This is it.*

*This is forever.*

We reached Elliott's side, and he stepped closer. Ray held his hand out toward Elliott, and he shook it, then they hugged.

"Take care of her, son," Ray whispered.

"Forever," Elliott replied.

I took Elliott's hands into mine, and we walked to the altar.

"Hi," he whispered.

"Hi," I replied.

"You're beautiful," he whispered.

"You're handsome," I replied.

"I love you," he whispered.

"I love you," I replied.

In front of all our loved ones, we promised ourselves to each other. We gave one another our hearts and souls. We began a new chapter to our love story that would last forever. We said 'I do' and we'd continue to say those two words over and over again. Through the dark days and the light, through loss and new beginnings. Elliott was my first love, and he'd be my last.

*I'm the luckiest woman alive.*

After the ceremony, we headed to the reception hall to celebrate our love. Everyone who meant anything to us were there with the brightest smiles on their faces. We honored Katie by lighting a candle in her memory, and having a table filled with keys as a token of our love for her. Then we proceeded to have the best night of our lives, because that was what she would've wanted most—our happiness.

When it came time for our first dance, Elliott and I both gasped as TJ moved to the microphone with a saxophone in his hands. "I know you both have a song picked out, and I'm sure it's perfect, but if you'd allow it, I'd love to play you one of my favorites."

"Please," I begged, tears in my eyes.

"Of course," Elliott agreed. We hadn't seen TJ play his music in years. I'd known he was working toward it with the help of great physical therapists, but we hadn't seen the outcome.

As he started to play the song, Elliott wrapped me in his arms and we began to dance.

"'At Last'," I murmured, speaking of the song TJ played. 'At Last' by Etta James. "This was his wedding song."

"And now it's ours." Elliott smiled, pulling me closer to him.

"This is the best day of my life," I said, swaying back and forth in his hold.

That night we laughed together, danced together, and ate our wedding cake with vanilla frosting number twenty-eight. Our lives weren't perfect, but we were beautiful imperfections together. He was mine, and I was his. Always and forever.

*At last...*

I was home.

# Elliott - Eight Years Later

"Daddy! Wesley bit me!" a small voice hollered, dashing into the bathroom. I sat beneath the sink, trying to stop the leaking pipe instead of hiring a professional. The little girl standing in front of me was the perfect mix of Jasmine and myself. Luckily, she got most of her mother's beautiful looks.

"I only bit her a little! She's being a big baby!" Wesley barked, barging into the room. He too, was a perfect mix of my wife and me. He received mama's sassiness, and her smile.

"Am *not*!" she cried.

"Are *too*!" he shouted.

"Whoa, whoa, whoa, time out." I placed the wrench down and stood up from beneath the sink. "What's going on? Katie, Wesley bit you?" I asked my daughter. With tears in her eyes, she nodded. I turned to Wesley. "Why did you bite her?"

"Because she bit me first, Daddy!" he cried, growing equally as dramatic as his twin sister.

I couldn't help but laugh. Having two four-year-old twins was a lot to handle. "How about you both hug and apologize?"

"But, Daddy, I don't want to apologize! I don't wanna be her friend no more," Wesley explained, crossing his arms with a huff.

Katie mirrored her brother's reaction. "Yeah! I don't want to ap-ap..." She stomped her feet, trying to push the word out.

I saw the irritation in her eyes and placed a hand on her shoulder. "Take your time, Sweetpea."

She inhaled deeply and exhaled slow. "I don't want to a-apologize either, Daddy!"

"Come on, both of you, sit down on the edge of the tub," I told them, and they did as I said. I kneeled in front of them. "What's the most important thing in the whole wide world?"

"Ice cream!" Wesley giggled.

"Yes, and after that?" I smirked.

"Family," Katie chimed in.

"Exactly, and we all know that sometimes we can get a little tired and grumpy, right? And we make mistakes, but when we are family what do we do?"

"We say sorry," Wesley grumbled.

"And love each other," Katie said rolling her eyes. When did my baby girl become an eye-roller?

"That's right. Because family is the most important thing, even before ice cream sometimes. So I need you both to hug one another and go back to playing, okay? Also, keep it down so you don't wake your mom or Leo, okay?"

"Ugh. Okay, Daddy," they said in unison.

They hugged for half a second before hurrying out of the bathroom.

"Wesley, stop biting me!" Katie shouted.

"You stop pinching me, then!" her brother replied.

*Well, that lasted longer than I thought.*

Like clockwork, Leo began to cry, and before I could go grab him from his crib, Jasmine was already there, lifting him up.

"You're supposed to be resting," I said, walking toward her and kissing her forehead.

"I'm not tired," she yawned, rocking Leo back to sleep. He was a little over a month old, and fifty times more mellow than the twins had ever been. The only time he cried was when he was hungry, needed a new diaper, or was awakened by loud noises.

"You're half asleep." I smiled. "Here, pass him this way."

She handed me Leo, and I rocked him back and forth. He was so small, so perfect. I couldn't believe the life we'd created, the dreams that came true.

We couldn't have done any of it alone, though. We had a tribe of people always standing behind us. Mom and Ray were only a phone dial away if we needed them. They were busy creating their lives together, but always made time to come help us with the kids if we called. Jason and Kelly also had their hands filled with two children of their own, so playdates with beers for the grown-ups were always fun. Their kids were almost as wild as the twins. *Almost.*

When we needed help the most, we'd stop by Uncle TJ's house and he'd make the twins listen to jazz and soul music for hours on end as he fell asleep in a rocking chair. He was well into his nineties, but swore he hadn't looked a day over eighty-seven.

Those people were my tribe. My family. My life.

I was so blessed.

Right as Leo was on the verge of rest, Wesley hollered. "Oh my gosh it's a flood!"

"Mama, can I put on my swimsuit?" Katie screamed, making Leo cry.

We headed to see the commotion, and there in the bathroom stood Wesley with a wrench in his hand and guilt on his face. "Oops? Sorry, Daddy," he murmured as the pipe under the sink was snapped and water was gushing across the wooden flooring.

"Oh my gosh, I'll turn off the water," Jasmine stated as I tried to soothe a howling Leo. As I went to scold Wesley, he shook his head.

"Remember, Daddy. Family says sorry, and I'm sorry. So, you can't be mad and you have to love me."

*Did he just throw my parenting lesson in my face?*

"I think it's time to get ready for bed," Jasmine said, grabbing the twins by their waists. "Before your father's vein in his neck pops."

She hurried them to bed, and then came back to help me clean up the floor. Leo stayed in my arms the whole time, and even with all the movements, he found a way to sleep. I lay him back in his crib and kissed his forehead. "Thank you for not being a twin," I whispered before returning to help Jasmine.

"I'll call a plumber tomorrow," I told her. "And I'll have someone look at the floors."

She yawned and shrugged. "No worries. It will all be okay, we'll have bacon in the morning."

I cocked an eyebrow. "A-are you sleepwalking?"

She yawned again. "I think I'm sleepwalking."

"Let's get you to bed." I wrapped my arm around her, and she tried to avoid slumber, but I lay her in the bed regardless of her refusal. I wrapped my arms around her body and held her close. "Sleep," I whispered against her ear.

"Sleep," she whispered back.

The twins were heard through the walls, still bickering. Whenever Jasmine tried to rise to check on them, I'd hold her tighter. "Sleep..."

She nodded. "Sleep..." She snuggled her small figure against me. "Our kids are devils."

"They are literally the worst humans to ever exist." I paused. "Let's have another one."

"Piss off." She laughed. "Would you choose this life again? If you had another chance, would you love me and these crazy kids?"

"Always. I would always choose this, choose you and the kids. I would always choose us."

"Forever and ever?"

"And ever."

She was so small and exhausted, and I swore I weighed five times as much as her, but she loved me just as much as I loved her. She was all beauty, and I was just me. Her skin was white as cream, and mine was painted caramel. My polar opposite. We weren't meant to fall for one another, but when we blended together we were some kind of beautiful.

"Elliott?"

"Yes?"

Her eyes were closed, and her lips brushed against mine. "Are you going to kiss me tonight?"

I smiled as my lips fell against hers, and I breathed her in. Of course I was going to kiss her. I'd planned to kiss her for the rest of forever. Our kiss was a promise for all that we'd find. For the family we made, for the adventures we'd discover. I kissed her for our past, present, and future lives.

Because of her, I lived again.

Because of her, I smiled.

Because of her, I was freed from behind the bars of my darkest days.

I'd spend the rest of our lives showing her my love through every single song that lived within me.

*The End*

# About the Author

Brittainy C. Cherry is an Amazon #1 Bestselling Author who has always been in love with words. She graduated from Carroll University with a Bachelor's degree in Theatre Arts and a minor in Creative Writing. Brittainy lives in Brookfield, Wisconsin with her family. When she's not crafting stories, she's probably hanging with her pets or traveling to new places.

### The Elements Series (All Complete Standalones)
The Air He Breathes
The Fire Between High & Lo
The Silent Waters
The Gravity of Us

### Other Books by Brittainy C. Cherry
Loving Mr. Daniels
Art & Soul
The Space in Between
Our Totally, Ridiculous, Made-Up Christmas Relationship

# Acknowledgements

Writing a book is hard. Writing this book was extra hard. Behind the Bars dealt with so many road blocks during the writing process. I've written and re-written this story so many times trying to find the best way to give Elliott and Jasmine the story they were asking for. This book almost broke me. If it weren't for a group of extraordinary individuals to hold my hand, I'm not sure I would've made it out alive. This is a story about strength, so let me quickly showcase where my strength comes from.

This book is for you, Mama. My 'Laura'. You are my rock, day in and day out. You are the voice of reason when I'm irrational, you are the calmness to my erratic sea. Thank you for always holding my hand and saying that everything always works out. You're right—it does. You have no clue how much you mean to me, and I'll spend the remainder of my life trying to show you. You are the music in a mute world.

To my sisters, Tiffani and Candace: You are everything good in the world. I know they say family isn't what you are born into, it's who you choose, but in this situation, you are both. You are my blood, you are my heartbeats, and I would choose you over and over again for the rest of my life. You are the Prue and Piper to my Phoebe. In the words of The Originals: "We stick together as one. Always and Forever."

To my brothers who will probably never read this: You are living proof that there are good men in this world. The world needs more good, kindhearted, funny, respectful, and loving men. Thank you for being exactly that. You all are a good thing.

To my papa: my cheerleader! Thanks for singing the praises of my books, even though it makes me blush and go, "Dad! Stoppp!" You're a hardworking man with an amazing heart.

To my agent, Flavia: You saved this book, and you saved me from crumbling. Thank you for reading re-write after re-write to help me in the late hours. From pushing me, and challenging me to put my all into the craft of storytelling. For believing in me—that's my favorite part:

your belief in me as an author and a person. Your belief in my writing when I struggled to see my own worth. Thank you for always standing by my side through every storm. When I think of strength, I think of you.

To my best friend. The Ann to my Leslie. The Princess to my Frog. I love you, Samantha. I love your heart and how it beats for love and justice, and all the beautiful things in the world. I love that you still love me even though I disappear during writing deadlines. I love that we sometimes hold full conversations with only memes. I love how somehow those are our most profound messages. I love you, and your husband, and your daughters more than words. If I could put a meme in this book for you it would be the 'Musk Ox' one from Parks and Rec. Obviously.

To Kandi Steiner—the girl who gets me more than most. Your messages of encouragement and words of wisdom stay so close to my heart. Then, during my breakdown about my cover, you swooped in and designed the most beautiful thing I've ever seen. Your heart is huge, and I love you so much. You are truly such a blessing to me, and I don't know how I became so lucky to call you one of my closest friends. We are the girls who feel everything, and I wouldn't have it any other way.

To Talon, Maria, Allison, Tera, Christy, Tammy, and Beverly: My favorite group of betas in the world. Thank you for pushing me. And thank you for not hating me for rewrites and having you read a pretty much different story from when you began. You are all the real MVPS.

A big, big thank you to my copy editors, Ellie at Love N Books, and Caitlin at Editing by C. Marie, and Emily at Lawrence Editing. All three of you went to war for me with this book. You've watched me break down and still, you smiled and showed up with grace and charm. You went above and beyond with your editing skills. Please don't ever leave me.

Virginia Alison—the best proofreaders in the world. Thank you for combing through every hair in this book. You both aren't just super sweet and amazing, you're also very gifted and I'm so thankful that you shared your time and energy with helping me.

And finally, to my readers: thank you. Without you, I'm just a girl typing to myself. Thank you for trusting me on the crazy journeys I take you on with these books. Thank you for believing in me, encouraging me, and pushing me to keep writing. There were so many days I've almost quit, and thankfully I had you all telling me to keep going. You are my lyrics. You are my strength. You are my key. You are my world.

Thank you for existing.

Thank you for being my favorite song.